What was this reactio

Shane's a good-looking guy—that's all, she told herself. Anyone would find him appealing to the eye.

"The twins fell asleep on line three of my story," she said on a bit of a stammer, trying not to stare. "You didn't get to say good-night."

She watched as he bent down to kiss each twin on the forehead and whisper, "I love you. Sweet dreams, my precious girl."

Aw. He was such a loving, doting dad. She'd known that, of course; she'd been watching him interact with his daughters for almost five years. But up close and personal like this, hearing the love and reverence in his voice, was something else.

"Let's go into my room," he said, leading the way and leaving the door just slightly ajar. "I can make us coffee or tea."

She felt her mind wander to the canceled wedding. "I was supposed to be in a much different hotel room right now. Drinking champagne. With a different man." She felt her cheeks flush. "Not that we're together, I mean." She sighed. "I should stop talking."

"Hey, it's okay. Your whole life turned upside down today."

She liked when he was understanding. And supportive. Yes, this Shane could stick around.

Dear Reader,

Stood up at her big outdoor ranch wedding, Ashley McCray is determined to confront her runaway groom and demand back every penny her family spent on the wedding. That's when the McCray Ranch foreman, widower Shane Dawson, gets an out-there idea: he's headed to the same town she is to drop off his twin five-year-old daughters at their maternal grandparents' house for a visit. The grandparents think he's doing a *terrible* job at parenting. They've even been talking about seeking custody. So Shane offers to drive Ashley to find her ex-groom if she'll give his girls pointers in acting like little ladies to appease their grandparents.

Ashley agrees and off they go on a very unexpected road trip across Wyoming. Along the way there are a few stops and many surprises, including feelings for each other that Shane and Ashley never anticipated…

I hope you enjoy this road trip book and Shane and Ashley's romance. I love to hear from readers, so feel free to email me at MelissaSenate@yahoo.com and check out my website for information on new books coming up.

Happy reading!

Melissa Senate

THE RANCHER
HITS THE ROAD

MELISSA SENATE

HARLEQUIN

SPECIAL
EDITION

Recycling programs
for this product may
not exist in your area.

ISBN-13: 978-1-335-59462-4

The Rancher Hits the Road

Harlequin Enterprises ULC
22 Adelaide St. West, 41st Floor
Toronto, Ontario M5H 4E3, Canada
www.Harlequin.com

Printed in Lithuania

MIX
Paper | Supporting
responsible forestry
FSC® C021394

Melissa Senate has written many novels for Harlequin and other publishers, including her debut, *See Jane Date*, which was made into a TV movie. She also wrote seven books for Harlequin Special Edition under the pen name Meg Maxwell. Her novels have been published in over twenty-five countries. Melissa lives on the coast of Maine with her son; their rescue shepherd mix, Flash; and a lap cat named Cleo. For more information, please visit her website, melissasenate.com.

Books by Melissa Senate

Harlequin Special Edition

Dawson Family Ranch

For the Twins' Sake
Wyoming Special Delivery
A Family for a Week
The Long-Awaited Christmas Wish
Wyoming Cinderella
Wyoming Matchmaker
His Baby No Matter What
Heir to the Ranch
Santa's Twin Surprise
The Cowboy's Mistaken Identity
The Rancher Hits the Road

Furever Yours

A New Leash on Love
Home is Where the Hound Is

Visit the Author Profile page
at Harlequin.com for more titles.

Chapter One

The groom was forty minutes late to his own wedding.

Shane Dawson, a guest seated on the bride's side at the lavish outdoor event at the McCray Ranch—*too* lavish, given what Shane knew about the ranch's finances—wasn't surprised. The question was: Would the guy show up at all?

From where he sat in the third row, Shane could hear Ashley McCray's parents, grandparents, aunts, uncles and cousins whispering and checking their phones for word from the bridal tent at the far end of the aisle, where the bride and her attendants were waiting. Shane's five-year-old twin daughters, Willow and Violet, junior flower girls, were sharing one chair to his right, glued to a game on his phone to keep them occupied. They'd been in the tent with the rest of the bridal party, but had apparently gotten so bored of standing around that the maid of honor had shooed them out and told them she'd call them when it was time.

At this point, that might be never.

The bride's great-aunt, nervously glancing behind her for any sign of activity in the tents, had unfortunately noticed that Willow's and Violet's fancy updos were coming out of their chignons and had summoned them over twice in the past half hour to fix their hair. She'd tsk-tsked the scuff mark on one of Willow's pink Mary Janes and the wrinkles in both girls' pink beaded flapper-style dresses, complete with fringe. A woman beside the twins had pointed out that Violet's fringe had gotten caught in the mechanics of the white padded folding chair and had spent ten minutes extricating his daughter from it, and now the fringe on the back was frayed.

The good news was that no one was paying any more attention to his "wild" children. They'd drawn plenty of attention earlier, mainly from a group of family friends of the bride's mother.

"Those little girls are pretty but lack decorum," one woman had said, shaking her head. "A little too wild."

"Are they family?" a blonde in a veiled hat had asked, eyeing the twins with haughty disdain.

"They're the foreman's daughters," a lady Shane didn't recognize whispered. "He's a widower," she'd added on a dramatic whisper.

"Ah," the blonde had said, her expression turning from disapproval to that all-too-familiar look that spelled "those poor girls." Then all their gazes had briefly landed on Shane with more pity than compassion.

"Those poor girls" were happy, healthy and loved. So what if they weren't quiet, perfectly behaved, pristine little robots as their own relatives—namely their maternal grandparents—thought they should be?

Don't think about the Shaws right now, he told himself, his tie tightening at his neck. His late wife's parents were full of unjustified criticisms over how he was raising the girls. Shane was doing the best he could. And the way he saw it, his best really *was* good enough. He was doing right by the girls. Yes, Violet liked to run instead of walk and mixed purple leggings with bright orange T-shirt dresses, her favorite color combination. Yes, Willow had a loud voice and a huge laugh—and no, he wouldn't shush her, particularly not in playgrounds, like her grandmother thought he should.

No one would stifle his girls. Not from their natural personalities. Not from who they were. Not from becoming who they were meant to be.

The problem was that after a weeklong visit with the girls last Christmas, the Shaws had emailed Shane a list of the girls' wrongdoings—everything from how Violet went flying down the stairs despite being told to walk nicely to the way Willow used inappropriate language for a little girl. Like "stupid dumbhead."

At the end of the email was an ultimatum about custody.

If you don't...if they don't...we'll be forced to consider whether they would be better served in our home and care...

A chill had run up Shane's spine even as he dismissed the "threat" as unwarranted. Racing down the stairs and referring to a classmate as a stupid dumbhead were hardly reasons for a judge to give custody of his daughters to their grandparents.

But the list was much longer than that. Violet had three fading black-and-blue bruises on her knees because of her need for speed. *If you won't teach the girls to walk properly and safely... Willow refuses to eat vegetables of any kind. You must know this isn't healthy...*

Again his tie tightened around his neck, and he slid in a finger to loosen it. He needed air—and he was *outside*.

If this wedding didn't get started soon, it couldn't *end* soon. And Shane could barely wait for that.

"Daaaaaaddyyyyyyy," Willow whined in her highest-pitched voice, her big green eyes moving from his phone to his face. "When's it gonna start?"

"Yeah, when?" Violet seconded, her matching green eyes never leaving the phone screen. "I want everyone to see Ashley in her gown already. She looks like a princess." She pumped a fist in the air at her game progress. "Yeah! Got you! That's twelve more points!"

"She does," Willow said with a nod. "A real princess."

Shane didn't want to imagine Ashley in her wedding gown. The moment he'd heard about the engagement six months ago, he knew it wasn't something to celebrate. Ashley was making a mistake. She was also a grown woman of twenty-eight, very intelligent, independent and thoughtful. So she *had* to know she was making a mistake—and was choosing to make it anyway. Shane had witnessed or overheard the boyfriend-then-fiancé disappoint Ashley several times. The few occasions that Shane couldn't bite his tongue, when he'd said something to Ashley, like *You deserve better*, she'd glared at him and snapped that he should mind his own business.

So that was what he'd done, all through the wedding preparations. And now here they were—waiting for the wedding to start, with Shane torn between wanting desperately to get it over with and also secretly hoping that something would happen to cancel it at the last minute.

Shane's daughters were now standing on their chairs, craning their necks to see if there was any action coming from the tents. Bridal to the left, groomsmen's to the right.

"Girls, down!" Shane whisper-yelled. Each girl sighed

and hopped down, more strands of honey-brown hair falling from their fancy updos.

Violet fell to her knees on the grass, a new stain appearing on the hem of her dress—and probably a fresh bruise just waiting to make an appearance in time to see their grandparents tomorrow. This was a school vacation week, and he'd promised to drop off the girls at the Shaws' home in Jackson Hole for a five-day visit. Where they'd no doubt assess the twins for any signs of better behavior—and then maybe follow through on their threats.

Don't think about that. Get through now.

Violet popped up with a giggle. Willow dropped to her own knees and also giggled. Then the twins high-fived each other.

He looked at his kind, interesting, smart, curious, big-hearted, beautiful daughters, his heart overcome with love for them. "I'm sure it'll start soon, girls."

Maybe the groom's eighty-thousand-dollar Range Rover had gotten a flat tire en route to the ranch. Maybe he really was just running late. Maybe the fact that he was now fifty minutes late to his wedding had nothing to do with cold feet.

Or maybe it was the result of a complete change of heart.

He pictured Ashley in the bridal tent, pacing, worrying, frantically calling and texting her fiancé of six months with Where are you?

"Yes, I'm sure it'll start soon," he repeated more for Ashley's sake than anything. It didn't feel appropriate to say the truth—that she might be better off if the wedding never started.

Suddenly, Anthony McCray, the bride's father, was kneeling beside him in the aisle. "How do you know, Shane?" he asked, panic in his deep voice. "Did you hear something? Do you know something? Did you see Harrington come in?"

Harrington Harris IV was the groom.

"I'm sure he'll be here any minute," Shane told his boss, whom he liked and respected. It was Anthony McCray who'd invited him since his daughter, not Shane's biggest fan, hadn't, even though she'd asked his twins to be her flower girls.

Anthony bit his lip and glanced over at the tents. No action. No movement. No sounds. "That's it," he said, his brown eyes worried. "I'm going to the groomsmen's tent to see if any of them know what's going on." He marched off, guests eyeing him.

A few minutes later, as Shane's daughters both lay on their chairs, heads where their knees should be, legs and feet up against the backrest as they counted clouds, Anthony hurried back past Shane's row. He whispered to his wife, but his voice was so naturally booming and deep that Shane could hear.

"None of Harrington's party has heard from him," Anthony said. "They've been texting and calling and get no response."

Shane could see Harrington's parents, over in the first row on the right side, standing and pacing, their phones out, their heads shaking. Every now and then, someone or a group of someones would come up to them, and Shane would see the parents shrug nervously. *Resignedly* might be the better word. Clearly they were used to their son's behavior and attitude.

Ashley should have been too.

But the woman was an optimist. Shane had gotten to know her pretty well over the past five years that he'd worked for the McCrays. She lived in a cabin near the big barn, where he naturally spent a good amount of time and where she worked as a groomer, horse trainer and all-around cowgirl to help out on the ranch, which hadn't been doing well the past six months.

Harrington Harris IV, whose wealthy family owned a very prosperous ranch and had made a fortune in oil too, hadn't worked a day in his privileged life. The running of the businesses was left to a management company.

Murmuring among the guests got his attention, and he turned around to see two of Ashley's bridesmaids walking down the aisle, their expressions stricken, tears in their eyes.

Uh-oh.

They got to the stage and cleared their throats, but all attention was already on them.

"I'm very sorry to report that the wedding is off," the redheaded bridesmaid called out.

Gasps could be heard all around. Including from Willow and Violet, who had leaped to their feet, eyes wide as they stared at the two women on stage.

"Unfortunately," the angrier-looking of the two bridesmaids added, "Harrington texted Ashley just a moment ago that he's very sorry, but he can't marry her. He thought he loved her but realized at the eleventh hour that he does *not*."

More gasps.

Oh, Ashley, Shane thought. He couldn't even imagine how she must feel right now.

His daughters' mouths were hanging open, their eyes darting to his, waiting for some kind of explanation.

"Apparently," the redhead said, "Harrington is already on the road to his family's summer mansion in Jackson

Hole, where he'll be 'working on himself,'" she added with air quotes and absolute disdain, "and determining what he wants to do with his life."

The two women sent a glare over toward the groom's side of the aisle, where there was lots more head shaking and whispering.

"Thank you all for coming," the other bridesmaid said, emotion clogging her voice, "but there will be no wedding today."

His daughters were now standing in front of him, their knees knocking into his in the narrow space between the chair in front of them and his own. "Daddy? Why didn't Harrington come?"

Before he could respond, Ingrid, Ashley's mother, ran toward the bridal tent. In moments she was back, flinging herself at her husband, who wrapped his arms around her. "She's not there! Her maid of honor said she ran out the back way after getting the text from Harrington. A few of the gals tried to find her, but she's not in her cabin or in the main house. Where could she be?"

Shane would wager a million dollars, not that he had a million dollars, that he knew exactly where Ashley was.

"Daddy?" Violet said. "What happened? Why isn't the wedding happening?"

"You heard what Cathy said," Willow told her sister. "Harrington sent her a text that he couldn't marry her."

"But why?" Violet asked.

"Yeah, why?" Willow said.

Being a dad—and a single dad, at that—was never easy. Moments like this, questions like this, were downright hard as he struggled to say the right thing, in the right way, on a level the five-year-olds could understand. He always strove to protect them while being honest. That balance was always near impossible.

He took a hand each and held on to them. "Sometimes people change their minds, even about important things. They realize something doesn't feel right, so they decide to do something else."

"Is Ashley sad?" Violet asked, her tone worried.

"She has to be, right?" Willow said. "Everyone kept calling this the biggest day of her life."

He squeezed both their hands and then pulled them in for hugs. "I'm sure she's sad. And when you're sad, you just have to let yourself feel what you feel, right?"

They both nodded. "When I see Ashley, I'm gonna give her a flower from the garden," Violet said.

"Me too," Willow said.

"That's a nice idea," he assured them.

As the guests continued to pile out, murmuring and whispering, and stopping to hug this person or that, Shane nudged the girls toward the aisle.

"Daddy, will you change your mind about being our dad?" Willow asked, looking up at him.

"Like Mommy had to," Violet said.

Both girls looked at each other, their expressions reaching into his heart and twisting. Their mother had died in a car accident when they were just three months old.

"Going to heaven isn't the same thing as deciding something," Violet said. "Right, Daddy?"

"Yeah, because she didn't *decide* to go to heaven," Willow responded.

"That's right," he said.

He wrapped them both in another hug. "I love you two more than anything in the world. I'd never change my mind about that. Never. That's a promise. And I always keep my promises, right?"

"Right, Daddy," they both said in unison, eyes brightening as they focused on his face.

"Can we go see Ashley to make sure she's okay?" Violet asked.

"Yeah, can we?" Willow seconded. "We can give her a flower and a hug."

Aww. *Take that, Beatrice Shaw.* His girls were thoughtful and sweet. He valued that over *walking nicely down the stairs.* "I have a feeling she needs some time alone right now. But it's really nice that you both care about Ashley."

Thing was, he cared about Ashley too, despite their squabbles and the tension between them the past few months. The real problem between them was that he knew too much, saw too much, heard too much. After an argument with Harrington on the phone or in person, usually in the barn or stables where he could hear loud and clear, she'd see Shane walking in her direction and hurry the other way, spots of red appearing on her cheeks. Sometimes she'd just shoot him a glare, lift her chin and march past him.

He'd go check on her. He was probably the last person she'd want to see right now, but he figured he was the only person who knew where to find her. And he felt compelled to make sure she was all right. Or as all right as she could be.

"Can we go to Katie's birthday party since there isn't a wedding?" Violet asked. "Or is the party over already?"

He pulled out his phone and checked the time. Their kindergarten classmate's sixth birthday party was from 1:30 p.m. to 3:30 p.m., with pizza and cake. "Actually, it's not starting for fifteen minutes," he said. "Let's go home, you two change fast, and I'll take you over to the party."

Their little faces brightened some more, and he was grateful that the complicated lives of adults were wiped from their minds, if only just for right now in anticipation of the party. They walked the ten minutes to their cabin, which had been the foreman's cabin for the entire fifty-plus years the McCray Ranch had been in operation. He glanced at the stables across the path from the big barn. Ashley was in there, no doubt, up in the loft, way in the back.

Another ten minutes later, the girls were in their brightly colored leggings and long-sleeved T-shirts and sneakers. He dropped them off in town at the party house, which was only a fifteen-minute drive, then hurried back to the ranch. While some people were still milling around, lots of cars were already gone. He didn't see the McCrays. Likely they were in the main house, getting a lot of support from family and friends.

He pulled back into his drive at the cabin, then walked the short path up to the ornate stables, Ashley's favorite place. She was in here, he was sure of it.

Now he'd just have to find the right words for her—a lot harder than with five-year-olds.

Ashley heard the stables door open and held her breath as she had every time someone had come in during the past forty minutes. They'd call out, *Ash? Ashley, you in here?* and she'd go stock-still, afraid they'd climb up the loft and peer way in the back where she was hiding in her secret spot. So far, no one had.

She still wasn't ready to talk to anyone. Not her parents or her cousins or even her favorite aunt, Daphie.

Years ago—when she was in high school and going through breakups or mean girl drama or her parents "didn't understand anything!"—she'd brought up a sleeping bag, down pillow and a go bag with provisions to get her through a few hours. After high school, the place had remained a refuge—and the supplies had stayed—but she'd never used it so much as in the past year, since she'd been dating Harrington. She'd found herself climbing up here quite a few times. She'd mull over what had pissed her off or made her feel uneasy or sad, and she'd come back down when it was either time to get back to work or she'd just plain rationalized away whatever had been bothering her, telling herself she was being "too sensitive" or could blame it on the "different worlds" factor between her and Harrison.

He was so cavalier about money, for example, pointlessly buying another vintage car for his collection or a champion racehorse and wanting her to be as excited when he knew she was worried about the McCray Ranch barely breaking even over the past couple of years. Anytime she'd bring it up, he'd say, "Ashley, just say the word and my father could fix everything. His accountant could transfer over a money market account as easily as he'd buy a few new suits at Brooks Brothers. You have nothing to worry about."

But the McCrays, Ashley included, had never been about *taking*. They worked hard, starting with Ashley's paternal grandparents, who'd started a small cattle ranch, grew it and passed it down to the next generation. Yes, there'd been ups and downs, but for the past ten years, things had been solid. Now, not so much.

And when she'd needed Harrington's understanding or support, he'd offer money. She'd try to explain what she *did* need from him, but he'd get impatient or antsy and make excuses to leave.

She should have counted how many times *that* had sent her up here.

Maybe she would have been the one to send a text changing her mind at the last possible second.

But instead she'd overlooked red flags, focusing on what she'd loved about Harrington, what was great between them—and much was, or had been. He had a big heart, and even though he could be clueless sometimes, he seemed to like when she'd point it out. He'd say, with wonder coming over his handsome face, that he'd never dated a woman who wasn't wealthy. That he was used to tossing his money and name around to get what he wanted. He talked a lot about how he never had to do that with Ashley—and in fact, how he knew that if he tried, it would turn her off. That had seemed to turn *him* on.

He'd sobbed for days when his paternal grandfather had died at the start of their romance, and she'd been there for him, bringing them much closer than they probably would have gotten otherwise. At the core, they were friends. Real friends. And she'd thought he did love her.

She'd clearly been wrong.

And now *everyone* knew it too.

She could envision her parents sitting at the kitchen table of their ranch house, worried sick over her, comforting each other, getting hugs from friends and family who were hanging around. Ashley's father had been talking about her wedding since she was a little girl, how she'd have her big day right here on the McCray Ranch and could invite her horse. She could hear him saying that in her head even now, and it managed to bring a small smile.

Despite how independent she was, Ashley was a daddy's girl, and the fantasy he'd stoked about her wedding, about finding her "one true love," had wound its way deep inside her. He'd been dazzled by Harrington as she'd been and had thought of her fiancé as her Prince Charming. Her father had said more than a few times that the only dreams he still had left were to walk her down the aisle, then hold his grandchildren someday. A few times she'd mentioned what Harrington had said about helping out in terms of money, and he'd gotten a bit angry—embarrassed, really—and waved his hand dismissively. *We McCrays built this place from nothing,* he'd say, *and we'll keep it going just like my grandparents did. Life is full of ups and downs, and now is a down. That's all. We don't take handouts.*

Her parents had raised her right, in her opinion. But because her father could be proud and had always been a man of tradition, he'd insisted on paying for most of the wedding, finally agreeing that the Harrises could take care of the videographer since it was a relative of theirs who still charged a small fortune.

Now it was her parents who were out a *real* fortune, piles of money wasted on a wedding that hadn't happened. Money they didn't have to spare. Her father had already sold parcels of land to pay for the wedding and keep the ranch afloat. She hadn't known about that until an aunt— not her favorite one—had slipped and mentioned it.

Ashley felt an ache both deep in her chest and close to the surface. She wrapped her arms around her knees, blinking back a fresh round of tears, waiting for whoever had come in to call her name, but there was only silence. Except for the sudden footsteps—which weren't retreating. Someone was coming—toward the loft.

She could feel her eyes widen as she heard a shoe hit a rung of the loft ladder. The sound got closer and closer. And then there was a familiar face and broad shoulders as Shane Dawson, the foreman at the McCray Ranch, climbed up and over, crouching over to where she was. He sat down along the wall about six inches away, arms around his knees like hers.

Shane Dawson was the last person she wanted to talk to.

"You'll ruin your nice suit," she said, wanting to beat him to the punch of saying whatever he'd come here to say. She knew what he'd come here to say, actually. And she didn't want to hear it.

"Eh, that's okay. It's rare that I ever need it." She could feel him eyeing the hem of her gown. "Straw adds a Western touch to the dress."

She gazed at her ruined gown, poked with straw, dirty in spots and snagged from climbing the ladder. Ashley and her mother and aunts had gone to at least five bridal boutiques in search of The Dress, but the prices had had Ashley shaking her head at them all. She'd ended up finding a beautiful gown online at half the price of the salons. She and her mother sometimes butted heads, but not over Ashley's pick. That day the dress had arrived, folded up and wrinkled, Ashley had tried it on and her mother had burst into tears at how perfect it was. Now tears stung Ashley's eyes and she blinked hard.

"I'm surprised you haven't said 'I told you so' yet, Dawson. I assume that's why you're here. Or did my father ask you to find me?" Figured Shane would think to climb up the loft ladder.

"Nope," he said, turning his head from against the wall to look at her for a moment. "The twins were asking after you, wanting to make sure you were okay."

Aww. "I love those sweetie pies." Violet, with a heart

bigger than Wyoming, and Willow, who knew every kind of horse there was. Ashley had taught the twins all about horses, and Willow in particular had always listened hard just the way Ashley had when her dad used to talk all things equine with her.

"I'm sorry about what happened, Ashley."

She glanced at him, appreciating that. That was really all she needed to hear. *Sorry. That sucks.* "Yeah, me too. I feel like I got stomped on—and it's no fun to get humiliated in front of two hundred of your family and friends."

She felt a warm, strong hand cover hers, and the simple gesture of comfort, of kindness when she needed it most, broke the dam. The tears came fast and furious. She reached for her go bag and pulled out a third box of tissues. Guess she wasn't cried out yet after all.

"I will say one thing, Ashley. He didn't deserve you."

Damned right he didn't. She'd thought they had something real and loving, but his text made it clear everything she thought about their entire relationship was a lie. Some kind of social experiment for Harrington, maybe. Slumming with the middle-class rancher's daughter. Getting a kick out of how she preferred picnics on the Harris Ranch's beautiful land over expensive restaurants. But then when it came right down to it, to their *wedding day*, she wasn't what he wanted. Wasn't enough.

He didn't love her.

Well, it was a little late to come to that conclusion, Harrington Harris IV!

She looked down at her exquisite engagement ring. Two carats, a perfect solitaire in a gold setting. She stared at it, anger building and building and— She grabbed the ring off her finger and flung it hard behind her.

"Um, Ashley," Shane said, looking behind them in the direction she'd thrown the ring. "That cost what? Ten thousand dollars?"

A feeling akin to horror turned her stomach upside down, and her eyes filled with tears. She could sell the ring to pay back some of the costs. She scrambled on her knees, pawing through the straw in search of the ring.

"I'll help," he said, kneeling down and feeling all over for the ring.

Ten minutes later, neither of them had found it.

Shane scooted over by the wall. "Calculating the bounce and probable direction…" he said, turning and digging his hands in the straw. "Got it!" he said without triumph, and she had to appreciate that. He held it out to her.

"I don't want to touch it," she said.

"I'll hang on to it for you." He put it in his pocket.

What had this day turned into?

She swiped at her eyes with the tissue and lifted her chin.

"You know what?" she said, anger radiating. "He's not getting away with this. He's gotten away with way too much the past year. He's going to pay me back—well, my parents—every penny that they spent on the wedding he didn't show up for. I'm going to hand him an itemized bill and demand payment. That ten-thousand-dollar ring won't cover a *fourth* of what my parents spent."

Shane raised an eyebrow. "You think that'll make you feel better? Personally, I doubt it."

"Yes, it will." It wasn't like Shane Dawson *knew* her.

Though sometimes she thought he did. More than once, he'd been annoyingly insightful after he'd caught the tail end of one of her and Harrington's arguments. He would always confirm that she'd been right, and for a moment, she'd revel in the feeling that she wasn't being "sensitive" after all. But then the rush would fade, and she wouldn't know what to do with her victory. The moment would end with her feeling more awkward around him rather than less.

And yet he *had* known exactly where to find her.

She glanced over at Shane, who eyed her back. He'd worked for her parents for just over five years. He'd caught quite a few of her most embarrassing moments. He knew too much about her as it was, and now he was a witness to her biggest humiliation.

Not being loved after all. Chosen and then put back.

Suddenly she felt…exposed. Even more vulnerable than she'd been before Shane's face had appeared over the platform of the loft.

She had to get out of here. She had to get away.

She bolted up, a piece of straw stuck to her wedding dress poking at her leg. She brushed it away.

She knew exactly where to go.

Chapter Two

Uh-oh. Shane knew that look on Ashley's face. Determination—but mixed with fear, worry and can-I-really-do-this?

She was going after Harrington. To present him with an itemized bill for the wedding.

Jackson Hole, where Harrington was on his way to, was seven hours across Wyoming. In her distracted state, Ashley was in no condition to drive.

Then again, her entire family would probably pile in the car with her.

"I suppose you'll be okay as long as someone else drives," he said. "Your mom? The aunt you often go riding with?"

"Daphie," she said, brushing more straw off her dress. "But no. I need to be alone. I need to think. To process. Digest. I really don't love driving on the highway, especially at night. Or in the rain. But I'll blast my playlists and podcasts, pick up some snacks." Her face brightened. "Yeah, I'll be fine. The road trip will help me…get over this—and result in my getting back my parents' money." She nodded to herself. "See you later," she said and started for the ladder.

He envisioned her on the side of the road in a rainstorm, car broken down, all alone…

And then he envisioned her finally getting to the Harrises' summer mansion, marching up to the door and knocking, and

Harrington not exactly being alone himself. Or amenable to seeing her. Or receptive to her demands for the money back. She wasn't thinking about any of this clearly.

"Ashley, I really don't think going after Harrington will make you feel better or—"

She held up a hand, then bent down and continued dusting herself off, straw falling to the loft floor. "Look, Shane," she said, glancing up at him in between wipes of her hands on her gown, "I appreciate that you didn't say 'I told you so' about him, but you're wrong about *me*. I *will* feel better when Harrington hands me a big fat check that will save the McCray Ranch. My parents spent stupid sums of money on this wedding that they didn't have. You very likely know that."

Shane *did* know that. For a few weeks, Anthony had kept his interesting math a secret from his foreman until Shane had found too many deficits. Money was going out faster than it was coming in, not helped by the fact that expected sales of cattle and land hadn't gone through.

"And a long road trip is exactly what I need," she said. "It'll be like the solo honeymoon I didn't expect to take."

She bit her lip, which was slightly trembling. Her face began to crumble. Tears slipped down her cheeks.

He grabbed the box of tissues and held it out for her.

"Whatever," she said, dabbing at her eyes, trying to put some steely resolve in her voice, her expression. It wasn't working. "I'm going and that's that."

"I hope you're planning to change first," he said.

"Of course I am. I *hate* this dress," she added, new tears forming in her hazel eyes. "I'm going to change, pack, let my parents know I'm fine and going on a mission, and then I'm leaving. Jackson Hole, here I come." She turned around and stepped backward onto the ladder and started climbing down.

Jackson Hole. Where he had to be tomorrow to drop off the girls at their grandparents' house. For just a little while, Ashley's situation had wiped that from his mind, but he was going to have to face the Shaws in just a couple of days. And their threat.

Wait a minute.

Huh.

An idea slammed into his head. An idea that could help out both him and Ashley. Maybe save his entire future. Save his *family*.

And hers—if Harris paid her back.

He thought of Ashley McCray in her straw-festooned, snagged, dirty wedding gown—and how she still managed to look elegant. She simply had a regal look about her. Even when she was grooming horses, Ashley looked great. She was what he supposed was called a "girlie-girl." She liked dressing up. Heels. Perfume.

And she was what the Shaws would call a lady. Polite, refined.

Oh, yes. She could help him. And in turn, he could help her. They could help each other.

"I have a bad idea," he called out. "A better bad idea than yours."

She climbed back up until just her head was visible over the floor of the loft. "And what could that possibly be?"

"I have to drop the twins at their grandparents' mansion tomorrow for spring break. Five days. What if *I* drive us to Jackson Hole—I'll drop you at Harrington's summer place, then take the girls to their grandparents."

She tilted her head. Bit her lip.

She looked at him. He looked at her.

Silence.

"I guess we're headed in the same direction, so it's not that bad an idea," she said. "The twins would be great, fun company."

Was that a diss? That *he* wouldn't be great, fun company? He supposed she *was* used to him pointing out her problems.

"There's a catch," he said.

Now it was her turn to raise an eyebrow. "Of course there is. What?"

"In return for me driving you seven hours so you can sit back and process, especially in the dark and in the rain, you'll teach my twins manners. I need them to be little ladies by tomorrow. By the time we arrive at their grandparents' house."

She stared at him in total confusion. "Why on earth would you want them to be little ladies?"

He looked away for a moment, a hard sigh escaping. "Because the Shaws don't think they're being raised right. 'Feral tomboys' is a favorite descriptor. They've dangled a threat to petition for custody."

She gaped at him. "*What?* Willow and Violet are two of the happiest, funniest, most curious, interesting little kids I've ever met. What's wrong with being tomboys?"

"I could hug you right now," he said, then could feel his cheeks slightly burning.

She smiled for the first time since he'd climbed up to the loft. "Huh. I guess we could *both* use a hug."

He tried to imagine hugging Ashley McCray—and couldn't. They just didn't have that kind of friendship. Not that they were friends, really. They just knew each other from the ranch. He just happened to know a lot about her personal life. She'd know about his too—if he had one outside of his role as a father. He'd moved to the ranch to take the job as foreman just a few months before he was widowed. He'd spent the past five years working hard and raising his daughters with absolutely no social life beyond relatives. He was friendly with the McCrays, but they'd always kept their relationship strictly professional.

"That's why I think we'd be good travel companions," he said. "We've both got a lot going on right now—so much that we'll probably be in our own heads most of the time instead of getting into dopey arguments about this or that. And I really do need your help, Ashley. Seriously."

She nodded and extended her hand, the earlier worry and unease gone from her hazel eyes. "It's a deal."

After making a plan with Shane to meet at his cabin in two hours—at 4:00 p.m.—so they could hit the road, Ashley slipped out the back door of the stables. She darted into the woods just a couple of feet away. There was a path she could take just on the other side of the tree line that would lead to the back door of the ranch house.

She did not want to be spotted by any guests still hanging around—and the wedding gown and updo would make her stand out big-time. She hurried along the path, her *peau de soie* pumps as ruined as her dress by now. Every now and then through a gap in the trees, she'd been able to see a few of her relatives hugging one another goodbye in the parking area, all holding a food container. Her parents must have had the dinners boxed up and handed out so they wouldn't go to waste. She had no doubt the wedding cake was still there, intact. She wished she could smash it.

Sigh.

It was over an hour since the wedding had been called off, and it looked like most of the guests had left.

As she pulled open the back door, she could hear people talking in the living room. Her parents. Her grandparents—both sets. Her three aunts—her mother's sisters—Daphie, who was recently divorced, Lila, who went nowhere without her two mini Chihuahuas, and Kate, who Ashley could hear threatening to sue Harrington for "breach of expectations."

She sucked in a deep breath and moved to the doorway of the living room.

"There she is!" Daphie exclaimed. "Oh, my Ashley," she added, rushing over and pulling her into a hug.

The hug felt so good. Ashley hadn't realized just how much she needed warm, strong arms around her. In seconds she was surrounded by embraces and hand squeezes and compassionate murmurs.

She'd thought having a purpose—going after Harrington for all the money her parents had wasted on the non-wedding—had perked her up, made her feel stronger. But suddenly, in the comfort of her family, all the hurt, all the humiliation, came flooding over her, and her eyes filled with tears.

"I'll kill him!" Daphie shrieked. "When I get my hands on that rat—"

"No, I'll kill him!" Kate said. "What an absolute—"

"Cowardly bastard," Lila added, shaking her head, a Chihuahua in each arm.

Her mother ran over, pulling her into a hug. "Are you okay?" she whispered, stepping back to peer at her daughter, her eyes so full of worry and concern. Ingrid McCray put a hand on either side of Ashley's face. "You'll be okay. You're strong. You're a McCray."

Her father nodded and hugged her next. "I'm so darn sorry, sweetums."

That did it again. The sight of her father's sweet brown eyes so filled with anguish for his daughter broke the dam.

"Someone get more tissues," Kate called. "We actually all went through two boxes already."

Ashley's mom darted off and returned with two boxes. Four hands thrust a tissue at her, and she used them all to dab at her eyes.

"I can't wait to tell that rat fink just what I think of him," Daphie spit, her curly red hair bouncing on her shoulders.

"Well, he ran away like the cowardly baby he is," her mother said. "He's halfway to Jackson Hole by now. Safe from our wrath."

"Not mine," Ashley said, lifting her chin, the tears drying up as her plan came back into sharp focus. "*I'm* going after that rat fink. I'm leaving for Jackson Hole in a couple of hours to demand every cent back that you two spent on the wedding."

"What?" her father said. "Ashley, honey, you don't have to do that."

"If she doesn't, I will!" Ashley's mother snapped. "And not for the money, for the principle! Okay, for the money too. How dare he!"

"I'll go too," Daphie said.

Ashley shook her head. "Actually, Shane is driving me."

"Shane?" her father asked. "Really? He offered?"

"Turns out he has to be in Jackson Hole tomorrow to drop off the twins at their grandparents' for spring break," Ashley explained. "So I'm going along."

Her dad was shaking his head. "Ashley, that rat bastard took enough from you. You don't need to waste even more of your time and energy going there to get the money back from him. I'll just sic the sheriff on him. Surely what he did breaks some old Wild West law."

Ashley almost smiled as she envisioned Harrington Harris IV being led away in handcuffs for leaving her at the altar. Until she imagined hearing him whine, *But I don't love her. How could I marry her?* And the sheriff agreeing and uncuffing him.

She sighed. "I want to. The ranch needs it. He's paying us back every cent. Shane's holding on to the engagement ring, which I'll sell when I get back. I need to do this, okay?"

Her parents peered at her, studying her the way they always did when she announced she was doing something a little "out there."

"I do feel more comfortable knowing Shane and his twins will be with you," her mom added. "They're a breath of fresh air—the girls, I mean."

Ashley laughed. "Not Shane?"

Ingrid McCray smiled. "I adore Shane Dawson. He's a great foreman. And he's a great dad. I just meant that Willow and Violet are a hoot. Shane is always pleasant, but he's not a comical five-year-old times two. Those girls will cheer you up for sure."

A great dad. She thought about why he needed her help with the twins on the road trip and almost blurted it out. But his issues with his in-laws were Shane's business, and she didn't think he'd want that getting around. Her parents could be trusted, but her aunt Lila was a huge gossip. Ashley glanced at her—she adored Lila, but the woman loved to dish. With the failed wedding, she was already hanging on every word to report back to her friends and acquain-

tances in the off-leash dog park where she took her Chihuahuas twice a day.

"Well, since Shane's driving you, I feel better about that
too," her dad said. "I'd trust that man with my life."

Ashley did like knowing she'd be in good hands. Safe
hands. "He *does* like to poke his nose into my business,
though," she said, thinking of the times he'd told her Harrington didn't deserve her.

"Mine too," Anthony McCray said. "But in my case,
that's his job. Do you know he refused to take a salary this
past month because of how bad the books were getting?"

Ashley gaped at her father. "Really?"

"That's nice and all," Aunt Kate said. "But Shane's wealthy,
right? His late wife's family is superrich."

"Actually," Lila said, one Chihuahua nuzzling her neck.
"His wife had a trust fund, but she never touched it. And
Shane left it alone for the twins when they come of age.
They lived on their own salaries—Shane's as foreman, and
his wife was a teacher, right?"

Interesting. "How do you know that?" Ashley asked. "I
mean, about his wife's finances?"

"Oh, it was big news when she married him," Lila said.
"That she married a ranch foreman and that they were not
living beyond their own means. That the wife went from
her parents' mansion with an indoor *and* outdoor pool to a
cabin next to a barn. Plus, I know one of her cousins and
got all the scoop."

"Huh," Ashley said again.

"I heard that Shane lets the grandparents pay for summer
camp and trips with them every summer to amazing places,
and he's fine with gifts for the girls," Lila added, "but on a
day-to-day basis, they live on his salary."

"Which he hasn't taken the past month," her father reminded them.

Ashley's busted-up heart softened toward the foreman a little more. Not that being proud and making his own way made him a saint, but that he turned down a salary to help out her father, to help their ranch survive, when he probably needed it… That was something.

Anthony McCray nodded to himself. "Now, *there* is a good man."

"It's good to know they exist," Daphie said.

Ashley crossed her arms over her chest. "Well, he may be a great guy, but I can't say I'm looking forward to sitting next to him in his SUV for the next couple of days. Shane and I are night and day. He's been tsking me all year over Harrington and our arguments." Ashley's chin wobbled. "And he was right too. I'm such an idiot." She covered her face with her hands, the tears threatening again.

Her mother put an arm around her shoulders. "No, honey. You were just in love. And Harrington won us all over. But now he's shown us who he really is."

Ashley nodded, dropping her hands. She sucked in a breath. "I'm getting back our money. I'm going to keep my mind focused on that. And I'll be fine."

"Sweetheart," her dad said. "You really don't need to go after the money or have anything to do with that lying coward again. We'll get through this—just as we would have had the wedding gone ahead. Let's just move on."

Ashley shook her head. "I need to do *something*. Something to help me deal with how stupid I feel. How angry I am. Family and friends flew in from all over the country. Cousin Ben wasted his army leave on a wedding that didn't happen. Harrington is going to pay us back."

"I get it," Daphie said. "When my ex walked out on me, I presented him with a bill for my suffering—twice-weekly therapy and *retail* therapy."

"I don't think it's the money so much as the last word Ashley is after," her eighty-two-year-old maternal grandmother said.

"Oh, Grammy," Ashley said, gently hugging the dear woman. "You've always known me so well."

But it was both. The money and the last word.

And maybe, if she was very honest, she'd admit that she was holding out a little hope that Harrington would take one look at her and tell her he was sorry. That he made the biggest mistake of his life by not showing up, that he just got scared, that of course he loved her and wanted to marry her.

Her chin wobbled again. How did a man spend a year with someone, share in her life, get close to her family and friends, propose, plan a wedding, whisper in her ear just the week before that he'd never been so happy, that he couldn't wait to spend the rest of his life with her, that she was his everything, and then decide days later that he was wrong about all that?

Maybe he would change his mind when he saw her again. And what if he did? What if he took one look at her on his doorstep, his "Sweet Ashley," as he always called her, and realized he'd made the biggest mistake of his life?

And if he *did* say that, what would she say in return? Did she actually want him back? If she *did* take him back, how could she necessarily believe anything he said at this point? How could she ever trust him again? He didn't show up to their wedding! He'd *texted* her that he didn't love her.

He made a fool of her in front of everyone she cared

about. How could she possibly want him to change his mind and love her again?

She happily accepted the fresh round of hugs she got from her family. The aroma of her grandmother's White Shoulders perfume—which had been her great-grandmother's trademark scent—made her feel instantly comforted.

And right now, she needed all the comfort she could get. Her entire life was up in the air. Of course her head was a jumble of crazy thoughts. She'd just have to see what happened when she arrived in Jackson Hole. How she felt. How he felt. Maybe she'd take one look at Harrington Harris IV and vomit. Tell him he was a low-down dirty rat coward and hold out her hand for the big fat check that would save her family's ranch.

And maybe she'd take one look at him and realize that their love story wasn't over. That all he'd have to do to get a second chance from her was admit he'd made a terrible mistake. That he knew now, with a little time to think, a little time apart, that she *was* the one for him. He'd beg forgiveness for the awful way he'd gone about getting to that point. They'd elope to Vegas, and she'd still make him pay for the wedding that wasn't.

Anything could happen.

Suddenly she was really glad she wouldn't be making the trip alone.

Chapter Three

Shane was due to pick up the girls from the birthday party at 3:30 p.m., but at 3:00 p.m. he received a phone call from Allison Waterly, the birthday girl's mother. There was an "unfortunate incident," and could he please come pick up the twins *immediately*?

Uh-oh.

He was in the middle of packing and quickly threw swim trunks in the suitcase open on his bed, his mental list of what he needed to bring zipping out of his head.

"Willow threw a cupcake at one of the other children," Allison said. "Hard. And she also refused to apologize."

Oh, Willow, he thought. *Why are you throwing cupcakes at anyone?*

"I don't know what led up to it," Allison continued, "but as an example for the other children, I'll need you to pick up the girls. Of course it's wrong to punish Violet for Willow's actions, but when I asked Willow why she threw the cupcake at Dylan, Violet shouted it was because he was a 'dumbhead idiot,' and we don't use words like that."

He sighed long and hard internally.

"I'll be right there," he said. "And sorry."

He headed down the hall, grabbed his keys from the hook by the door and went out to his SUV, glancing over at Ashley's cabin about a quarter mile down the path. She was likely in the middle of packing too.

He'd been second-guessing himself for offering to drive her to Jackson Hole. Maybe he should have encouraged her to stay home. He didn't think confronting the ex was a good idea or a good use of her time and energy when an email would do—and document her request just fine. But now, en route to pick up the girls, he was reminded of how badly he needed Ashley's help with them. When she taught them manners, he could ask her to cover *why they can't go around throwing cupcakes—hard—at children. Even if they're "dumbhead idiots."*

He sighed again and got in his SUV and drove out. When he arrived at the Waterlys' home and headed up the walkway, the front door opened. He could see the twins sitting on the entry bench, bright red parting gift bags in each of their hands. They popped up when they saw him coming.

Allison gave him the same look of pity that the McCray relatives had when they learned he was a widower. "Willow did finally apologize to the boy she threw the cupcake at," she said, giving both girls a satisfied nod.

"And I also apologize," he said to the woman. "I know managing a party full of kindergartners is hard enough without having to call a parent for early pickup."

"No worries, Shane. Thank you for coming, girls."

He gave each twin a sharp look.

"Thank you for having us," they said practically in unison.

Allison smiled, and with an arm around each girl, he ushered them out, the door closing behind them.

"We'll talk in the car," he said.

They weren't exactly hanging their heads on the way to

the SUV, which meant Willow felt justified for what she'd done, and her twin agreed.

Once they'd pulled away from the house and were on the road, Shane eyed Willow in the back seat. "Okay, tell me what happened."

In another glance in the rearview mirror, he caught Willow's face fall, her lower lip slightly tremble. She looked at her sister. Violet eyed her, then frowned and looked down.

Huh. He gave them a few seconds.

Willow kept her head down now. "That dumbhead stupid idiot Dylan said that it's weird that we don't have a mother like everyone else." Her voice was low, practically a whisper, and he could tell that she was trying not to cry.

"And what did you say?" he asked. He realized a second too late that he should probably say something about the stupid and dumbhead and idiot, but what they were talking about seemed more important than shutting them down over word choices.

He wondered if their grandmother would agree, given what the issue was. If Beatrice Shaw were in the car with them right now, would she chastise them for their language? Or would she be more focused on what had upset Willow?

Especially because it involved their mother. Beatrice's daughter.

Willow was still staring at her lap. "I said we *do* have a mother. But that she died."

Violet bit her lip. "And I said that our mom is in heaven. And that means she's always with us."

"You know what that dumbhead stupid idiot said?" Willow asked, scrunching up her face in anger. She met his eyes in the rearview mirror. She was on the verge of crying.

"Hang on a sec," Shane said, pulling over. He set the car

in Park and turned around to face his daughters. "What did he say?"

Tears filled Willow's eyes. "He said that our mom is *not* with us because she's *dead*."

Violet's eyes filled too, her face crumpling. "And he said that dead people aren't walking around or making pancakes or doing anything."

"And that's when I threw my cupcake at him," Willow said.

Shane got out of the car and opened the rear door. Both girls hopped out. He knelt down and they came in for a hug. "Your mom *is* always with you. She is." He pulled back a bit and touched his hand to the region of his heart. "She's in here. For me and for you two. Always."

"I knew Dylan wasn't right," Willow said, her face brightening.

"He's never right," Violet added.

"You know, you wouldn't have gotten in trouble if you'd just told him that. When you get mad, use your words. Your voices. Next time, if you have something in your hand, like a cupcake with frosting, don't throw it at the person you're mad at. First of all, you won't get to eat it that way. Am I right?"

The girls both laughed.

"And no matter how mad you get at someone, throwing things at them is wrong," he added. "It's like hitting. Not allowed, okay? And neither is using bad words. You can tell someone they're wrong without calling them names. Understand?"

"Yes, Daddy," Willow whispered. "I'm sorry." Her sister echoed her words.

"I love you girls so much," he said. "And I have a surprise for you."

"We're not in trouble?" Violet asked, her sweet face brightening.

"You already got in trouble," he said. "You were booted from the birthday party. It's settled, as far as I'm concerned."

Both their narrow shoulders sagged with relief.

"Let's get back in the car and I'll tell you the surprise," he said.

They raced in and buckled up. He pulled back into traffic. "How would you like to take a road trip—with Ashley? And me, of course."

He knew the answer before he asked, of course.

"Yay!" Willow said.

"Yay!" Violet seconded, pumping her goody bag in the air.

"Where are we going, Daddy?" Willow asked.

"You know how I'm taking you to your grandparents tomorrow?" Shane asked, eyeing them in the rearview mirror. "It turns out that Ashley has to go to Jackson Hole too. So we're all going to drive together. It's a long trip. We'll leave in about a half hour and stay overnight at a hotel. But there are rules for the road trip."

"What rules?" Violet asked.

"I want you two to be kind and respectful to Ashley," he said. "By respectful, I mean that you shouldn't ask her questions that she might not feel comfortable answering."

"About her wedding?" Willow asked.

"Exactly," Shane said.

"What shouldn't we ask her?" Violet asked. "And what *can* we ask?"

"Well, you can ask her if she's okay. You guys were there at the wedding. You know what happened. That the wedding *didn't* happen after all. So it's fine to ask her how she is. But I don't think you should ask her questions about why he didn't show up. Stuff like that. She might not want to talk about it, okay?"

He got two solemn nods.

"Is Ashley very sad?" Willow asked.

"She's definitely sad," he admitted.

"We can draw her pictures to cheer her up," Willow said.

"And give her candy and a toy from our goody bags," Violet added, holding up the bright red gift bag.

"That's really nice," he said. "So when we get home, we'll pack for the trip. You'll be at your grandparents' house for five days, so double-check your suitcases that you have play clothes *and* dress-up clothes."

He'd do a final check before they left.

"And scrunchies," Willow said. "Nana doesn't like when our hair is in our faces."

"Or when we're loud," Violet added.

"Or chew with our mouths full."

"Or run hard in the house."

"Well, since you know all that, it'll be easier to remember not to do those things, right?"

"I never remember," Willow said.

Violet nodded. "Me either."

"It's *important* to remember," Shane said. "It means to think before you act. I know it's not easy—for adults *or* five-year-olds. But try, okay? Sometimes, even when something isn't important to you, it's still important to someone else, like your nana, so you do the thing for *them*."

"Okay, Daddy," they both said.

"You know what my favorite thing is about going to Nana and Pops's house?" Violet asked.

"What?" Shane said.

"They have so many pictures of Mommy. All over. They even have pictures of her when she was little."

"I love looking at those pictures," Willow said.

Shane's heart constricted in his chest.

Almost five years after losing Liza, looking at photos of her still wasn't easy. He figured it never would be. He'd loved her very much. They'd had a good marriage. There had been ups and downs, like everyone had. But they'd been solid. And happy.

And just like that, she was gone.

He wasn't about to lose the girls too. Not when he could do everything in his power to keep them. If that meant guiding Willow and Violet to be little ladies on the way to Jackson Hole so that they'd impress—or simply *not horrify*—their grandparents, so be it.

"You take good care of our girl," Ashley heard her father say to Shane as the last of the bags were stacked in the cargo area of Shane's SUV.

Oh, brother. She wasn't one of the horses or cows. She wasn't ranch equipment. Their foreman was simply giving her a ride because he needed her help. But she knew her father was comforted by the idea of his trusty foreman watching out for "our poor baby," which her aunt Kate had actually referred to her as earlier, so she let it be.

She *was* grateful she wasn't making this trip alone. Shane had his downside—butting into her business, getting know-it-all-y—but he *was* trustworthy, and she felt absolutely safe with him. And he came with two absolutely adorable bonuses. She loved that Violet and Willow were already buckled into their booster seats in the back, their faces full of excitement about the trip—because Ashley was unexpectedly coming along. Their sweet heroine worship of her always made her smile, but right now, it was a real balm to her busted-up heart.

And finally, after another round of hugs with her parents, aunts, uncles, cousins and grandparents, the SUV doors closed, the engine started—and they headed down the long drive.

Shane had mentioned he had to make a few quick calls since he hadn't planned on leaving for Jackson Hole today, but the grandparents had been thrilled to hear the girls would be arriving early and he'd been able to change his hotel reservations for the overnight stay.

The seven-hour road trip would be broken into two days of driving, giving Ashley a lot of time and space to think and process. They'd be on the road for a little over two hours today, arriving at the lodge Shane had booked in Bison Creek for a late dinner and maybe a swim in the heated pool before the twins' 8:30 p.m. bedtime. Then they'd hit the road again bright and early, stopping to see a couple of sights along the way, and arrive at the Shaws' home by late afternoon.

Then he'd drop her off at Harrington's.

Shane had planned everything, from the route to the timing to kid-friendly places to stop for breakfast and lunch tomorrow and a petting zoo just a half hour outside Jackson Hole. How she appreciated having him take the reins. To not have to do any of this brain work and research herself—figure out the route and where to stop, not to mention driving for hours by herself without knowing how things would go when she reached her destination. Having him as the driver didn't change that—she still didn't know how things would go when she arrived—but at least she didn't have to concentrate on driving while she worried about it. He'd also let her know he'd put the engagement ring in the safe in the ranch's office.

While she'd been packing, he'd texted the entire itinerary to her along with: I'll wait, of course, while you and Harrington talk. Shouldn't take long to tell him off and get your money back. Then we'll drive home.

She hadn't mentioned that she might not be returning home with Shane. That she and Harrington might want to *really* talk. See how things felt with the pressure of the wedding off the table… Which was why she now found herself thinking that she probably should have brought the ring with her. In case it was slipped back onto her left hand.

She hadn't mentioned that to anyone.

She could barely admit it to herself that she felt a stirring of hope.

"Are we there yet?" Willow asked in a very exaggerated whine.

Violet giggled.

Ashley turned around and grinned. "Um, we've got today and most of tomorrow to go."

"I was kidding!" Willow said, her big green eyes twinkling. "Daddy said we're not allowed to ask that."

"That's right," Shane said, smiling at his daughters in the rearview mirror. "Every parent's favorite rule of the road."

Now the girls were whispering. Something about candy?

"Ashley, since you might be sad," Violet said, "do you want something from our goody bags from the birthday party we went to?"

"Oooh, whatcha got?" Ashley asked. "And it's very nice of you two to be concerned about me and want to cheer me up with treats. Thank you."

The girls beamed at her.

"Three fun-size Snickers," Willow said.

"And four Dum-Dum lollipops," Violet added.

Ashley smiled. "I will definitely take a Snickers. Any cherry lollipops?"

She heard more whispering—loud whispering, which made her smile. "You give her a Snickers," Violet said. "And I'll give her a lollipop 'cause I have cherry."

Once she had her treats, the girls went from quiet to whispering again. She caught Shane glancing at them in the rearview mirror. With a *look*. Ah—she knew what that look was probably about. He'd instructed the girls not to ask her questions. She thought about telling them that they could ask her whatever they wanted. But then again, she'd probably take their earnest questions to heart and get all upset again.

Father knows best, she thought. *Let it go. Eat your Snickers.*

They played a round of I Spy. And I'm Thinking of a Number between One and Twenty. At Ashley's turn to think of a number, Willow guessed sixty and Violet ninety, since both girls could now count up to one hundred by tens, and they all laughed. Then the twins started singing the chorus from their favorite song, and Ashley joined in, which earned her serious bonus points since she knew the words. Then they asked Shane to put in their favorite kiddie mystery podcast.

Five minutes later, she turned around to ask them where they both thought the runaway dog in the podcast was hiding, and she was surprised to see Willow and Violet conked out, fast asleep.

"Wow, they're out cold," she whispered to Shane.

He smiled. "No need to whisper. They sleep through the blasted rooster every morning—unlike me—so you won't wake them by talking. It takes a lot of energy to be them. They nap easily and sleep hard at night."

"I wonder if *I'll* ever sleep again," she said, letting out a sigh. "My entire life is up in the air."

"In the air? What do you mean?"

"I *mean*… I can't really know what will happen when I get to Harrington's."

He glanced at her and she caught the confused look on his face. "You *know* what will happen. You'll hand him the bill for the wedding, he'll pay without hesitation because it's probably the equivalent of a weekend getaway to the Harrises, and we'll be on our way."

"Well, yes, I'm definitely going to ask for the money. But there's always the possibility that Harrington and I will decide to work things out."

A quick look at Shane revealed his face kind of scrunching up. He pulled over on the service road and put the SUV in Park.

"What are you doing?" she asked. "What's wrong?" She instinctively looked back at the twins, but they were as fast asleep as they'd been two minutes ago.

He dropped his hands off the wheel and slightly turned to face her. "You've got to be kidding me, Ashley. You *are* kidding me, right?"

What was he talking ab—

Oh.

The light bulb went off. He was talking about Harrington. About her saying that things might work out between them.

Clearly he hated Harrington. That much had been clear from the way he'd always pointed out the guy's every… imperfection. But she'd never given much weight to his opinion on that point before, and she wasn't about to start now. It was her relationship, so her feelings were what mattered.

"Shane, you don't go from about to marry someone to magically losing all your feelings for that person because they…" *Left you at the altar. Humiliated you—in front of your family and friends and people you never met, since the Harrises had invited a bunch of their own close friends.*

Said in a text that they realized they didn't love you.

She glanced down at her lap, her heart so heavy she might slump over.

"Right," he said. "But you don't hope to get back together with that person either."

She bit her lip, uncertainty *and* a flare of anger shooting up in her gut. Why was she talking to him about this?

"Oh?" she asked with as much sarcasm as she could get into the tiny word. "What do you do, then?"

"You deal with how bad it hurts. And day by day it'll get easier. Until one day, you'll realize you don't feel like you were drop-kicked into a herd of running cattle. You'll feel more like yourself."

Her gaze shot to his face. *Kind of specific there, Dawson.* It occurred to her that he might be talking about himself. How *he'd* dealt with heartbreak.

She certainly wasn't going to argue with him that he didn't understand that kind of pain. He'd lost his wife to a terrible car accident on a rainy night. The mother of his two baby girls. Violet and Willow had only been three months old. For five years he'd been raising them on his own. Yes, he had family close by—she'd met his kindly parents many times when they came to visit him and the twins. But on a day-to-day basis, he was alone with two little girls, all their lives changed in an instant. And he'd been grieving all that time. It couldn't have been easy.

"Let me ask you something," he said suddenly. "What did you—what do you—love about Harrington Harris?"

She felt herself bristle. "I could list fifty of his good traits. But loving someone is about much more than why they're a good person. It's about chemistry and how the person makes you feel, how you *feel* about them. It's about the inexplicable. And yes, the list of traits, of course."

"Let's hear the top ten traits of Harrington Harris IV," Shane said, starting up the engine and pulling back onto the road.

She shot him a glare. Yes, she was defensive. But rightly so. How dare he? She didn't have to justify herself to him.

To herself, maybe. But not to anyone else.

She cleared her throat. "On our first date, we were on our way to dinner when he saw a stray dog limp into the woods and asked if I'd mind if he went after it to bring it to a vet. It took us two hours to find the dog. Harrington carried him out, wrapped him in a blanket in his car, and we took him to the vet. Over a thousand bucks later, Harrington found a foster family for him until he could heal, and that family ended up adopting him and named him Woody."

Shane scowled. "Did you make that up?"

"The name? Of course not. They named him Woody after being rescued from the woods."

"No, I mean the entire story. Your ex-fiancé doesn't strike me as the type to give up the surf and turf and hundred-dollar bottle of wine to save an injured stray."

Ashley gaped at him. "You think I made it up? That I sat here and lied to your face?" Now she was indignant.

"Just doesn't seem like him."

"That's because *you* don't know him. You saw him around the ranch when he came to see me or pick me up or drop me off. You overheard bits and pieces of our private conversations and came to all kinds of unfair conclusions. Harrington is a good guy. Yeah, he can be impatient and a little self-absorbed sometimes. But no one is perfect."

He kept his eyes on the road. "I suppose not."

Ashley straightened up in her seat and looked out the window. She should steer the conversation to small talk. "Wow, we're only in Weaverton?" she asked, noting the sign for the town limits.

"We've been driving for twenty-five minutes," he said.

"Gonna be a long trip."

"Yeah," he agreed, still scowling. "No argument from me on *that*."

Now *she* was scowling.

Chapter Four

Shane had not said a word about Harrington Harris for the past hour and twenty minutes, though he'd been dying to. He'd wanted to *what-about* Ashley every five seconds.

What about when your fiancé didn't attend your father's sixtieth birthday party at the ranchers' association lodge because "something suddenly came up" and then you found out that the "something" was drinks with a friend he saw all the time?

What about when you'd been telling him how you didn't like when he answered for you, kept talking over you and interrupted you three times during dinner with his family, and his response was "Wow, I didn't realize you were so sensitive"?

What about when you mentioned you had a craving for fettuccine Alfredo at the Italian restaurant you were headed to on a date, and while getting into his Porsche, he'd said, "Um, Ashley, isn't that really fattening?" and then looked down at your hips and added, "You seem to take after your mother's side, and she and your aunts are all a little..."

Shane had overheard that gem while walking from the barn to where a truck had pulled up with a delivery. He'd given Harrington a death stare, but the brat hadn't even had the decency to look embarrassed. He'd just shrugged and given a *Well, it's true* look back, while Ashley stood stock-still, taking it in before exploding on Harris. She'd given him a piece of her mind and snapped that he could go to dinner alone, and Harrington had looked pained as if he couldn't fathom what he'd said wrong.

He doesn't deserve you, Shane had said for at least the tenth time since they'd started dating, staring Ashley right in the eyes before she'd told him to mind his own beeswax and then stomped off into the stables.

Now he glanced over at her in the passenger seat. They'd made small talk on and off, whether about the weather or Jackson Hole itself, but she'd mostly stayed quiet, looking out the window or playing Wordle and Spelling Bee games on her phone. She was a good speller. Another plus for helping the girls "be their best selves" for the grandparents.

"Ooh, is that our hotel?" Ashley asked, sitting up straight and pointing up ahead where the Bison Creek Lodge, with its steeply pitched green roof, came into view. As they got closer, he could see that two white cats were asleep on the padded swing hanging on the porch, and two small dogs— pugs or French bulldogs, he wasn't sure—were gnawing on rawhide bones on a little rug under the swing. There'd been nothing much on the freeway for the past thirty minutes, and then the white fencing of the lodge appeared, welcoming visitors up its long drive through gorgeous grounds that were both rustic and manicured at the same time. The lodge looked like a luxe log cabin.

"Are we here yet, Daddy?" Willow piped up from the back. Then both girls broke into giggles in the middle of yawns.

He hadn't realized they'd woken up. "I'll allow that since, yes, we are here!" Shane said as he parked in the gravel lot.

Ashley turned to smile at the girls, then got out of the SUV and glanced around. "What a gorgeous place."

The twins unbuckled and hopped out, rushing to Ashley's side. "Yay!" the girls said in unison.

As Shane loaded up the dolly with their bags, Violet and Willow kept up a nonstop commentary on everything they saw and everything they thought. Ashley seemed charmed by them and answered all their questions.

"Let's head in," Shane said, pulling the dolly. "We'll have dinner and see what's fun to do after for a bit before your bedtime."

"But we just woke up," Willow pointed out. On a yawn.

"I have a feeling you two will be zonked by eight thirty," he said.

Ashley held open the door and they went inside the lodge's inviting lobby. Shane checked in, surprised to learn their rooms were connected by an adjoining door. The girls would definitely like that; Ashley might not. Violet and Willow were entertaining and kept you on your toes—but they weren't great to have around when you wanted some peace and quiet.

A smiling porter took the dolly and led the way through a set of hunter green French doors down a hallway. Rooms 106 and 108 were on the first level. The porter opened both doors and pulled in the dolly, and after Shane tipped him, he left. Ashley went into her room and knocked on the adjoining door, which Shane opened.

The girls popped their heads into Ashley's room, swiveling their heads to note the differences between hers and theirs.

"I love both rooms," Willow said.

Ashley said that she did too. They were painted a pale terra-cotta with framed prints of Wyoming landscapes on the walls. Ashley's room held a double bed, and Shane's had a double and two cots, all with fluffy-looking blankets and pillows. Each room also had a small love seat, a desk and a round table and two chairs by the gated patio.

"Me too!" Violet said. She zipped back and forth.

"I have a fun idea," Ashley said to the twins. "Why don't you two bunk with me tonight? It'll be a girls' night."

The twins actually jumped up and down and clapped. "Can we, Daddy?"

"Sure can," he said. Huh. Guess she hadn't had enough of them yet. Then again, they had been asleep most of the ride here. As the twins ran into Ashley's room to explore every nook and cranny, he whispered, "You sure about your little guests?"

She nodded. "Very. I adore the twins. You know that. And I can start assessing what lessons they might need," she added on a whisper. "So far, I don't see any behavior that warrants actual correcting. Nothing an eagle-eyed grandparent could get upset about."

For a moment there, he'd blissfully forgotten about the Shaws. But they were the reason he'd struck the deal with Ashley, and he sorely needed her help. "The Shaws get upset about everything, though. Even overexcitement bothers them. The way they shrieked when you invited them to share your room? That's a no-go with Nana and Pops."

"Anyone who lets himself be called Pops surely has a warm side," she said. She'd met the Shaws in the harrowing days after Liza's death, but just in passing on the ranch grounds, really.

"True. He's much easier than Nana." He glanced at the alarm clock on the bedside table. "Let's figure out dinner.

Then maybe they can hit the pool for a half hour. You'll be able to do some serious assessing, trust me."

"Sounds like a plan," she said with a smile and went into the adjoining room, then came inside. "So we'll just switch rooms."

He took his bags into the other room. As the doors between the rooms shut, her very simple statement struck him. He was so used to taking care of everything on his own—from managing the McCray Ranch as foreman to the day-to-day of raising his daughters. It was nice to have someone else make a phone call and get something done.

The front desk attendant had mentioned the lodge's restaurant was open till nine and room service was available. He grabbed the menu and looked through it. All he needed to see was that there was a kiddie section. Sold.

He knocked on the adjoining door. Ashley opened it—and he was rendered speechless for a moment.

Maybe because she was *right there*. Just inches away. But he was also suddenly struck by how pretty she was. He was always vaguely aware of her beauty; it would be impossible not to notice. Ashley McCray was tall and strong, with long silky light brown hair shot with gold and hazel eyes with gold flecks like a cat's. She had fine, delicate features and a sexy small mole beside her lip.

Jeez. She offered to do one thing to make his life easier and all of a sudden he was noticing her mole? Her catlike eyes? How long and lean and full-breasted she was?

He glanced down fast at the menu. "Uh, I thought we'd order room service. Decent menu. I'm thinking of the mushroom burger and steak fries."

"Ooh, can I have some of your steak fries, Daddy?" Willow asked, rushing over to see the menu.

"Me too!" Violet said, catching up with her sister. "And can I have chicken tenders?" She turned to Willow. "If you get the mac and cheese, we can share."

"I want the mac and cheese, Daddy," Willow said.

Big surprise. "Done and done. And yes, I'll share my fries."

He handed Ashley the menu.

"What are you getting, Ashley?" Willow asked. "Do you like burgers?"

"Do you like pizza?"

"Do you like ham-and-cheese sandwiches?"

"Do you like chocolate ice cream?"

Shane gave Ashley his best *I told you so* look. Then remembered she was too familiar with that look of his as it pertained to *her*. "Anything look good?"

"The whole menu's great," she said. "And yes to all your questions, girls. I like just about everything."

Willow scrunched up her nose. "Even broccoli?"

"Love it. Roasted with a little drizzled butter and salt—heavenly."

The girls made faces at each other.

"Hey, girls," Ashley said. "Do you know that princesses across the world have a special princess rule?"

They stopped moving and talking and stared at her with wide eyes. "What rule?" they asked in unison.

"Well, princesses must represent their kingdoms. That means when they're around other people, no matter who, they have to act a certain nice and polite way. Otherwise, people might say, 'Oh, the princess is messy or noisy or rude, so I guess everyone from her kingdom is like that.'"

Willow tilted her head. "So how do they have to act?"

"Well, you know how I said I love broccoli? Especially

with drizzled butter and salt? And you two looked at each other as if I were from another planet?"

They both nodded.

"Royal princesses would want to be nice and respect what other people like or dislike. So they would simply smile. Or maybe they'd say, 'Isn't that interesting!'"

Willow and Violet turned to each other. "Let's practice it!" Willow said. "I like string beans, but not when they're mushy."

Violet started to giggle, then cleared her throat and smiled. "Isn't that interesting!"

Shane burst out laughing. "Perfect."

"Yup," Ashley said. "You've got it, girls. And speaking of vegetables, I'm going to order the pasta primavera. It has a delicious cream sauce and spring vegetables."

"Isn't that interesting!" Violet said with a big smile.

Shane shook his head on a grin. "I'll call the front desk to order. Why don't you two wash your hands?"

Ashley nodded and slung an arm around the twins. "Come with me, girls. Oh, and I'll have you loving broccoli before the night is over."

"Do you think Ashley has magic powers?" Willow whispered to Violet as they zipped into their room.

"I think so," Violet whispered back.

Shane smiled, catching Ashley's gaze before she headed into her room behind his daughters. She sure seemed to—when it came to the Dawson twins.

So far, so good. Ashley knew exactly how to impart etiquette lessons to the girls in a fun way they could understand and enjoy. And he and Ashley seemed to be back on good footing again. Friends. Or maybe just temporary partners.

Or something.

* * *

It was the Dawson twins who had the magic powers—to make Ashley forget, to get her mind off herself and everything that had happened today. They were so charming and comical and sweet and, yes, whirlwinds, they didn't leave a lot of room for her to brood or sulk…or even be annoyed at their father.

As if she'd make up the story about Harrington dropping everything to rescue Woody the stray dog. As if she'd fall for someone who didn't have a heart. *Marry* someone without a heart.

How dare Shane Dawson?

She sighed as she remembered that she *hadn't* actually married Harrington Harris. Because he hadn't shown up for the wedding.

Great. Just great. A minute ago, she'd been laughing at something Willow said. Now she was pushing pasta primavera around her plate with her fork, her appetite waning. All she could think about at this moment was sitting at the vanity in the bride's tent earlier today, staring at herself in the mirror, at her beautiful veil that was now crumpled in a ball up in the stables loft. The slow, then very fast realization that her fiancé wasn't coming to the wedding.

"I only like the broccoli a little bit," Willow said, her mouth full of the bite of pasta primavera she'd agreed to try. "Even with the good sauce. Is that okay to say?"

Ashley turned her attention to the little girl sitting beside her at the round table by the sliding glass doors to the balcony of the room. She and the Dawsons were just about finished with their room service meals. Willow's twin was staring at her too, waiting for her verdict. Even Shane had paused with his fork midway to his mouth, awaiting her response.

"Willow, I'm really proud of you for trying it," Ashley said. "Do you want to know something?"

"Yes, I do!" Willow said.

I do. I do. I do...

Violet leaned forward, as did her sister.

Even Shane leaned forward a bit, Ashley noticed.

"Every time you take a bite of food," Ashley said, "there's a special thing you have to do. You have to chew with your mouth closed."

"Daddy tells us that all the time," Violet said—her mouth full of a steak fry. "But how will we talk and eat at the same time?"

Ashley glanced at Shane with a smile. "*That's* the special thing. You can't. You can only open your mouth to talk after you swallow! It's a good rule. Want to know why?"

The girls leaned forward again.

"Let's say I took a big bite of my pasta and then kept talking while I chewed. You'd have to watch my dinner jumble around in my mouth. Yuckeroo, am I right?"

Willow seemed to think about that, and then her face fell. "That dumbhead stupid idiot Dylan talks with his mouth full."

Violet nodded at her sister. "He's the dumbest stupid-head."

"If he is," Ashley said, "you definitely don't want to do something he does, right?"

Both girls brightened.

"I'm only going to talk when my mouth is empty from now on!" Willow said.

"Me too," Violet seconded.

"Good." Ashley forked a big bite of her dinner. Chewed. Didn't say a word. Swallowed. "See, easy!"

"I want to try!" Willow said.

The Dawson twins spent the next few minutes chewing with their mouths firmly closed.

Ashley glanced at Shane, who was watching with something of a mystified look on his face, like he'd just seen a unicorn and couldn't quite believe his eyes. "So, girls, tell me. Why don't you like this Dylan? It must be bad, because you've called him some pretty harsh names."

"Oh, he totally deserves it!" Violet said.

"He does. He made me throw my cupcake at him at the party today. And we got sent home early."

Ashley glanced at Shane. She hadn't heard about this.

"Well, girls, we had a good talk about that," Shane said quickly. "Want to check out the pool?"

Their eyes lit up, whatever led to Dylan getting reamed by a cupcake forgotten.

Interesting that Shane didn't want to rehash it. She wondered what that was about.

"Come on, Dawson girls," Ashley said. "Let's go change into swimsuits."

The girls scrambled out of their chairs and ran for their room.

She probably should call them back and teach them to push in their chairs and walk nicely to their room. But why shouldn't they run? Why shouldn't they express their excitement?

She'd have to talk to Shane about that, about instilling manners and a little grandmother-approved etiquette without squashing their personalities and typical five-year-old behavior. There had to be a balance for teaching good manners without constantly addressing their behavior and correcting, to the point where the girls were afraid to be themselves.

This might be a little harder than she'd thought.

The next hour was a lot of fun. The four of them found the indoor pool and had a great time slipping into the heated water. They all stayed in the shallow end, the twins dunking underwater, Shane tossing each girl up and catching her, Ashley throwing plastic rings for them to find at the bottom of the pool.

And because they were in the shallow end, she couldn't help but notice Shane Dawson's body, the top half mostly. Broad shoulders. Muscled chest and arms. Quite a few times she found herself staring and had to drag her eyes off his physique. She was used to seeing him in his Western-style button-downs and jeans or a heavy jacket all winter.

Now he was practically naked.

It was a good thing she barely liked the man or she might actually consider him...attractive. It wasn't as if she could miss that hard chest with defined abs and fine dark hair traveling along his abs and disappearing under the waistband of his swim trunks.

Or his face. Which was quite handsome.

Luckily, just then, Willow came splashing up triumphantly with her red ring Ashley had thrown for her. Attention diverted.

Once it neared the twins' bedtime, they all got out of the pool, all smiles, grabbed their towels and headed back to the rooms. Aww, she figured they didn't ask to stay in the pool longer because they were excited to bunk with her. Shane said he'd take care of bedtime, but Ashley wanted to try it, not that she knew what it was or involved besides tucking them in. She'd never been a babysitter growing up.

"The girls will fill you in on the routine," he told Ashley as he stood in the adjoining doorway between their rooms. "Right, you two? No skipsies."

Ashley laughed. "Like toothbrushing?"

"Exactly," he said.

A half hour later, after Ashley had had a quick shower, the girls had their baths, got changed into their jammies, which were T-shirts and sweat shorts, and Ashley was combing their pretty honey-brown hair, which fell all one length past their shoulders. Had she ever combed anyone's hair other than the horses?

"It's nice to have you comb our hair," Willow said, glancing shyly at Ashley as she slid the comb through her sister's locks.

Violet nodded. "Daddy always brushes our hair after baths and in the mornings before school, but it's nice to have you do it."

Aww. Her heart melted. Ashley could still recall her mother combing her hair, braiding it, gathering it into endless ponytails—but these girls had been motherless since they were babies.

"I like doing it," she found herself whispering back, so touched by these two. "All righty," she added. "How about you hop under the covers?"

They slid into their side-by-side cots across the room from Ashley's bed. Ashley had given them a choice of being read to or hearing a made-up story, and they picked the made-up story. She barely got two minutes into a tale of a horse named Helena when she realized both girls were asleep, an arm curled around their "lovies," a fabric doll for Violet and a squishy stuffed horse for Willow.

She knocked on the adjoining door.

"Come on in," Shane called out.

She opened the door and almost gasped. Shane was sitting on the love seat in worn jeans and a black T-shirt, his hair damp from his own shower.

What was this reaction to him?

He's a good-looking guy—that's all, she told herself. Anyone would find him physically appealing.

"The twins fell asleep on line three of my story," she said on a bit of a stammer, trying not to stare. "You didn't get to say good-night."

"They're so active, I'm used to them falling asleep sometimes as I turn around to grab a book. I'll go give them good-night kisses," he added, standing. His presence was suddenly so...overwhelming. Shane was tall, six foot two, she'd guess, with those broad shoulders.

She moved over by the door to give him some privacy with his daughters. She watched as he bent down to kiss each twin on the forehead and whisper, "I love you. Sweet dreams, my precious girl."

Aww. He was such a loving, doting dad. She'd known that, of course; she'd been watching him interact with his daughters for five years. But up close and personal like this, the love and reverence in his voice, was something else.

"Let's go into my room," he said, leading the way and leaving the door just slightly ajar. "I can make us coffee or tea." He gestured to the single-brew coffee maker and the offerings beside it.

"Perfect." It had been one hell of a day, and though she should opt for caffeine-free, it wasn't like she'd get to sleep for hours anyway. "I'd love the tea—caffeinated."

He brewed two foam cups, one after another, and brought over the nondairy creamer and sugars. They sat side by side on the small two-person love seat, their drinks in front of them on the little square table.

Ashley wrapped her hands around the hot cup, letting the steam soothe her before taking a sip. She felt her mind wander to the canceled wedding. And where she'd expected to go afterward. "I was supposed to be in a much different hotel room right now. Drinking champagne. With a different man." She felt her cheeks flush. "Not that we're together. I mean…" She sighed. "I should stop talking." She hadn't meant to say any of that.

"Hey, it's okay. Your whole life turned upside down today."

She sipped her tea and peered at him. She liked when he was understanding and supportive. Yes, this Shane could stick around.

"You were going to Italy for the honeymoon?" he asked.

She nodded. "Starting off in Rome, near the Trevi Fountain. Then Florence, then Venice. Then day trips. For a few seconds while I was up in the loft in the stables, I actually thought about going on the trip solo. But I'd be miserable. And lonely."

"How *are* you doing?" he asked, holding her gaze.

She gave a small shrug. She'd been so occupied the past hour that she hadn't been focused on the fact that she'd been left at the altar. She remembered the whole sequence of events, starting with one of her bridesmaids whispering in her ear that she'd heard from the groom's tent that Harrington hadn't arrived yet, to the resultant confusion, the worry that something had happened to him en route. Then the slow, sickening realization that he was a half hour late. And finally, the text message that said he wasn't coming.

"Not great," she said. She hadn't known it was possible

to feel such visceral pain and numbness at the same time. "One minute I feel like crying and the next I feel like maybe I dodged a bullet. I guess you think I did."

He turned slightly to face her. They were so close on the small love seat. "What matters is that you feel like hell, and there's no way around that except to let yourself feel every feeling—even when *what* you feel is confusing and in conflict. You'll go up and down for a while, Ashley."

She sighed. "I just… I don't…" She leaned her head back against the cushion. There was always the possibility that she and Harrington would work things out…

Was that what she wanted? Half of her said *yes*. Half of her said *no way. That jerk can go jump in a crocodile-infested lake.*

She just knew she was confused.

And hurt.

She bit her lip. "It's why I'm glad I've got those two funny little roommates. They cheer me up, take my mind off myself."

He reached over and took her hand, the warmth, the contact, the gentle squeeze so comforting that a burst of sadness welled up from deep inside and she almost burst into tears.

Instead, she leaned her head on his shoulder and closed her eyes. She felt him stiffen for a moment, and she almost sat up straight, but he slung his right arm around her, the heavy weight of it feeling so good. She was in such need and this time she couldn't stop the tears.

"Let it out," he whispered.

And so she sat there with her head on his shoulder and cried.

Chapter Five

Shane sat stock-still on the love seat, Ashley still leaning her head on his shoulder, though her tears seemed to have stopped.

He wasn't used to comforting a woman.

The last time a woman had cried in his presence was his wife. The twins had caught some very ordinary infant virus and she'd been scared, as he'd been. They'd hovered over the bassinets, slept in the nursery to check on the babies every half hour, terribly worried new parents, weighed down with responsibility for two precious lives with big fevers.

That was five years ago. Except for two cowgirls at the McCray Ranch, and Ashley, of course, he hadn't spent much time around women. He certainly hadn't dated, much to his mother's disappointment the past year. *It's probably time you got yourself out there again*, she'd say gently. *Something to think about anyway*, she'd add with a hand on his shoulder.

He still didn't feel ready, though. He'd loved his wife. He'd loved their lives, the excitement of welcoming twins, of being new parents. And then slam. Gone in an instant. No goodbyes. One second Liza was there, the next she wasn't.

He'd been laser focused on his baby daughters. On doing right by them. He wasn't a mother, would never be, but he'd come to realize he didn't have to be. That he was their father and he'd be a damned good one. He had great support in his family, and he wasn't alone and didn't feel alone.

Even if the Shaws' threats sent chills up his spine.

His girls and his job—that was what he focused on. If he thought about sex, it was about missing his wife and their *ahhhs* when the twins finally went to bed. He didn't look at women in the grocery store aisles or around town and have a thought in his head about them.

He didn't know if he'd ever be ready to be with someone else.

Even if, like his mother had said, five years was a long time to be alone.

He wasn't alone.

He certainly wasn't right now. With Ashley sitting so close. Her head a gentle weight on his shoulder. He could smell her shampoo, a clean, coconut scent. And he was extremely aware of her in a way he'd never been before.

That he wasn't comfortable with. Neither of them was in the market for romance, particularly with *each other*.

He could use some air.

"Want anything from the vending machine in the lobby?" he asked. He was itching to stand up, to move, to extricate himself from Ashley's nearness, but of course he wouldn't. He'd sit here, be a support, until she was ready to move herself.

She lifted her head suddenly. "I wouldn't mind a candy bar. Snickers. And Cheez-Its."

Phew. He looked at her and smiled. "Back in a jiff. If you're okay."

"I'm okay," she said in a small voice that went straight to his heart.

Ashley was hurting, and that was all he needed to know, needed to respond to.

They could both use a five-minute interlude so he could remind himself of that, he thought as he stepped in the hallway, the door shutting behind him.

Unexpectedly intense, he thought, trying to emotionally distance himself from whatever was going on with him—where Ashley was concerned. Trying and failing because he couldn't get her face out of his mind.

A few minutes later, just being out of the room, the simple act of pressing in the buttons for the snacks and watching them fall with a tiny thud, had him feeling better. Holding her Snickers and cheese crackers and a bag of white cheddar popcorn for himself, he headed back to the room. His phone vibrated in his back pocket, and he stopped to fish it out, balancing the snacks against his midsection.

His boss. Or in this case, Ashley's dad. He had a feeling Anthony McCray was calling strictly as a father, not a rancher.

"Hi, Anthony," Shane said, stepping out an exit door to the side of the lodge. The cool April air felt good on his face, in his hair—in his lungs.

"How's my girl?" Anthony asked. "Give it to me straight. I just called her and she said she's okay, that the twins are cheering her up, that she went swimming and had excellent pasta, and something about a Snickers?"

He smiled and looked at the bounty of treats he was clutching. "I just hit up the vending machine. Snickers and Cheez-Its. I'll be honest, Anthony. She's hurting and confused. But that makes sense, given what happened."

"I could kill that coward," Anthony said, the pain in his voice, the worry for his daughter, evident. "I'm not so sure she should be going to see him at all. I don't care about the money. I never did."

I'm not so sure either.

"Just rest assured that Ashley's in good hands with us, Anthony. Remember that trips are often about the journey instead of the destination. The drive is letting her get away, to have some time to really think and process. And to have fun company in my daughters, who are keeping her very busy. And then there's me to keep her head on straight." He paused. "Not that I have any right to tell her what to do or think, but, well, you know what I mean."

"I do. And I'm grateful. You have my complete trust, Shane. Ingrid and I take a lot of comfort knowing she's with you and the twins. You'll call me if I need to know anything?" Anthony said hesitantly. "I know she's a very capable grown woman, but if she needs us, we're there, okay?"

"Absolutely," he said.

With that, they disconnected and Shane headed back inside the lodge. He let himself into his room to find Ashley standing in front of the sliding glass doors to the patio, arms wrapped around herself, staring out at the darkness. The moon was almost full, lots of stars visible. He wondered if she was wishing on one. Wishing that when she finally arrived at the Harris family summer mansion, she and her ex would get back together.

He mentally shook his head at himself and told himself to stop judging. She loved Harrington, clearly. To the point that she'd been about to marry him. And like Ashley had said herself, those feelings didn't go away just because the person did.

He knew that from firsthand experience.

But like he'd told her dad, some time away to really think

or just *feel* would do her good. Maybe by the time they arrived in Jackson Hole, she'd want to punch Harrington in the stomach just like he and her parents did.

"I come bearing snacks," he said as he stepped farther into the room. He set everything down on the square table in front of the love seat.

Ashley turned around. "Just what I need. I'll get us water from the mini fridge. Or maybe a mini bottle of wine. There's red and white."

"I'll split the white with you," he said.

She smiled and got the waters and the little bottle of wine, pouring half into two foam cups. "Classy with a *K*," she said, holding up her cup.

He held up his, wondering what she'd toast to.

"You do the honors," she said. "I'm plumb out of anything wise to say."

"To figuring it out," he offered.

She took a breath and slowly nodded. "Yeah. To figuring it out. That's what life is all about."

"Right," he said, taking a sip of the pretty bad wine.

She did too, then sat down and grabbed the Snickers. "So what's this about Willow hurling a cupcake at someone at the party?"

He felt himself stiffen, his thoughts jumbled. He took his time sitting down beside her, spending a bit too much time opening his white cheddar popcorn. Talking about this would mean talking about Liza, and he didn't want to. The subject of the girls not having a mother kept him up at night as it was. Mostly because he couldn't see himself ever dating. And no dating meant no stepmother. He didn't want to talk about any of it. He had enough going on right now to stop him from sleeping.

"Want some?" he asked, holding the little bag toward her.

"Nah, but thanks. I'd offer you some of my Snickers but I ate the entire thing already."

He smiled, then felt it fade as he recalled Allison calling him, relaying the incident. His fierce little girls, trying to protect their own hearts at age five, even if they went about it the wrong way.

He sighed inwardly, suddenly unsure if he himself was going about anything right. How he parented. How he handled the loss of their mom and kept her memory alive for Willow and Violet. "Dylan, who you heard all about," he blurted, "said it was weird that they don't have a mother. And when they told him it wasn't weird and that she was in their hearts, he said she wasn't because she was *dead*."

Now, why had he come out with that? He could have deflected. Could have changed the subject to their route for the morning's drive and the sites he wanted to stop at that he thought the girls would enjoy. Instead, he'd answered her question.

Because you want to know what she thinks, he realized.

Ashley's mouth dropped open. "Stupid dumbhead idiot."

"Right?" he said with as much of a smile as he could muster, which wasn't much of one, though he liked that she was on the twins' side.

"If there's a positive to the comments and questions they'll get about their mother, it's that it's out in the open, that the girls are thinking about how they feel—and dealing with it."

"That's a good point," he said. "I instantly go into protection mode, but they really can't be protected from the truth. Their mom *is* gone."

"And now their grandparents want to take away their dad?" she said, anger in her voice. "What is that all about?"

"When it comes right down to it, that's what they'd be doing, so it's how I know they're not thinking clearly or about what's best for the girls. That's it not really about Violet and Willow at all. We're coming up on the five-year anniversary of Liza's death. The grief that never goes away is at work here."

She turned to face him more fully, curling her legs behind her. "What do you mean?"

"The Shaws are hurting. The loss has settled in their bones, as it has mine, as a terrible fact. So with the anniversary coming up, I think they want to see more of Liza in the girls. More of themselves too. But when they look at them, all they see is me. And ranch life."

Ashley stared at him, seeming to take that all in.

"The Shaws always felt like they lost their daughter to a different world and way of life," he continued. "They liked that she became a teacher, but not that she lived on her salary and within her own means. They wanted her to live in a fancy condo, and instead she paid rent for a one-bedroom above the bakery on Main Street. And when she married me instead of…" He paused, realizing what he'd been about to say.

"Instead of someone like Harrington," she finished for him.

He nodded. "They couldn't understand it. I once overheard them ask her, 'But, sweetheart, what is Shane bringing to the table?'"

He shook his head, remembering the anger mixed with shame he'd felt in that moment over what he couldn't give the woman he loved. Liza's parents were both old-money rich. *His* parents would survive on their paychecks from his mother's job as a hairstylist and his father's as a farm machine mechanic. The Dawsons still lived in the small house they'd raised him in. Besides the retirement plan he'd set up for them, Shane had long started a savings account called Mom and Dad, and whenever he collected enough, with a little help from solid investments, he'd hire a contractor to build them a porch or he'd send them on vacation to Disney World or wherever they wanted to go. Liza's parents had five homes. Two in Wyoming. They spent most of their time at the "summer" home in Jackson Hole because their son, who had toddler twins of his own plus a new baby, lived there, and they felt wanted and needed and helpful in a way they hadn't felt the first year after Liza died and they'd lived primarily in Bear Ridge.

He realized that Ashley was staring at him, her head tilted a bit, waiting for him to finish his story. "Sorry," he said. "Got caught up in memories."

She reached for his hand and gave it a soft squeeze, the small gesture a comfort but that damned awareness of her anything but.

Get Ashley McCray out of your head, he ordered himself. *Stop noticing her. Stop thinking about her. Stop.*

He turned away slightly, slipping back into the memory of overhearing the Shaws ask Liza what he brought to the table. "I remember holding my breath, wondering what she'd say. This was just a day after we'd gotten engaged. We'd driven to Jackson Hole to tell them the news in person, and they were pleasant enough to me, but that night, when I'd left the room, I heard them ask her that question."

"What did she say back?" Ashley asked.

"She said, 'He makes me really happy.' And her mom said, 'Oh, honey, a puppy could make you happy too. A husband needs to bring a future.'"

"Oh, God," Ashley said.

He nodded. "Liza ripped into them." He smiled at that memory. "She said that love was everything. That moving to the McCray foreman's cabin, with the chickens and ducks hanging out in the front yard, and raising the family she was excited to start there had her heart bursting with absolute joy."

"Aww," Ashley said.

"Her dad said, 'Well, at least Finnigan likes the good life. That'll dictate his choices.'" He shook his head again on a laugh. "That's Liza's brother. He's a good guy, and he and his wife FaceTime with the twins every week, but he lives in a different world. Their parents' world. Which is fine."

"So the Shaws want the girls to be the Liza they lost when she married you," Ashley said. "But it sounds like she was always her own girl, own woman, own person."

He nodded. "That's why I think it's about their grief. They want the twins to be a reflection of the daughter they expected, even if she turned out to be a rebel." He smiled again. "They think the twins are all me, but they're a lot like Liza. Clearly."

"I'll do whatever I can to help," Ashley said. "If the twins have to learn to be little ladies to get through visits with their grandparents, we can make that happen."

This time it was he who reached for her hand and gave it a squeeze, but he didn't let it go. He stared at her hand in his. "Thank you. I do need help, Ashley."

And then suddenly they were just looking at each other. That damned awareness of her, how pretty she was, how sexy, how much he did need her help, was at the forefront. There was something different in her hazel eyes. The past year she usually looked at him with wariness, as if she expected him to hurl a truth at her that she didn't want to hear. But now there was something softer in her gaze.

She bolted up. "Well, I'd better turn in. This has been some day."

Relief mixed with disappointment. He could sit here all night and talk to her. But he needed the space, and it was obvious she did too.

"It has," he agreed, standing too. "Good night, Ashley."

"Night," she said, moving toward the adjoining door.

"Oh," he called, "expect to be woken up around six a.m. The girls' eyes pop open and they're raring to go."

She turned and smiled. "Good. Last thing I need is to lie in bed and think."

Same, he thought. *About you too now, apparently.*

She hurried into her room.

Leaving him with that damned awareness that didn't let up even with a door between them.

The girls did wake up at 6:00 a.m., and since Ashley had slept fitfully, she was both raring to go herself that early and zonked. But as she'd told Shane last night, she certainly didn't want to lie around in bed thinking about anything. Including the undeniable fact that she was attracted to Shane. After she'd left his room, she'd slipped into bed, expecting the day to come crashing down on her. The canceled wedding. The crying. The mission to get her money—and maybe her ex-fiancé—back.

But she'd found herself flipping from her back to her stomach to her side, thinking about Shane and all she'd learned about him. She and Shane had never been what anyone would call friends; they were simply acquaintances at the ranch who rarely spoke or interacted since there had been little need. As the horse groomer and de facto stable manager, though that part really fell under Shane's job, she'd leave notes tacked up for him on the stable bulletin board or she'd email him with anything the grooming department needed or she wanted special ordered. He was the busy foreman with two young daughters. She was the engaged daughter of the ranch owners, and they'd all kept their relationship more professional than overly friendly. That hadn't stopped him from butting in, of course.

He doesn't deserve you...

And now that she had a little more context for Shane, a deeper understanding of him, he seemed less like a buttinsky and more like...someone who cared.

She thought about everything his wife had given up to live in Shane's world, choosing to live on a teacher's and foreman's salaries—in a two-bedroom cabin on a medium-sized ranch that was having financial difficulty. But look at what she'd had. Shane as her husband. Two precious baby daughters. A career she'd loved. A lifestyle that suited her soul.

Ashley tried to think of Harrington giving up his Porsche for a pickup. He had a pickup, of course, but a souped-up one that had cost more than Ashley earned in two years.

Very briefly last night, when she'd been tossing and turning, she'd found herself wondering what it would have been like if Shane had moved just a few inches over on the love seat and turned to face her. Putting them in kissing distance.

Oh, snap out of it, she told herself. *You're not really attracted to Shane. He's just...a very big comfort to you right now. He's the one here for you. Offering his shoulder. Literally.*

He got you treats. He listens. He...really does seem to care.

Now Ashley sent a shy glance his way. They were sitting on a bench in the lodge's backyard with their take-out coffees from the restaurant, where they and the twins had gone for breakfast. It was almost 7:00 a.m. and they'd be hitting the road soon, but at the moment they were enjoying the April sunshine and watching the girls run around in the playground. There were two other families out there, both with children around the twins' age, and they were all playing nicely together. No "dumbhead stupid idiots" being thrown about—or cupcakes. Violet was coming down the curving slide, and Willow was climbing up the ladder for her third turn.

"I imparted a couple of lessons in the morning routine," she said, then took a sip of her hazelnut coffee. "Little things like making sure they—and by 'they' I mean Willow—put the cap back on the toothpaste. Taking a moment to brush their hair—they both had serious bedhead."

When the girls had burst into his room, ready for the restaurant, he'd said, "I like your ponytail, Willow. And the way your hair is tucked behind your ears, Violet." The girls had given him big smiles. She'd liked that he hadn't said, "Oh, how pretty you look," or, "How elegant." He kept the focus of his compliment where it should be.

"They hate brushing their hair on the weekends or vacations," Shane said, sipping his own coffee. "They didn't give you a hard time like they do me?"

She smiled. "Nope. But I'm a novelty."

"I loved when Willow told Violet she was talking with her mouth full in the restaurant," Shane said. "They might not remember all the time, but for her to bring it up means they're thinking about it. At least Willow is."

Ashley smiled. "And I loved Violet's 'Oh, right! I forgot.'"

Ashley had asked the girls how they liked the breakfast, which came from the buffet, and when they didn't ask her in return, she reminded them that it was nice to ask others about themselves and show curiosity and interest. Between the hair and the corrections, that had felt like enough instruction for an hour-long period after waking up.

"At least out here, on the playground, they can be as loud and wild as they want," Ashley said, just in time to hear an earsplitting shriek from Violet as two slightly older girls pushed her and Willow on the tire swing, the twins belly-over, arms dangling down. They were laughing and playing very well with others, and they could shriek all they wanted.

Shane let out a sigh. "The Shaws have a play set in their backyard. When I've dropped them off in the past and the girls have played out there, Nana and Pops were constantly shushing them and telling them, 'Not so fast, not so loud.'"

Ashley took that in. She thought it seemed ridiculous to expect little girls to be quiet when they were outside on a play set. There was a reason people used the expression "indoor" and "outdoor" voices. Outdoors was where it was supposed to be okay to be loud. But Shaws' house, Shaws' rules. That was the way of the world. "I'll talk to them about that as we get much closer to Jackson Hole, about being considerate of their hosts, even if it's hard to remember to use their indoor voices outdoors," she added with a grin.

"This is a big relief," he said. "Having a partner on this. And someone the twins want to please. Not that they don't want to please me or their grandparents, but hearing the little corrections and advice from you adds a special quality that hearing it from Nana and Pops and their boring old dad can't compete with."

"You're definitely not boring," she blurted out. She felt her cheeks flush.

"I'm not bored, that's for sure. No time for that. Plus, those two," he said, pointing at the twins on the tire swing, "make that impossible. Every minute they're awake is an adventure."

She turned to smile at him, touched at how reverent a father he was, how devoted. "I'll bet. And a grand adventure." She felt her smile fade as she looked at the woman sitting on a nearby bench holding a baby in fleece pj's. The young mother lifted up the baby and said, "See Daddy pushing your big brother on the swing? Upsie-daisy," she added, bringing the baby down and then back up.

Ashley bit her lip, her eyes on the woman, on the baby, that wistfulness coming over her. "I guess that wasn't going to be me anyway," she said.

"What do you mean?" Shane asked, following her gaze to the mother.

What the heck? Why had she said *that*? One embarrassing statement led to another, apparently.

Or maybe she simply found Shane Dawson a little too easy to talk to. She used to find him judgy. But now he seemed more like the friend she hadn't considered him to be before.

A friend she was way too attracted to.

"Harrington wanted to put off starting a family," she said, their conversations about that echoing in her head. "I wanted to try for a baby right away." Her shoulders sagged and she looked away—from the young mother, from Shane. She took a sip of her coffee to try to get her equilibrium back.

"He wanted to wait a couple of years, till you were settled in your marriage?" Shane asked.

"More like he wanted to wait until we were thirty-five and had jet-setted to every hot spot across the world. When I'd bring up wanting a baby as soon as possible, he'd say, 'Ashley, do we *really* want that kind of responsibility in our *twenties*? Kids are great, but they control your life. Let's have a lot of fun first, and then when we've been everywhere, done everything, seen everything, experienced everything, we'll be ready for a child. Okay?'"

"Did you say okay?" he asked.

"Not at first. I kept trying to explain how a child would enhance our lives. But he just couldn't see it. And the person who isn't ready wins. It's just the way it is."

"You two want different things, Ashley. Jet-setting to Istanbul or Japan or Paris or wherever isn't your dream. Settling down, starting a family, is."

Could her shoulders sag any more? "But if he isn't ready, and I love him, then what's wrong with waiting till he's ready? That's called *compromise*. It's what marriage is about."

Even *she* winced at the defensiveness in her voice.

And the fact that she'd used present tense.

"Compromise is vital," Shane said. "But so is sharing the same goals and values and dreams with your spouse. That makes compromise a bit easier. If you want the same things, the compromising is just in the details."

She felt a lonely chill that had nothing to do with the crisp April breeze. She bolted up and looked around for the twins. "I'm gonna go play with the girls for a bit before we pack up." Tears stung her eyes and she blinked them away.

Then she lifted her chin and hurried over to the swings,

where Violet and Willow were high up in the air, chatting and laughing.

"Ashley, look how high I am!" Willow shouted.

"And me!" Violet seconded.

That chill was melted by their big smiles and exuberance. She did want to be a mother—and now, not later. Not when she was thirty-five.

She didn't want to travel the world.

She wanted a husband and child and a family dog and her job as horse groomer and trainer and cowgirl at her parents' ranch.

You want what Shane had, she thought. *What he still has*, she amended. *A family.*

She glanced back at him on the bench. He was looking right at her, his expression part apologetic for upsetting her, part neutral for being…right.

Ugh, he was making her think too much when she needed to process. She wasn't even sure that made sense. Processing *was* thinking. Hadn't they toasted to *figuring it out*?

But, but, but. Now she was all turned around and upside down and wasn't sure about *anything*.

Maybe she and Shane could make it the rest of the way to Jackson Hole without talking.

Chapter Six

They'd been on the road for just over two hours when they stopped for donuts, the best in Wyoming, according to *everyone*—locals, food critics and online reviews from visitors coming and going from the national parks. Shane agreed. He never passed through the tiny town of Bixby without going into Bess and Daughters Donuts and coming out with a few dozen to hand out and keep for himself.

As they entered the small bakery-café, the delicious scent of warm, sugary confections filled the air. Bess and her adult daughters could be seen through the glass-fronted wall between the kitchen and café in various stages of baking—mixing and sliding big trays of donuts into the ovens. As the foursome waited in line—there were at least ten people ahead of them at this random time of 10:13 a.m.—the twins studied the display containing around twenty different flavors.

"Oooh, I want chocolate with different-colored sprinkles!" Violet said.

"I want strawberry with cream. Do they have that, Daddy?" Willow asked.

Shane peered up at the huge blackboard listing the daily offerings and specials. Reading had just started clicking for the girls, but the big menu was overwhelming even for him. "Strawberry with cream with or without sprinkles?"

"With!" Willow said. Both girls grabbed hands and inched up in line, their anticipation and excitement over something so simple making Shane smile.

Ashley cleared her throat, her gaze on the twins.

Then again.

And one more time.

"Oh!" Violet said. She leaned close to her sister and whispered, "We're supposed to be interested in others."

Willow turned to Ashley. "What kind of donut are you getting, Ashley?"

Ashley gave the girls a smile, then perused the blackboard and peered around the person in front of her toward the display case. "I'm thinking the carrot cake donut."

The girls stared at each other for a moment. "How interesting!" Violet said.

"Yeah, how interesting!" Willow seconded.

Shane burst out laughing. "That *is* interesting."

"I love carrot cake!" Ashley said. "How could I resist a donut version?"

"What kind are you getting, Daddy?" Willow asked. "Your favorite? Cider?"

"You know it," he said. "And a box for your grandparents too. I'll get a dozen different kinds."

"Nana likes cider donuts too," Willow said. "Chocolate ones."

Violet nodded. "And Pops likes chocolate ones with cream inside. But there's always too *much* cream."

"I'll make sure to get those in their box," Shane said, giving both girls' heads a caress.

Twenty worth-it minutes later they were back in the

SUV, the girls' donuts consumed at a picnic table out front, a big blue box of a dozen for the Shaws in the cargo area. But the vehicle wouldn't start. Shane tried again. Nothing.

"Uh-oh," he said. "Starter maybe?"

He tried one more time. Dead as could be.

A half hour later, Bixby Auto came to tow the SUV to their shop. They said they'd be in touch within a couple of hours—sorry, but they were already backed up this morning. Shane almost wished they hadn't had their donuts yet so they could easily pass another hour. But they were full and ready to be on the road.

They were back at the picnic table, the twins counting people coming and going and sitting nearby. There wasn't much around in Bixby other than a beautiful nature preserve with a very cool footbridge that the twins loved walking on. That would pass some time.

Shane suggested it, and Ashley said it sounded great. Then her eyes widened.

"I just realized something. Do you know who moved to Bixby a few years ago? My cousin Miranda. She and her husband, Michael, were at the wedding too. You remember them, right?"

"Sure do," he said. The couple had both been ranch hands, working for room and board at the McCray Ranch while Miranda went to school at night for her teaching degree. "Miranda got a teaching job at the regional high school, and they bought a small cattle ranch."

Ashley nodded. "I'll give them a call and see if they're around today. We might be in luck since it's Sunday. I can apologize for them driving all that way to the wedding and getting a sitter for nothing." She sighed. "They had a baby just six months ago. Roxanna—Roxy. So sweet."

"We don't have to call them," he said gently. "They might put you on the spot, asking questions."

He realized he was being protective of Ashley.

"I don't mind. Miranda and I got close when she worked at the ranch, and they did come to the wedding. The twins won't remember Miranda or her husband, but they're assured a fun time if we go over to their place. Plus, I think they have chickens."

The twins would love nothing more than to watch chickens and maybe collect an egg. "Sounds good to me," he said.

"And you know, maybe spending a little time around a baby will make me realize I'm not ready to be a mom," she added, seeming lost in thought for a second.

He highly doubted that. Babies had a way of sneaking their way into hearts no matter how screechy or stinky they were.

As he watched her head a few feet away beside a tree to make her call, that same blast of protectiveness came over him. Maybe he just felt responsible for her. He'd promised her father he'd watch out for her, hadn't he?

A minute later she was back. "Miranda and Michael are going to come pick us up—they'll be here in fifteen minutes. Girls, Miranda is my cousin, my dad's sister's daughter. Miranda and her husband used to work at the McCray Ranch, and now they live here in Bixby. We're invited to meet their baby and chickens and stay for lunch. Oh, and did I mention they have two puppies?"

She was so good with the twins, so aware of their age and interests. She approached all conversations with them so thoughtfully. He'd known she had a great rapport with

Violet and Willow from her interactions with them at the ranch, but he hadn't known just how bighearted she was.

"Puppies *and* chickens!" the girls shouted in unison.

Shane grinned. "Say no more."

As Ashley went on to tell them about what she knew about the chickens and dogs, Shane held up his phone and went over to the same tree Ashley had just left. He pressed in the speed dial for the Shaws.

Beatrice Shaw, aka Nana, answered. "Shane, everything all right? We're not expecting you till five."

Yeah, five o'clock wasn't happening. "We're in Bixby at the moment. We stopped at that famous donut place, came out and my SUV wouldn't start. It's at a local auto shop. They're not even going to call me to diagnose it for a couple of hours. So depending on what it needs, I'm not sure we'll make it to Jackson Hole until late tonight. Or late morning tomorrow."

Silence and then a long sigh. "I made reservations for four at Donatella's at six. I'll need to cancel, *obviously*."

For *four*. Guess he wasn't invited to the Shaws' favorite restaurant this time. Not that he'd want to go to that stuffy place anyway. At least they had a children's menu with a few basics. The girls would always eat spaghetti and meatballs.

"You know, Shane, if you had a reliable vehicle, this wouldn't have happened. You really can't drive the girls around in an old junker. It's not safe. *Obviously.* And now the start of our time with the twins is completely thrown off."

If she said that word one more time…

"I apologize for that, Beatrice. But the SUV is perfectly reliable and barely five years old. Things *do* happen."

"Yes, I'm well aware," she said. "Well, even if you get your car back this afternoon, there's no sense arriving late at night. And in the morning you'll have a five-hour drive, and I suppose you'll stop a time or two. I'll expect you between two and three."

Fine with him. It would give Ashley a bit more time to prepare Violet and Willow to be on their best behavior. "I'll text you as we get closer to let you know an exact time."

And with that, they disconnected. Shane couldn't get off the phone fast enough.

He headed back over to the picnic table, where Ashley was answering questions about chickens. "Change of plans. Since we don't know when we'll get the SUV back, we're not expected at Nana and Pops's house till tomorrow. So we'll be spending the day and night around here. We'll have lunch with Miranda and Michael and meet their pups and chickens, and then we'll figure out the rest of the day."

Fifteen minutes later, a red minivan arrived. Miranda and Michael were both twenty-six, both redheads, though Miranda's hair was long and Michael's very short, and both had big warm smiles. Michael waved and went around to the passenger side to take their baby from the rear-facing car seat.

Ashley, her arms around the twins, took care of the introductions. The girls said shy hellos.

"And this little darling," Michael said, kneeling down slowly in front of the twins, "is Roxanna. She's six months old. We call her Roxy for short." Shane wasn't surprised the baby had a head full of red hair herself.

"She's so cute!" Willow said.

"And teensy!" Violet added.

"What's your favorite donut?" Willow asked, looking from Miranda to Michael before sneaking a look toward Ashley to see if she approved of Willow's attempt to show interest in others.

Shane held back his laugh.

"Chocolate with sprinkles," Miranda said.

"Did you know that Bess's has carrot cake donuts? That's my favorite," Michael added.

The twins looked at each other, then turned back to Michael. "Isn't that interesting!" they said at the same time.

With that, they piled into the Lorings' minivan and fifteen minutes later were at their ranch, a small cattle operation with a long driveway and beautiful land, surrounded by white fencing. Two pups were in a large pen at the side of the house. They barked their hellos.

As Miranda parked, Shane turned to the girls in the back row. He explained that they'd have to ask to pet the puppies, ask if they could touch the chickens, ask, ask, ask. Got it?

They got it, they insisted, seat belts off and raring to get out.

Michael gave the girls the lowdown, then opened the pen, and the pups came rushing out toward the twins, who'd dropped to their knees and were instantly smothered in puppy love.

Yes, this would be a good detour. For all of them.

Except maybe Ashley, who was now holding baby Roxy in her arms and looking at her with such wonder, such reverence. It was clear she couldn't wait to be a mother, no matter what she'd agreed to in order to suit her former fiancé.

At this point, it was anyone's guess what would happen when he dropped her off in Jackson Hole.

* * *

What a day.

Ashley had to admit she was glad Shane's SUV hadn't started and would actually be in the shop overnight because she had that rare feeling that she needed to be exactly here right now, with precisely these people. With her cousin Miranda, whom she'd immediately reconnected with as if they hadn't spent the past few years apart except for rare family get-togethers. There were some people with whom you could just pick up where you left off, with that same closeness, and it was like that with Miranda.

And with Shane and the twins. Every time her gaze would land on Shane, when the group was having lunch in the ranch house or when they visited the chicken coop or were playing with the pups or taking a tour of the ranch, she'd feel a warm familiarity, a sense of trust that told her she wasn't alone in the world. Of course, she had her family, who always had her back. But this was something different, this unexpected connection to Shane. He'd meet her gaze and give her the slightest nod with such warmth that she'd feel something stirring in her chest.

"Okay, I have to ask," Miranda said when the two of them were alone, taking a walk in the fresh April air on the ranch property. Well, not quite alone—baby Roxy was fast asleep in a carrier strapped to Miranda's chest. They were about a half mile from the house, the sky above bright blue with fluffy clouds, the temperature mild, in the low fifties. "Did Harrington not show up because he could see something was going on with you and Shane?"

Ashley stopped in her tracks, her mouth dropping open. "What?"

"Well, clearly something is. And yesterday was your wedding day, so…"

She'd always loved how Miranda just said whatever was on her mind, put it out there. But this was crazy talk!

"Nothing's going on between us," Ashley said. "And nothing was going on yesterday or last week or months ago or ever in the five years I've known Shane Dawson. Miranda, come on."

"I'm not accusing you of having an affair," Miranda was quick to explain. "I just mean that anyone looking can feel your chemistry. Maybe Harrington noticed."

Ha! If Harrington had noticed there was something brewing between her and Shane, it was their *animosity.* But Harrington wasn't one to notice those kinds of things. She frowned, wondering why someone—namely herself— who noticed everything didn't pay attention *that*.

Ashley linked arms with her cousin and resumed walking. "The only thing going on between me and Shane is *why* we're on this road trip together in the first place. We both kind of need each other right now. I'm an emotional mess and he has my back. He's got an issue with his late wife's parents and needs my help in improving the twins' manners before he drops them off at their house. So we've both got some big stuff going on, and we're helping each other out. That's why it seems…" She trailed off, biting her lip.

Miranda smiled. "Seems what?"

"Like we're closer than we are. That's all!"

"Or you're just getting close, period," Miranda countered.

Ashley wanted to argue, but she had to admit that it had certainly felt that way last night. "I suppose we are. He's so easy to talk to."

"And look at," Miranda added with a grin. She wiggled her eyebrows, and Ashley laughed.

But the undeniable sex appeal of Shane Dawson was no laughing matter. She found him so attractive that it was kind of getting in the way. It was difficult to appreciate him as the good friend he was becoming when she thought about…kissing him. Touching him. Being held by him.

"I don't mean to make light of what happened," Miranda said. "I know you must be hurting bad." She tugged Ashley closer via their linked arms. "I'm so sorry, Ash."

"Yeah," she said, sucking in a breath. "It does hurt. But it helps that I'm doing something. I'm gonna get back every penny my parents spent on the wedding." She'd told Miranda about her plan earlier. "And I guess I was thinking that Harrington would take one look at me and realize he'd made the biggest mistake of his life."

Miranda stopped walking, her expression so compassionate that Ashley almost started crying. "Do you think that's what will happen?"

Ashley looked up at the sky at the cloud slowly moving by. "I don't know. I mean, he didn't show up for his own wedding. He told me—via text—that he realized he didn't love me." She let her head drop back, the stark truth of that making her chest hurt all over again. "Like I said, I'm an emotional mess. I don't know anything."

"Well, I'm glad you're not alone—making this trip by yourself," Miranda said as they resumed walking. "That you're with someone you can lean on."

"Me too," Ashley said. She hadn't realized how much she needed that until she found herself with Shane's support.

A fussy wail came from the carrier, and Miranda glanced down, caressing the baby's pink-capped head. "Aww, what's the matter, my sweet? Need a change of position?" She knelt down for safety, unbuckled the harness and scooped Roxy out.

"Aww, she's so precious," Ashley said. "Can I hold her again? I love that baby shampoo smell." Ashley had gently rocked the baby for a good half hour while Miranda and Michael had fixed lunch.

Miranda transferred Roxy into her arms, and again, Ashley was mesmerized by the sweet face, the curious, alert blue eyes looking up at her. The tiny nose and bow lips. How could she have thought that waiting till she was thirty-five to have a baby was something she could possibly do? Just another thing rationalized in the supposed name of compromise. Where was Harrington's compromise? He hadn't met her halfway. He'd never said, *Since you want to start a family right away and I want to wait seven years, why don't we agree on three and a half years?* What she wanted didn't seem to matter.

Why was that okay with you? she asked silently, her gaze on the baby, her yearning so evident her knees almost wobbled.

"Harrington wanted to wait till we were thirty-five to start a family," Ashley blurted out.

"Ash, can I be really honest with you?"

Her eyes swung up to her cousin's.

"I didn't get a great impression of Harrington when I met him at your engagement party. I know you might get back together—and if that happens, I'll regret having said this. But he just seemed so self-absorbed, talking about himself, his big plans. I don't think I heard the word *we* or *our* come out of his mouth. Even when he was right beside you."

Ashley felt the air whoosh out of her lungs. She held on to the baby a bit more tightly. Miranda was right. One hundred percent right. Ashley had long been aware that Harrington, despite his good side, was focused on himself, but she'd attributed that to his being wealthy beyond belief and living in a different world where he always got what he wanted.

"He does have good points," she rushed to say, tears stinging her eyes. "The way he'd look at me when we were alone, the things he'd say. He'd make me feel so special. And he did have a big heart. I'd seen evidence of that time and again."

Did you make that up? she recalled Shane asking after she'd told him about Harrington working so hard to rescue the stray dog.

"I'm sure he did, Ash. You agreed to marry him, after all. You're smart, independent and incredibly grounded. You'd never let yourself get swept off your feet by anything superficial, so I know you loved him for good reasons. But the way he left you at the altar, what he said in that text... My God."

Ashley bit her lip and handed the baby back to Miranda, too emotional to have that precious life in her arms. Once Miranda had her daughter back in the carrier, Ashley wrapped her arms around herself, feeling so...vulnerable. Exposed.

"I'm sorry, hon," Miranda said. "I don't mean to add to the heavy weight on your shoulders. I know you have a ton on your mind."

Ashley laid a hand on her cousin's forearm. "It's okay. It's more than okay, really. It's necessary. The truth hurts but it's *everything*. Shane tells me the truth too. It's why I like having him around."

"Now, Shane I like," Miranda said. "Always have. From day one. Michael feels the same."

I like him too, she wanted to say, but that made her feel even more vulnerable, so she kept it to herself.

Chapter Seven

"Daddy, can we get doodle puppies too?" Violet asked as he tucked her and Willow in at eight thirty that night.

The twins were in the Lorings' guest room and were sharing the double bed. Shane and Ashley would camp out on the huge sectional sofa in the living room, each on one end. He was looking forward to that—spending some solo time with Ashley. He'd rarely gotten to talk to her one-on-one over the course of the fun, busy day. He'd see her across the room or on the other side of the chicken coop or patting the Lorings' two horses in the barn, and sometimes she'd seemed on the sad side. Or maybe just lost in thought. He'd checked in a couple of times with a private text, just asking how she was holding up. She'd gotten through yesterday—and the disaster of a wedding day—and her mind had to be a jumble today, even with all the distractions.

"I actually want chickens more than puppies," Willow said. "Puppies can't lay eggs. And it was fun to find the eggs in the coop."

"Let's get both!" Violet suggested.

"Hmm. Pets are a lot of work," he said. "And we're a pretty busy family. But maybe in the future."

For the next few minutes, Shane answered their questions about what the future meant, when it started and how long it lasted.

Willow yawned and wrapped her arm around her lovey. "Maybe in the future you'll marry Ashley."

Violet yawned too. "And then she'll be our stepmother. Lianna at school has a stepmother and she makes awesome lunches."

Shane's throat closed up. This was unexpected. They'd never said anything about wanting a stepmother before.

"If you marry Ashley, then she'll have a wedding," Willow said, her eyes fluttering closed.

"And she won't be sad," Violet added, clutching her own lovey.

"You two like the idea of a stepmother?" he asked tentatively, not sure he should put too much stock in the sleepy-time conversation. Sometimes the twins talked about things in the abstract that he took much more seriously than they did. He'd spend hours contemplating their comments and questions only to find out in the morning that those deep ruminations during the bedtime routine had been completely forgotten. But sometimes, their questions were forefront the next morning, the center of their hearts. It was hard to know. Especially this. About his getting married again.

"We like Ashley," Violet said.

"We love Ashley," Willow amended.

Violet nodded her agreement on that. "Tell Ashley goodnight, Daddy."

Within seconds, both girls were fast asleep.

He sat there, on the edge of the bed, barely able to breathe, to move. They'd never talked like this about anyone before. Not sitters they'd particularly enjoyed their time with. Not even their beloved kindergarten teacher, Ms. Henry, who was single.

But he was sure the subject wouldn't come up in the morning. There would be too many other things to think about, like the anticipation of Michael's promised chocolate chip pancakes and bacon, getting to pour the puppies' kibble into their bowl for their own breakfasts and collecting the eggs in the chicken coop. If the girls were too distracted to remember what they'd said, then all the better. The idea of remarriage wasn't a thought in *his* head, so he'd prefer it wasn't in the girls' either.

There was a soft tap on the door—Ashley.

He stood up, his legs a bit shaky. He sucked in some air and got himself together. "They're out cold. They said to tell you good-night."

"Aww, I wanted to tell them a story, a continuation of the adventures of Helena the horse."

He smiled. "There's always the long car ride tomorrow."

She smiled too, her pretty face lighting up, and he was struck by the desire to kiss her. To feel her against him.

That would not be happening. She was in way too vulnerable a place. With everything going on right now, worrying about the McCray Ranch as its foreman, watching out for Ashley on this journey—both her personal, emotional journey and the road trip—and the impending arrival at the Shaws' home, where they could make good on their threats to sue for custody of the twins, Shane was in no headspace to start something. Particularly with a woman who'd been left at the altar yesterday. A woman he *was* supposed to watch out for—not take advantage of. If she seemed…drawn to him—and he did get that sense— it was because he was her support system right now. That was all. He represented safety. And there was nothing safe in kissing. It could lead somewhere downright dangerous for two vulnerable people.

"Want some coffee?" she asked. "I'm gonna make herbal tea. Miranda has a thousand kinds."

"Actually, I'd like herbal tea too. Pick something for me."

She smiled again and headed for the kitchen, Shane following her and trying to keep his eyes off her moving body, from the sway of her hips in those jeans to her silky long hair down her back.

"I love this farmhouse," she said as she rummaged through the tea selection. "So cozy. Just right."

He agreed. The house was small and just one story, but it had interesting nooks and crannies and managed to be a bit sprawling with three bedrooms, including Roxy's nursery. Shane had lived in ranch housing his entire adult life and had never had a house of his own, but one like this would do nicely. It really was just the right size. The Lorings had mentioned during dinner that they planned to add a family room in the coming year—and another baby. Shane had never thought about moving, whether building or buying a house of his own, because he'd lived his daughters' entire lives in the foreman's cabin. He couldn't imagine wanting to live anywhere else. It was steeped in good memories—sad ones too—and so many important firsts had happened there.

Yet now that the girls were five and they could all use more room, maybe it was time to think about their own place. It would certainly give the Shaws less to complain about. *They don't even have their own home. The cabin is steps from the barn—they live beside cows...*

Once their tea was ready, they decided to split a carrot cake donut and sat down on the sofa. Miranda and Michael's bedroom was at the far end of the hall, so they didn't have to worry about waking them. Ashley had mentioned she'd volunteered to care for the baby anytime Roxy woke up during the night so the couple could get a good night's sleep.

Shane took a bite of the donut. "Huh, this *is* good. I'll have to tell the girls."

"They crack me up," she said. "They've really taken to the 'Isn't that interesting!' comeback in just the right tone. And they're such great sports about the etiquette lessons. I sneaked in a bunch today. They really enjoyed paying the Lorings compliments. 'What a nice house! What a cute baby! I love your red shoes.' And they now like asking, 'May I do this? May I do that? May I pick up that white chicken? May I check for eggs?'"

He grinned. "The Shaws will like that too."

"I'll admit, I wasn't as strict as their grandmother would probably approve of when it came to how they acted outside. I know the Shaws don't like when the girls run and stomp and shriek, but if they're outdoors, I can't see telling them to walk instead of run or lower their voices. I couldn't bear to squash their exuberance while they were exploring the ranch."

"Same," he said. "When we're closer to Jackson Hole and it'll be easier for them to remember, we can give them some basic rules about the Shaws' house that we'd like them to follow. In their grandparents' backyard, they will have to pipe down. Not run at top speed. Then back home, they can go crazy all they want."

She nodded. "They're such great kids. I just adore them."

That went straight to his heart. "They adore you too. They told me so when I was tucking them in."

"They're so full of life and love," she said, wrapping her hands around her mug of tea. She took a sip and seemed lost in thought for a second. "I'm definitely not waiting till

I'm thirty-five to have a baby. Spending the day with Roxy in all her baby glory cemented that for me."

"And if you and Harrington get back together?" he asked and immediately regretted it.

She didn't exactly bristle but she did seem taken aback. "Well, he and I will certainly have a lot to talk about. I mean, at the most basic level, the trust is gone. That has to be dealt with first."

"Ah, so you'll work up to the fact that you want very different things in life, value different things, want a different lifestyle. You'll work on the trust first, then get into equally important fundamentals."

She stared at him and put her mug down. Then her face kind of crumpled. "I don't know what I'm saying or thinking or doing. I don't know anything."

Oh, heck. His intention was to get through to her—not hurt her or break her spirit. He inched closer and took her hand, holding on to it with a gentle squeeze. "I'm sorry that I keep lobbing this stuff at you. I happen to think a lot of you, Ashley. So I guess I'm feeling extra protective. Plus, I promised your dad I'd look out for you."

Her eyes twinkled for a moment. "Aww. I could see him making you promise just that."

"He did. But I've been doing that long before yesterday."

She only half frowned at that. "Yes, you have, haven't you? I didn't like it then, and I still don't. But I'm glad you are, if that makes any sense. I need it, even if I don't like it."

He smiled and was about to move back over a bit to give them some space when she turned to look at him. He realized that their lips were about an inch apart. And they were just staring into each other's eyes, neither saying a word.

He was barely breathing. Ashley seemed both expectant and nervous.

Remember, you're not allowed to kiss her. That's not looking out for her.

But *she* kissed *him*. She leaned in just enough for their lips to touch, her eyes closing, and her soft mouth on his almost did him in. In that moment, all he could do was feel and not think, and he kissed her back. And then she parted her lips and pressed closer to him, her arms slinking around his neck, her lush, full breasts against his chest.

It took everything in him to pull back. "I want this, Ashley. Trust me. But I *don't* want to add to your confusion. I don't want to be the cause of even more confusion."

She bit her lip and looked at him, then looked away and slid over a bit. She picked up her tea and took a sip. "I did just say I didn't know what the hell I was doing or thinking." She sighed. "But that was one hell of a kiss."

Understatement. "Yeah, it was."

She took another sip of her tea and nodded—as if to herself. "What happens on the road trip *stays* on the road trip."

He stared at her for a second, then picked up his own mug. He felt like a necessary bucket of cold water had been poured on his head. What she'd just said was a stark reminder that their real lives were elsewhere. That she *didn't* know how she felt or what she was thinking or where her heart was. Anything could and probably would happen on this trip. They were out of their usual element, on an adventure, both headed for uncertainty when they reached their destination, both on unsure footing. Ashley would have to find her way to herself. And he had to fully focus on the looming threat the Shaws represented. Nothing that happened on this road trip should be analyzed; nothing could be set in stone. A kiss was just a kiss. Nothing more.

Which meant that when it came to his own heart, he had to watch out for himself. He couldn't mistake this for the start of something.

He wasn't even considering bringing romance into his life.

Shane stood up and grabbed the pillows and blankets that Miranda had set out for them. He put a set next to Ashley and grabbed the other, then set up his bedding on the long section of the sofa. Ashley did the same on the chaise.

But the very short distance between them did nothing to make him stop wishing she was curled up next to him.

Ashley had finally dozed off when she woke to the sound of a baby fussing, a short cry. She sat up, disoriented, and for a moment, she had no idea where she was. Until she noticed the long form of a man stretched out on the sofa, a blanket half covering him.

Shane. Fast asleep.

She felt her eyes widen in remembrance of that unexpected kiss and forced her gaze off him, her heart pounding.

She was about to dash into the nursery, but Miranda had told her that if Roxy woke in the night, Ashley should give her a chance to soothe herself back to sleep before rushing in. Ashley waited a beat, her attention drawn back to the man sleeping just a few feet away.

For a moment, she was mesmerized by the sight of Shane lying there on his side, his dark hair tousled, his head resting on a crooked arm on the pillow. The long eyelashes against his cheeks. The strong, straight nose, the chiseled jawline. And those shoulders and arms that the blanket wasn't covering.

She sucked in a breath, recalling how she'd felt in those arms.

He stirred, moving a bit, and she felt a little panicky for a second, but he remained asleep.

Phew. She was not ready to face him. Not at—she glanced at her phone on the coffee table—1:42 a.m. Not after that kiss that she didn't know what to make of.

Just when she thought baby Roxy had gone back to sleep, another little cry came from the nursery. Ashley peeled off her own blanket and tiptoed into the room. "I've got you," she cooed to the beautiful baby.

She heard footsteps behind her and hoped it was anyone but Shane. Hours after that kiss—that incredible, hot kiss—she'd still been thinking about it, feeling the imprint of his mouth on hers, remembering his passion, the desire in his blue eyes. If he hadn't stopped them from going further…

Complicated—on so many levels. And *complicated* was something neither of them needed.

She settled down in the glider chair with Roxy in her arms, glancing toward the doorway to see who'd also woken up.

Shane.

He stood in the doorway in his sexy Wyoming Cowboys T-shirt and sweats and tousled dark hair. And again, the memory of their kiss came over her.

She felt a flush come over her entire body and gave the baby a gentle sway.

Focus on Roxy, not the man in the doorway.

"Is she hungry? Wet?" he asked, getting right down to business.

"Hmm. Miranda said she didn't need a middle-of-the-night bottle anymore. And she's not wet. She seems to be going back to sleep." Roxy's eyes were fluttering closed. But then they'd open slightly, then close again.

"I can't believe what I don't remember," he said, coming into the room and sitting down in the padded chair by the window directly across from her. "Every stage, every year seems to push the last one farther into the recesses."

This was good. Easy conversation about the baby they were up in the middle of the night to care for. Nothing about the kiss.

Maybe I dreamed it, she thought. It *had* been dreamy.

But no, she'd been wide-awake, every cell in her body on red alert.

Get back to the conversation, she chastised herself. *Stop thinking about it!* "Defense mechanism maybe," she said. "New parents don't remember getting up five times in the night, making bottles while half asleep, changing diapers. That way, they'll want to do it all over again with baby number two and so on." Just like childbirth. She smiled. "I can imagine having four of these tiny marvels. Yeah, four."

"Four?" he repeated with a smile. "I can tell you that *two* is a lot."

She laughed. "Well, at the same time, sure." She chuckled. "Like I'd know. But I *hope* to know."

She'd done it again. Opened herself up for a comment about how getting back together with Harrington wouldn't get her what she wanted since Harrington wasn't interested in *one* baby, let alone four. She waited, bracing herself for it. Truth was, she cared what Shane Dawson thought. She respected him, and his opinion had started to matter.

"You'll be a great mother, Ashley," was what he said.

She was so surprised that tears stung her eyes. The conviction in his tone touched her even more than the words themselves. She looked over at him, so handsome, the kiss pushing its way into her thoughts again, and she forced herself to look down at the baby, to keep her focus on where she at least knew she wanted to go. Shane Dawson wasn't going to be part of her future except as foreman of her family's ranch.

What happens on the road trip stays on the road trip...

It had to. For both their sanity. Like the kiss.

Why *had* she kissed him? And she had—she'd made that first move.

Because of the moment. Their growing closeness. And her attraction to him.

If she was attracted to another man, surely that meant she should let go of Harrington and any thoughts of a second chance with the guy she'd expected to marry.

What happens on the road trip...

On the other hand, maybe kissing Shane had been about their toast when they'd shared that mini bottle of white wine in the lodge suite last night. To figuring it out. She didn't have to know how she felt about every little thing. Every big thing either. She just knew she couldn't bury her head in the sand. Better to put herself out there and find out this or that than burrow under the covers, even if that was what she also wanted to do.

"That means a lot," she said almost on a whisper, the emotion in her voice another surprise. Just what was this man doing to her? She turned her attention to the sweet weight in her arms and gently rocked Roxy, who was now asleep again. "I'll put her back in the crib. I hope she doesn't wake up while I transfer her."

"You've got the magic touch," Shane said. "She fell back asleep in like three seconds."

Oh, Shane. If Harrington had twin five-year-olds, he would have said, *Let me do it. I'm a pro*, and practically grabbed Roxy out of Ashley's arms to show her how it was done. To show her *up*.

Roxy went into the crib without a stir, just a little arm shooting up by her face, her bow lips quirking, her chest rising up and down in her orange pj's. *You are a wonder*, Ashley thought, watching the baby sleep.

She turned around to find Shane *right there*. Standing not three inches behind her, peering into the crib and holding up a palm for a high five.

But when she reached up her hand to tap his palm with hers, he held it. While looking right into her eyes. His other hand went to her chin, tilting it up. Kissing distance once again.

And then they both leaned in at the same time.

How could this kiss be even hotter? she wondered, snaking her arms around his neck. She couldn't get close enough to him. He inched away again, but this time he took her hand and led her out of the nursery.

There was a recessed area between the living room and kitchen, and he led her there, pressing her up against the wall, his mouth, his tongue, his hands exploring her. If anyone came out of a bedroom, whether a grown-up or a five-year-old, they could disengage fast and pretend like they'd been heading for the kitchen. But still, they were being risky.

She could feel his erection against her inner thigh, and a burst of heat spread through her belly. His hands were underneath her T-shirt, slowly moving up to her breasts, where they stopped to cup and rub, and then her shirt was lifted up, his mouth following.

She could melt to the floor. He lifted her up, and she wrapped her legs around his hips as he kissed her so passionately she wished she were naked.

"What I would give to make love to you right now," he whispered.

"Me too," she whispered back. "But we're playing with fire in a lot of ways."

"I keep waiting for a door to open," he said.

"I know. It's kind of killing the moment."

He laughed and took her hand and led her back to the big sofa. "I'd snuggle up with you, but we'd fall asleep and big eyes would find us that way in about three hours."

Ashley grinned. "And we'd wake up to the sound of the twins saying, 'Isn't that interesting!'"

Shane laughed again and pulled her against him, giving her one last passionate kiss. "Good night, Ashley."

"I think I'll be able to sleep now," she said.

"I know what you mean. It's like something has been… released."

"Yeah. This," she said, wagging a finger between them, "is still very confusing and probably a bad idea. But…yes. We're clearly attracted to each other and we're going through a crazy time, so here we are…"

He touched her face and slid back under the covers. She did the same.

But she didn't fall asleep for a long time.

Chapter Eight

Shane awoke the way he often did—to a twin or two jumping on him and asking, "Daddy, are you awake?"

"Oh, I think he is now," Ashley said from the other side of the sofa. He turned his head to see her sitting up with a grin, and the girls both scrambled over to her. She slung an arm around each. "Morning, sunshines."

"Morning, Ashley," they said in unison. She must have taught them that yesterday morning because he'd never heard them say it together like that. Some mornings, they didn't say it back to him at all, particularly on school mornings.

"How did you sleep?" Willow asked very politely.

Shane stared at his daughter. Wow. Ashley had worked wonders.

"Did you have any dreams?" Violet asked her.

Ashley gave each of their chins a little squeeze. "I slept very well, thank you for asking. How about you guys?"

"Very well," they both repeated.

"And yes, I did have a dream. A really good one."

"What was it about?" Violet asked.

"Yeah, what?" Willow seconded.

Ashley glanced at Shane with a sly smile. "You know how sometimes you can't remember the dream, you just know it was good? It was like that."

Ah. He had a feeling she'd had the same dream he'd had, which wasn't fit for anyone's ears but theirs. In his dream, he and Ashley had continued their hot encounter, her legs wrapped around his waist. They were at the Mc-Cray Ranch, though, in the hayloft, and things were hazy and fuzzy and weird the way dreams could be. But it was a very good dream.

"Morning, everyone!" called Michael, walking into the living room with baby Roxy in his arms. Miranda was behind him in a fuzzy pink chenille bathrobe.

"Morning!" the twins called out.

"How did you sleep?" Willow asked Michael.

He tilted his head and smiled. "Very well, thank you. And you?"

"Very well," Violet answered for her.

Miranda grinned at the girls. "You two are so polite! I hope you've rubbed off on Roxy. I'll be hitting you guys up to babysit when you're older, for sure."

The girls both clapped and ran over to Miranda to hug her.

"Who wants my world-famous chocolate chip pancakes?" Michael asked.

That got a round of excited yeses. Shane's phone buzzed with a text—the auto body shop letting him know he could pick his SUV up anytime after 8:00 a.m.

They all made a plan—quick showers, and then Shane would help with breakfast while Miranda and Ashley tended to Roxy and brought the girls into the chicken coop to collect eggs.

The shower cleared his head but did nothing to wash away the memories of the kiss or middle-of-the-night encounter, and he was glad for it.

Fifteen minutes later, dressed and ready to make a lot of

pancake batter, he passed Ashley in the hallway on her way to shower. He wanted to grab her in his arms and kiss her, but of course, he couldn't with everyone around. They settled for giving each other knowing looks, which did something funny to his belly. Neither was pretending last night hadn't happened. Or saying it shouldn't have.

He wasn't ready for this—a romantic relationship. But he was going to see it through, wherever it might lead. Maybe none of this was "real" and they'd go their separate ways when they reached Jackson Hole. Maybe she would get back with the cad. Maybe he'd be busy in court with the Shaws, fighting to keep his girls. But right now, whatever was happening with him and Ashley felt good. He couldn't say whether it was right or wrong. But it was definitely good.

He was adding a handful of chocolate chips to the batter, Michael beside him in his Wyoming's Best Dad apron, when Ashley came into the kitchen. She smiled at him, both shyly and hotly, poured herself a cup of coffee and then left with Miranda and the twins to visit the chicken coop.

"I love life," Michael said, sliding a tray of bacon into the oven. "One minute Ashley is stood up at her own wedding and the next she's found a good guy. I'm happy for you both."

Shane held up a hand. "Whoa, there. We're just traveling to Jackson Hole together. We're not a couple."

Michael laughed. "Uh, sure."

"No, really," Shane said, frowning. "We're not. We're supporting each other through a hard time for us both. We're... friends."

Friends? Did friends kiss so passionately that Shane almost lost control? Did friends wrap their legs around friends' waists while backed up against a wall?

"I repeat—uh, sure." Michael grinned and checked the batter. "That looks great. The griddle's ready, so pour away."

Shane ladled six pancakes onto the griddle, watching the bubbles form, the aroma making his mouth water. He'd rather focus on the pancakes than Michael's line of conversation.

"Hey, I just call it like I see it," Michael continued. "There's something serious going on between you two. It was like that with me and Miranda when we met. She'd just come out of a bad relationship, and I was taking care of my sick mom and barely hanging on. Neither of us was looking to get involved, but we didn't really have a say."

Shane frowned again. "You must have had a say."

"Nope. Every time I'd see Miranda around the McCray Ranch, I'd forget what I was doing or even what day it was. She'd ask me to help her with something, and I'd realize I'd do anything for her. I fell in love before we even started dating."

Hey, no one said anything about love. Or dating.

Shane shook his head. "Ashley and I are on separate missions to the same place. That's all. We'll likely be going our separate ways once we reach Jackson Hole."

"Yeah, I doubt that," he said. "Miranda mentioned that Ashley's going to talk to that jerk about getting paid back for the wedding. And that maybe they'd get back together. That's not happening. The last part, I mean."

"How can you be so sure?" Shane asked. He also wanted to be sure, but he wasn't. Ashley had fallen for Harrington once, and maybe working things out with him was more important to her than he realized.

"Because of you," Michael said.

Shane gaped at the guy. "Me? I'm not anyone here, Michael."

Michael shook his head. "It's amazing when someone can't see what's happening in their own life. But that's what makes it so interesting."

Shane flipped the pancakes, narrowing his eyes. "You and Miranda taking bets?"

Michael laughed. "Never. We love you guys. You were very good to us when we worked for you. And Miranda has always adored Cousin Ashley."

Huh. This was worse. Michael was sincere. Which meant he believed every word he said.

What happens on the road trip stays on the road trip. No matter what, he had to remember that. What Michael was seeing wasn't "real life." His and Ashley's everyday lives. This was just an emotionally heightened time for both of them, and they were leaning on each other. Giving in to their attraction to release some of their anxiety and frustration. Whatever was between them was nothing more than a distraction.

Yes, he thought, stacking delicious-smelling pancakes on a big serving plate.

It's a distraction.

But then the chicken coop crew came back in the house, the twins rushing into the kitchen to show Shane the green and blue eggs they'd found, and he and Ashley locked gazes. A look that held so many different emotions he couldn't begin to count each one.

Okay, this might be more than a distraction. But he had no idea *what* it was.

"Girls, time to go!" Shane called out, glancing around.

Ashley expected to hear four feet come pounding into the living room, where the well-fed group was waiting to hit the road and head for the auto body shop so that Shane could pick up his vehicle. It was 7:50 a.m. and the car would be ready at 8:00 a.m. But the twins were nowhere to be found.

And the longer they stood here waiting to leave, the longer she'd daydream about what had gone on during the night with Shane. *A lot* had gone on.

So far, they hadn't talked about it. But she'd catch Shane looking at her, so much in his blue eyes, and she knew he was thinking about it. Like she was.

But thinking about him was…confusing—and threw a major monkey wrench into what she thought she was doing on this trip. What she was supposed to be doing. She had to stop thinking about last night and focus on getting back on the road. To their destinations. To their missions. To the reasons they were here in the first place.

Where were the twins? she wondered, craning her neck to see outside. She didn't hear them either.

"Violet and Willow, to the living room, pronto!" Shane called out.

Silence.

"Maybe they're saying goodbye to the dogs," Ashley said.

She and Shane walked into the living room, expecting to see the girls on the floor with the doodles, but the dogs were in their beds. No sign of the twins. They'd already said good-bye to the chickens, so Ashley knew they weren't outside.

"Willow! Violet!" he called again. "Let's skedaddle!"

It's too quiet, Ashley thought. *Something isn't right.*

"Let me go look in the room they stayed in," Ashley said and headed down the hall.

Ah. She heard whispering in the hall bathroom. She knocked.

Sudden silence.

Then a flurry of whispering.

"Um, just a second," Violet said through the closed door. Nervously.

"Everything okay in there?" Ashley asked, getting worried.

"No," Willow said. "Violet looks funny."

Funny? "Girls, let me in, okay?" Ashley asked.

The door opened and Willow poked her head out. She was biting her lip.

The door opened wider and there was Violet, standing on a step stool in front of the mirror, a pair of nail scissors in her hand.

And "bangs" cut into her long brown hair, except the bangs were about four inches above her eyebrows. And woefully uneven.

Oh, boy.

"Violet, honey, you cut your hair?" Ashley asked, even though the answer was obvious.

Violet's eyes filled with tears, and she turned around on the stool. "I wanted to look like Miranda."

Miranda had long hair too and a swish of bangs—which ended just above her eyebrows. And were perfectly even and looked great.

Violet's hair looked…as Willow had put it: funny.

Ashley heard footsteps, and suddenly Shane was standing outside the bathroom.

"Everything okay?" he asked.

Now it was Ashley who bit her lip. Nana wasn't going to like this haircut.

Yes, hair grew. But not fast enough to be back to normal before they reached Jackson Hole.

Violet looked sheepishly up at Ashley, who nodded, and Violet opened the door wide and burst into tears.

Shane stared at his daughter with the crazily cut bangs. He didn't say a word.

"I wanted to look like Miranda," Violet said, tears streaming down her cheeks. "But I look like a stupid idiot."

She jumped off the step stool and cried, her head hanging. Willow was looking at her father with big eyes, as if holding her breath while she waited to see what he'd say.

Yeah, I'm right there with you, kid, Ashley thought.

Shane knelt in front of Violet. "Honey, listen to me. I never want you to call yourself names. Okay? No matter what you do. You wanted to look like Miranda, so you cut your hair. It's not the end of the world, right?"

"But I don't look like Miranda," she said, the tears streaming harder.

Shane tipped up Violet's chin, his expression compassionate. "Well, I suppose you learned that if you want a hairstyle like someone else, you could ask them where they get it cut, and I can take you there next time."

"Oh," Violet said. "But what do I do now?"

"I can straighten out the bangs," Ashley said. "But mostly, you'll just have to wait for them to grow. A few weeks is all."

"A few weeks is a really long time," Violet said. She stepped closer to Ashley. "Can you really fix my hair?"

Ashley pulled the girl into a hug. Violet sagged against her, wrapping her arms around Ashley. "Sure I can. I can't make them longer, but I can make them straight."

She stood up and glanced at Shane, who whispered a thank-you.

With Willow watching with big eyes, Shane hoisted Violet onto the counter. Ashley took the scissors and snipped just enough so that the bangs were even without hacking into them any farther.

"There," Ashley said, stepping back. "That looks even now."

Willow nodded. "It does, Violet."

Violet took in a breath. "Thank you, Ashley."

"You're welcome," Ashley said.

As they were about to leave the bathroom, Violet threw herself at Ashley for another hug. The little girl didn't say a word. Ashley hugged her back. Aww, now she was going to cry.

"We've really got to get going," Shane said. "Why don't you two go say your goodbyes to the goldendoodles?"

Violet and Willow hurried away.

"You handled that so well," Ashley whispered. "You could easily have gotten upset, given that they're due at their grandparents' this afternoon."

"The twins don't need my worries heaped on them. Violet made a mistake, and she'll absolutely learn an important lesson from it. Never touch scissors to her hair herself."

Ashley smiled. "Definitely."

He gave her hand a squeeze, and they joined the group in the living room, the twins sitting with the dogs, patting away and telling them they hoped to visit again soon.

"Okay, Dawson girls," Shane said. "Time to head out."

Miranda held open the door. As the twins were about to walk through, she said, "I like your bangs, Violet. They're like mine." She gave her hair a swish.

Violet let out something like a gasp. Her entire face brightened, and she gave her own hair a swish. Then she smiled at her sister and out they went.

"Oh," Violet called back. "Thank you, Miranda!"

Ashley glanced at Shane and grinned. The girl might arrive at her grandparents' with bangs very high up on her forehead, but at least her manners were A plus. She turned to Miranda. "Don't tell anyone, but you're my favorite cousin for a reason."

And then, finally, they all got in the car. The Lorings dropped the McCray-Dawson crew at the auto body shop, where Shane's SUV was all ready to go. Ashley wouldn't have minded if the shop had called about a delay, even another whole day. They'd had a great time in Bixby, even including the hair mishap. *And* even though their detour had included some unexpected romance with Shane Dawson. No matter how she tried to compartmentalize what had gone on between them, to rationalize, to tuck it into something easy, she couldn't.

After goodbye hugs with Miranda and Michael, a promise from both sides to text and swap photos, and a kiss dropped on baby Roxy's capped head, they were back on the road.

Oh, I should mention, Miranda had whispered in her ear as they'd hugged. *The right guy is the one driving you to the wrong guy. Just my fifty cents*, she'd added with a smile.

More confusion. Had her former fiancé done the wrong thing to do the right thing—for himself, and really, if she thought about it, *her* too, since he'd made it clear he didn't love her? Or had he simply gotten cold feet so bad that it had messed with his mind, his emotions? If that was the case, perhaps they could just try to be together without the pressure of an engagement.

Maybe it wasn't that Harrington didn't love her but that he just wasn't ready to get married. The past couple of days, that was what had been knocking around her head and her heart. He'd been about to take a huge step, make a major life commitment, only to realize it wasn't what he wanted.

She wasn't sure if she was letting him off the hook by rationalizing or if she was just really thinking hard about the whole thing.

Luckily, Jackson Hole was a good five hours away and they'd be making at least one stop for everyone to stretch their legs. They'd arrive in town around 2:00 p.m. She'd have plenty of time to think, to feel, to consider all the angles. And given that they'd be driving with the girls, there would be no hanky-panky between her and Shane, no conversation about themselves. She could focus on herself, on what she needed.

She slid a glance at the gorgeous, sexy, kind, warm, funny man in the driver's seat. She had to tear her gaze away from his profile, his shoulder, his forearm, his hand on the wheel. The hand that had touched her so intimately last night.

Yeah, she was already doing a bad job of focusing on herself. Or maybe she had that backward.

Chapter Nine

At 1:00 p.m., they made their second stop since leaving Bixby—the first being Bess and Daughters Donuts for another dozen for the Shaws and a few individual ones for themselves. This time, they pulled into the gravel parking lot of a beautiful park with a few well-reviewed food trucks, a petting zoo, a duck pond and two enchanting footbridges. Ashley got out and glanced around, the grounds managing to seem both rustic and manicured at the same time. The moment the girls' feet hit the gravel in the lot, they raced for the bridge just a few feet away, looking at the ducks swimming below and pointing and chattering excitedly.

"Now, Nana and Pops would have a lot to say about that," Shane said, locking the SUV. "They didn't ask if they could go—they just took off and at full speed. Granted, they didn't have to cross the parking lot and the footbridge is three feet in front of us, but still."

"Well, maybe Violet and Willow factored that in," Ashley said, eyeing the girls leaning over the wide stone railing to better see the ducks. "If they did have to cross the lot, I think they would have asked. And they're *right there*," she added.

He nodded, keeping his eyes on his daughters. "But that jogger coming in their direction had to move out of their way or risk being mowed down by speeding five-year-olds. The Shaws would have called them back, made them sit down on that bench and given them a lecture."

Ashley could see he was conflicted about whether he should too. "Well, what would that lecture be?"

"I know exactly what the Shaws would say because I've been with them when they've scolded the girls for running ahead. They'd say, 'Decorum, girls. Remember we taught you that word. That means you conduct yourselves like the little ladies you are. You ask permission to go to the bridge. You hold hands for safety as each other's partners. And you walk nicely. And once there, you admire the ducks quietly. No shouting and being loud and disturbing other people's enjoyment of the park.'"

Ashley thought about all that for a moment. "I think when they're with their grandparents, that's just the law of the land. The girls are expected to behave a certain way and that's fine. It's a little stuffy and highfalutin, but again, their house, their rules. You don't have to have the same rules."

He nodded. "The past couple of years it's been tough trying to make them remember that different rules go for different places. But now that they're five and have just a couple months left of kindergarten, they're used to rules being enforced. There are school rules and home rules and grandparents' rules and all-the-time rules."

"Like talking with their mouths full. They seem to understand that it's an all-the-time rule."

"Right," he said as they started heading over to the bridge. "Meanwhile, running down the stairs at their grandparents' and leaping off the second step and making a thud is a no-go there. At my cabin, it's fine. I think over lunch, we should have that talk with them." He glanced over at them. "Just explain it again in a way that's not overwhelming." He stopped for a moment, his gaze on his daughters. "I want them to be who they are, not constantly stifled. I love who they are."

Ashley could feel his love for his girls radiating from him. She touched his arm for a moment. "I think they'll be just fine. They've got big personalities. Yeah, they'll get their feelings hurt or they'll get criticized and corrected. But no matter what, those girls' personalities, their curiosity, their exuberance and their big hearts will always shine."

He gave her hand a squeeze, and the sudden touch— his warm, strong hand, the *connection*—brought back a vivid memory of last night. She blinked it away and kept her gaze on the twins.

She could hear Violet saying that she wished she could have a pet duck and Willow saying she'd want a swan. "Think Nana will say something about Violet's bangs?" she asked Shane.

Shane sighed. "Definitely. Beatrice won't find it amusing in the slightest, not that I did. But Violet cutting her hair was perfectly age appropriate. And every time she looks in the mirror, she'll see that cutting her own hair was a mistake."

"Their grandparents don't take that into account?"

He shook his head. "The past couple of years, they've been full of criticism. Like, 'The twins have to learn, period. You're too lenient, too soft, and you're not teaching them how to behave in the world.'"

"They're so hard on you," Ashley said. "Honestly, it's unfair. To you and the twins."

"I appreciate that," he said, holding her gaze for a moment.

Reminding her about last night…

"Daddy, Ashley, do you see the ducks?" the twins called, jumping up and down and pointing and leaning over the stone railing again.

"They're so beautiful," Ashley said as they joined Violet and Willow. "I love the one with the green bill."

"So, guys, what does everyone want for lunch?" Shane asked. "I read that the taco truck here has amazing tacos. And really great strawberry lemonade."

"I want tacos!" Violet said.

"Me too!" Willow seconded.

Shane took orders—chicken for the twins and spicy beef for Ashley and strawberry lemonade for everyone—and then headed for the truck.

"Oooh," Violet said, turning to the left. "It's a wedding!"

Ashley turned too. Sure enough, a bride and groom were being photographed on the far side of the bridge. Ashley looked down and noticed a small group off to the side all dressed up, though there weren't any chairs set up. The couple must have gotten married somewhere else and come here for photos.

She thought of her beautiful white gown—still beautiful, even decorated with straw—crumpled in her closet, her veil still up in the stables loft. Her bridal party, in their matching pale pink satin dresses and *peau de soie* peep-toe pumps. Humph—she'd make Harrington reimburse her maid of honor and bridesmaids for that big expense too.

The groom dramatically dipped the bride, the photographer clicking away.

Harrington used to like doing that, dipping her for a kiss. It used to make her feel so special, the drama he brought to even the quickest of kisses. She inwardly sighed, seeing herself in that bridal tent, staring at herself in the mirror, noticing the worry and tension in her face when she began to realize that Harrington wasn't coming. That he wasn't just late.

"Ashley, when you marry Daddy you can take pictures here!" Willow said.

Ashley was immediately shaken from her thoughts—because she'd almost choked on air. *Marry Daddy?* What?

"I think Daddy and Ashley should definitely take pictures here," Violet said. "I hope they get the ducks in the pictures too."

Ashley realized she was staring—hard—at the twins, trying to make sense of what they'd just said. Should she correct them now? Wait for Shane to handle it? Why on earth would they think she was marrying their father? Where had that come from?

"Violet, Willow," she began hesitantly. "Your daddy and I aren't getting married."

"We know you're not getting married *now*," Violet said.

"Yeah, not right *now*!" Willow added with a big grin, the *now* getting a couple of extra syllables.

Phew. Her heart slowed back down to normal.

"We just meant someday," Violet added.

Someday. Ashley suddenly imagined herself in the foreman's cabin, the Dawson home. She saw herself curled up on the sofa in front of the crackling fireplace, snowflakes coming down, as she flipped through a photo album of her and Shane's wedding, the girls beside her, smiling and full of remembrances of the big day. Oh, and in this little winter fantasy, Ashley was eight months pregnant with Violet and Willow's little sister or brother.

What on earth? she thought again. *Now I'm seeing myself married to Shane Dawson? Pregnant with his child?*

Back to reality, Ashley.

"Well, you know what happened a few days ago," she said. "I was supposed to get married, but it didn't happen."

Willow nodded. "Because Harrington didn't come."

"Right," Ashley said. "So, I'm probably going to take my time getting over that, you know?"

"Do you still feel sad?" Willow asked.

"I feel…confused," Ashley said.

"Why?" Violet asked.

"Because planning a wedding is a big deal. And when the groom doesn't show up…well, that's a bigger deal. It raises all sorts of questions."

The girls both nodded.

They'd met Harrington several times when he'd come to pick her up. She wondered if they'd liked him.

Oh, heck, yes, she was going to ask.

"What did you two think of Harrington the times you met him?"

"He was always nice to us," Willow said.

Violet nodded.

Well, at least she had that. He'd been nice to children. She hadn't picked a complete cad.

She inwardly sighed, watching the bride and groom, who'd moved down below where the pond was.

"Tacos for everyone!" Shane called as he approached a nearby picnic table. "Come and get it!"

Ashley's heart fluttered, as did her stomach with a bunch of butterflies. That was new too. This fluttering. The attraction, she was getting used to. Liking this Shane Dawson, the man she'd come to know on this road trip—*that* she'd accepted. But what was this schoolgirl excitement about him coming over with tacos?

Oh, please, she thought, hopping up as the girls ran over. *You were just picturing yourself living in his cabin, married to him, expecting a baby. You've got...feelings for the guy. Accept* that.

Problem was, admitting to herself that she did have feelings for Shane Dawson was a little too scary right now. Too much too soon. Too fast.

The tacos were as good as the online reviews said they'd be. Shane had dragged out this stop in the park for as long as he could, spending a while at the petting zoo, going back to the ducks for a bit, returning to the table for refreshments, wanting to delay the inevitable: the final leg to Jackson Hole. Where he'd have to hand over the girls till Friday, get a lecture of his own from the Shaws and then wait for the impending assessment. *We're sorry, Shane, but we've warned you. The girls are not being raised right, and so you leave us no choice but to petition for custody...*

His stomach rolled.

Oh—and then there was dropping off Ashley at Harrington Harris's summer palace.

His stomach rolled again.

"Ashley, is that a beaver?" Willow asked, pointing at a woodland creature on their way back toward the parking lot.

Ashley peered at it. "Sure looks like it. I see buck teeth!"

"And it has a big flat tail," Violet said excitedly.

"Last one to that tree is a rotten potato chip!" Willow shouted, racing for a big oak with huge and dramatic horizontal branches. It was the perfect climbing tree.

"Last one to the top is a rotten cheese stick!" Violet said, starting her climb.

"Careful, girls!" Shane called. "Watch your footing."

"Trees are so irresistible to kids," Ashley said, tilting her head back to see the girls climb higher and higher.

Shane got out his phone and snapped a few photos, leaning close to Ashley to show her a particularly good one, where he'd caught both girls climbing, the excitement on their faces a thing of beauty.

"I've seen you sitting on a branch pretty high up in that big maple near the stables," Shane said to Ashley. "Quite a few times, actually. It's like the outdoor version of the stables loft for you."

Ashley smiled. "I didn't think anyone knew about my outdoor hiding place. I climb up pretty far behind dense leaves."

"My Ashley McCray radar is pretty strong."

She tilted her head, looking at him for a moment. "Seems so. I guess I didn't realize this whole past year of my relationship with Harrington that you were looking out for me."

"Always," he said, and the connection between them locked his eyes to hers. He couldn't look away if he tried.

"Look at me, Daddy!" Willow called at that exact moment, and he had to smile to himself. Only his daughters could wrest away his focus from Ashley's hazel-gold eyes, her pink-red lips…

He glanced up to see Willow alarmingly high up. Too high. Violet was several feet below, sitting on a limb and looking intently at a leaf. He saw Willow reach for a branch above her head—and miss. She screamed as she slipped, her arm sliding against a branch as she dropped—hard— to the ground.

Shane's heart stopped, then started pounding. He ran over, Ashley right behind him. Willow lay on the ground, looking half shocked, half in pain, the wind knocked out of her.

"Willow!" Violet yelled and looked panicked as she jumped down from her perch, landing on her knees. She rubbed at them, then ran over.

Willow was crying, her face red, and she wasn't moving. "My foot hurts, Daddy. It hurts really bad."

"Oh, no," Shane said. He peered at her ankle, visible above her little orange socks. It was already swollen. "Let's get you to Urgent Care, honey. It might be broken." He scooped her up, careful not to touch her ankle.

They all hurried to the SUV, Willow sobbing in his arms.

"Ashley, will you reach into my pocket and grab the keys?" he asked.

She did and unlocked the doors and held the back seat door open as Shane settled Willow in her booster seat and got her buckled. Ashley got in beside her and buckled up as Violet scrambled into her own seat on the other side.

Once in the driver's seat, he grabbed his phone and typed in: Urgent Care near me. There was one just seven miles from here. Thank God.

He heard Ashley murmuring softly to Willow. A glance in the rearview mirror showed she was holding Willow's hand. He registered that as very thoughtful before another look in the mirror showed Willow's face contorted in agony.

His heart pounded harder.

All he could think as he drove as fast as he could without risking an accident was that his baby girl was hurting.

Because he'd been too busy flirting with Ashley instead of watching his daughters, who he knew were up in that tree.

He could kick himself. Maybe if he'd been watching, paying attention, he could have been a bit closer with his arms ready to catch her.

Instead his daughter landed with a thud on the ground, her ankle reddened and swollen.

He mentally shook his head. There was nothing the Shaws could ever say that would be worse or more critical than what he was yelling at himself right now.

Ashley and Violet sat side by side in the Urgent Care waiting room, Violet playing a game on Ashley's phone, Ashley's gaze darting to the Exam Rooms door every five seconds. She kept hoping Shane and Willow would come through, but a half hour had passed since they'd disappeared inside with a nurse, and there was no sign of them. Violet had tears in her eyes when they'd first arrived, her sister sobbing and wincing in pain, but the phone game seemed to be working to distract her from the wait.

"Do you think her leg is broken?" Violet asked nervously, putting the phone on her lap. "Eli Overman broke his leg from jumping off the monkey bars, and he wasn't even that high up."

"It could be a sprain or it might be broken. We'll have to wait and find out. But either way, the doctor will know what to do. Willow might come out in a cast or a brace to keep her foot secure."

"I'll sign her cast," Violet said with a nod.

"Me too—if she has one. She might only have a brace or something called a boot that comes on and off."

Violet's eyes got all misty again, and she seemed to shrink into herself.

"Want to sit on my lap?" Ashley asked, holding out her arms.

Violet immediately scrambled over, settling herself and turning inward. Ashley put her arms around the little girl, resting her cheek atop her silky hair with the very short bangs for a moment.

The door to the exam rooms finally opened. Violet, who'd normally rush over to her father and twin, seemed nervous and hesitant and stayed on Ashley's lap. Shane's gaze darted to Violet. Unless Ashley was imagining it, he seemed a little upset at the sight of her there. *Stop it, Ashley. Of course he's upset and tense and stressed—it has nothing to do with you.*

Willow was all smiles now. "Guess what? I have to wear this! It's called a boot. It'll keep my ankle steady as it gets better. I have to wear it for six whole weeks. Daddy said that's the rest of school!"

Violet hopped off Ashley's lap and walked over to her twin. "It doesn't hurt anymore?"

"It does a little. But not like before. The doctor wrapped it up with a superlong bandage. It's under the boot."

"No crutches?" Ashley asked. "That's a relief."

"Sure is. She can walk on it in the boot only." He turned to Willow. "And what did the doctor say about taking care of your ankle? About being nice to it? Gentle? Not running or jumping?"

Willow giggled. "He did tell me to be *extra* nice to my ankle. And I will. Pinkie promise!"

Shane smiled and extended his pinkie, which Willow wrapped her own around. "There, that's a solemn promise made." He turned back to Ashley. "Thanks for staying out there with Violet." He walked over to Violet and gave her hair a gentle ruffle. "You okay, honey?"

"Yup," Violet said. "Now that Willow is okay."

He smiled at his daughter and held up his hand for a high five.

Yup, Ashley had had it 100 percent right about his girls' big hearts. And Shane's.

"Okay, we can get back on the road," he said with a soft clap.

He was definitely stressed. About the grandparents' reaction? About the injury? That it happened at all on his watch?

Something else?

You're a little too invested in what Shane Dawson is thinking and feeling right now, she realized. *Because you care about him. And his daughters.*

A lot.

Instead of sitting between the girls like she had on the way to Urgent Care, she got in the front seat. As they pulled out of the lot and got on the highway, the big entrance sign noting Jackson Hole made her tense. Soon enough, they'd be going their separate ways.

Suddenly Ashley didn't like the thought of that.

After a half hour of driving, the quiet in the car had her turning around to check on the twins. They were both asleep. No surprise there, given the drama. Shane had been either quiet or keeping his line of conversation to Willow's injury.

"I figure we'll make one more stop an hour before we're set to arrive," he said. He'd made a quick call to the Shaws, gratefully getting their voice mail, and had left a message updating their ETA, which wasn't too far off course despite the Urgent Care visit. "A coffee shop or convenience store for some refreshments. We can have that talk with the twins about rules for their grandparents' house."

Ashley could only imagine the extra ire and ammunition the Shaws would have now. Even if the girls behaved like "little ladies," the sight of them, Violet with her scraped knee from jumping out of the tree and her extremely short bangs, and Willow with her big black boot on her left foot, would tell their own story—a story the Shaws would interpret their own way.

"You okay?" she asked.

He glanced at her and nodded, his expression softening a bit, which was a relief. "Just worried. About the ankle and the Shaws' reaction. 'Why weren't you watching them? Why weren't you paying attention? Sure, it's just a sprain, but it could have been much worse.' Followed by head shaking. And decisions." He seemed to shiver a bit.

"I wish I could help in some way," she said.

"You have. You've been an incredible help, Ashley. Every step of the way."

She felt her smile reach deep inside. And then, because he seemed lost in thought, she let him be. If he needed to release some tension or talk anything out, he would. And she'd be there.

But she wouldn't be in a few hours. She'd be at Harrington's, which suddenly felt so…wrong.

She had to see him, though. She had to get her parents' money back. Her bridal party's money back. Not to mention even a little of her dignity.

She had to tell him off.

And then something would happen—either he'd break down and tell her that he *did* make the biggest mistake of his life in leaving her at the altar, that the sight of her, standing before him, made him sure of that, and could they please have a second chance without the pressure of the wedding…

Or he'd look at her without any emotion, assured he'd made the right call, and say, *No problem, Ashley. Here's a check*... Maybe he'd apologize but say he'd done the right thing by ditching her, that they weren't meant to be.

Tough luck, kid. Them's the breaks. And close the door in her face.

One of those things would happen.

Now it was her turn to shiver, despite the perfectly comfortable temperature in Shane's SUV, the beautiful April weather outside.

She had a lot of thinking to do. And barely any time left.

Chapter Ten

Shane had been planning to stop in the heart of Jackson Hole, at the park the girls loved so much with the four arches made out of shed elk antlers and the incredible views of the mountain ranges. But given Willow's sprained ankle, he'd opted for a coffee shop near Town Square, where the girls could have chocolate milk and he and Ashley could get some necessary caffeine boosts. They parked very close to the café, Willow managing to walk fine in her boot.

At a table outside with their drinks and two treats to split, Shane had reiterated the rules for the Shaws' house. Indoor voices even outdoors. Walking instead of running, particularly in the house and down the stairs. Not jumping. Saying *please* and *thank you*. Using Ashley's tips and tricks, such as "Isn't that interesting!" in response to the grand-parents saying they enjoyed something the twins thought was *the worst*. No name-calling of anyone, even when referring to someone they didn't like, such as Dylan from school. They were to allow Nana to brush their hair and put it up in ponytails. And they were to show interest in others, asking questions that weren't too personal.

"Can we ask Nana and Pops about Mommy?" Violet said, taking a sip from her box of chocolate milk.

Willow tilted her head, staring at Shane, waiting for his answer.

Shane's heart gave a little ping. "Of course you can."

"I like when people ask us about Mommy, but they never do," Violet said.

Willow nodded. "I guess they think we don't want to talk about her, but we do."

"Yeah," Violet said. "We only don't like when people say something mean. Like that stu—" She paused, Shane's words from exactly one minute ago obviously sticking with her. "Like Dylan."

Sweet success. Instead of "stupid idiot," she'd used his name with a little venomous lilt to her voice. Fine with him.

"The kid from the birthday party?" Ashley asked, her gaze soft on the twins.

Violet nodded. "He said it was weird that we don't have a mother. But it's not weird."

"It's not weird," Willow agreed. "It's just the way it is."

The wisdom of five-year-olds sometimes rocked Shane to the core. He reached over and gave both their hands a squeeze across the table. "I think Nana and Pops feel just like you do about Mommy. Your mother was their beloved daughter. Just like you're my beloved daughters. I think they'd love to talk about her. Especially with you two."

The twins' little faces brightened.

"When we're back home at the McCray Ranch," Ashley said, "I'd love to hear what you know about your mommy. I can tell you what I know too."

Violet smiled. "We don't remember her, but we have a lot of stories about her from Daddy."

"We both have Mommy's green eyes," Willow said.

"And we both love horses just like Mommy did," Violet added.

Ashley's eyes were misty. "Well, you guys know how much I love horses too. I remember that your mother had a favorite horse named Duck. I thought that was very funny."

The twins laughed. "Duck!" Violet said. "Daddy told us about that horse. She was brown and white."

Willow nodded. "And a big fluffy white tail, right?"

"Yup," Ashley said with a grin.

The girls had their special smiles on their faces—which told Shane they were lost in thoughts about their mother. When they had those smiles, he knew they were at peace, that they were enchanted by what they knew about their mother, what they'd learned over the years, what they'd heard.

Ashley, as usual, was a master when it came to the twins' hearts and souls. How she always had the right thing to say at the right time amazed him.

Violet scooted close to her sister on the bench and cupped her hand around Willow's ear, whispering something. Usually Shane could hear their "whispers" loud and clear, but not this time.

Violet looked at Ashley. "Want to know a secret?"

"I already know it," Willow said with a nod.

Ashley glanced at Shane, her eyes still misty. She leaned forward on the bench. "I do want to know a secret."

"We like that you knew Mommy and remember her," Violet said. And then she hurried around the table and threw her arms around Ashley.

Willow got up and very slowly walked around too in her boot, doing the same from the other side of Ashley.

"Oh, my heart," Ashley said, tears spilling down her cheeks now. "I'm glad to know that secret. Thank you."

The girls beamed and went back to their seats, their attention taken by a young teenager zipping by on a skateboard. They sipped their chocolate milks and watched him make sharp turns, eyes wide.

"Parenthood," Shane whispered to Ashley, who dabbed under her eyes with a napkin. "It's something else."

"I really can't wait to find out," she whispered back.

His heart pinged again, this time at the idea of Ashley finding out because she was the mother of some other guy's child. A guy she hadn't met yet. Certainly not that cowardly serial disappointer Harrington Harris IV.

Ashley with someone else. As much as Shane wanted her to be happy, he didn't like the idea of her happy with another man.

Unsettled—and he'd been unsettled enough—he plastered on a neutral expression. "Well, everyone ready?"

When that was the last thing he was.

They headed inside the coffee shop so the girls could wash their treat-sticky hands. As he and Ashley waited, something suddenly occurred to him. Something he didn't like one bit.

"So, I guess I'll be dropping you off at Harrington's now?" he asked. "I suppose I should have asked earlier if you'd arranged to see him."

He could feel his scowl deepening.

She frowned herself. "Actually, I haven't gotten in touch with him at all. I figured I'd do that when I arrived. But now that I'm here…" She bit her lip and let out a breath. "I'm just not ready."

He was relieved but worried for her. She was conflicted, her beautiful eyes reflecting that.

"I have an idea," he said. "Why don't you stay in town while I drop off the twins? Walk in the park, do a little shopping, whatever eases your mind. I'll text you when I'm leaving the Shaws' house. Maybe by then you'll have made some decisions, and I'll come pick you up."

He felt little stabs poking at his chest. He didn't want Ashley anywhere near Harrington.

But this certainly wasn't his decision. He'd said his share on the trip here. She knew how he felt about her getting back together with the guy. What she'd do was up to her, and he had to accept her choice.

"That is definitely the plan," she said, perking up some. "I'll do exactly that. Stroll the park and check out the shops. Maybe have two or ten more iced coffees."

He reached his hand to hers and gave it a squeeze. He had no idea what was going to happen. With anything. But he knew, right here, right now, that he couldn't bear the thought of Ashley McCray with another man. Particularly her ex-fiancé, but any other man.

Except him.

But was he ready for a relationship with her? Right now, he was too focused on the Shaws' threats and the holy hell they were going to rain down on him about Willow's injury and Violet's haircut. The scrapes on Violet's knees. The faded bruise on Willow's arm from falling off her bike last month. And those were just the immediately visible issues. Then the twins would open their mouths. Move. And…

"We're ready to go, Daddy!" Violet said as the girls came out the restroom.

He sure wasn't.

"Nana! Pops! We're here! We're here!"

Surely the Shaws would appreciate the twins' excitement at seeing them, Shane thought as the girls raced out—and

Willow was fast in that boot—of the SUV in their grand-parents' driveway, forgetting everything he'd told them twenty minutes ago in town.

Beatrice and Charles Shaw appeared in the doorway of their stately stone house, the Grand Tetons rising in the distance behind it. Shane was always struck whenever he saw the Shaws because there was so much of Liza in them. Beatrice's hair was a deep auburn, and though Liza's had been long and wavy while her mother's was a precise bob to her chin, the similarity in color and texture always caught him off guard. Liza had had her father's green eyes, her mother's perfect nose and alabaster complexion. And height from both tall Shaws.

Beatrice was in her signature outfit, a twinset (he'd learned what it was called from Liza) with dressy pants, and flat shoes with some sort of crest on the toes. Tasteful jewelry, tasteful makeup. Charles, as usual, was dressed in tan chinos and a crisp button-down shirt, this one plaid. Beatrice always had a snooty look about her, but Charles radiated warmth. Liza had had his ready smile.

Violet dashed up the bluestone walkway and threw her arms around her grandmother, then her grandfather, Willow going quite a bit slower in her boot.

The good news? Violet had been so fast running from the car to her grandmother that Beatrice couldn't possibly have noticed the budding hairstylist's bangs. The Shaws' attention was on Willow—her foot, to be exact. Shane hadn't mentioned the reason for the delay in the voice mail.

"What on earth?" Beatrice said, giving Violet a quick hug and then stepping forward to peer at her twin.

Violet remained on the porch. "Willow sprained her ankle and has to wear that boot for six whole weeks!"

Beatrice's gaze traveled from Violet to Willow. She stared at her granddaughter. Well, she'd definitely noticed the hacked bangs now.

"Girls! Welcome!" Charles said. "We're so happy to see you and have you stay for a few days!" He rubbed his chin for a moment. "Hmm, Willow, let me guess… You were running superfast and tripped and landed funny."

"Guess again!" Willow said, making her way to the porch.

Beatrice scowled, her gaze on the black boot.

"You were climbing high at the playground and took a tumble," Charles said.

Willow grinned. "It was actually a tree!"

"And where was your father while you were falling out of trees?" Beatrice muttered.

"Talking to Ashley," Violet said so guilelessly that Shane couldn't fault her for ratting him out. He *had* been talking to Ashley.

"Ashley?" Beatrice said, her chin rising as she shot a quick glance Shane's way. "Who, pray tell, is Ashley?"

"Ashley McCray!" Willow said from the porch.

"Oh, yes," Beatrice said. "The rancher's daughter."

Shane felt himself bristle. That sounded so dismissive. *The rancher's daughter.*

"Ashley's a horse groomer," Violet said. "And her fonsay didn't come to their wedding."

"Her fonsay?" Beatrice repeated.

"Fiancé," Shane offered, his collar tightening even though the first two buttons of his own button-down shirt were open.

"I see you have a new hairstyle," Charles said quickly to Violet as if sensing they should get off the topic of Ashley pronto.

Thank God for Charles. Or actually, maybe not. Beatrice hadn't even gotten to Violet's hair yet. Now she would.

Violet beamed. "I did it myself. I wanted to look like Miranda."

That got Beatrice's attention. The chin lifted just slightly again, and her eyes slightly narrowed. "Miranda? *Who's* Miranda?"

"She's Ashley's cousin. We stayed with her and Michael when Daddy's car was broken."

"Oh, yes, that," Beatrice said. "I almost forgot about the broken-down vehicle." Another glance of disdain was sent Shane's way.

"Ashley came with us on the trip," Violet said. "When he leaves here, Daddy's going to take her to her fonsay's house to get back her money!"

Oh, boy. That was a loaded sentence. Full of things for Beatrice to home in on. To the point that she didn't even correct Violet's pronunciation.

"For the wedding," Willow explained.

For a moment, Beatrice just stared at the girls with a strange expression. "My goodness. How...vulgar," she added under her breath.

But Shane heard it. A burst of anger grew in his gut. There was nothing vulgar about Ashley McCray or her intentions. He stared daggers at Beatrice, which she didn't seem to notice because her attention was moving from Violet's bangs down to her knees. Her scraped knees.

Beatrice walked over to him. "Is Ashley your girlfriend?" she asked in a whisper, her voice cold—but curious.

"She's a family friend. My boss's daughter," Shane said unnecessarily. "We were headed to the same town on the same day, and it made sense for me to give Ashley a ride. The girls adore her."

Beatrice didn't respond. She walked back over to the porch, where Willow had climbed up. Violet was behind her, doing a cartwheel.

Don't knock out a window, he prayed. Or maybe she should. Kick out the whole pane. It would give them something else to talk about.

Beatrice turned to the twins. "Well, I don't know how I can possibly take you two to Climbing Kingdom now." She shook her head with yet another look of disappointment at Shane. "You girls specifically asked to go there on this vacation, but now we can't."

"What matters is that you two are here!" Charles cut in fast. "We're going to have a great bunch of days."

"Yes, of course we will," Beatrice said with a smile at her granddaughters. Then she turned to Shane, the smile gone. "We'll take it from here. Bye now. Girls, say goodbye to your father."

Dismissed. Fine with him. The less time he had to spend with Beatrice Shaw, the better.

The twins came over and hugged him tight. "I'll pick you up on Friday morning, okay? You listen to your grandparents and remember the rules I told you about."

He caught Beatrice raising an eyebrow. They had another round of hugs, and then he held up a hand in goodbye to the Shaws and walked over to his SUV.

Beatrice followed. "A word, Shane."

He turned, dread rising in his throat, desperate to get out of there.

Charles was leading the twins around the side of the house to the backyard, where they had a play area.

Beatrice waited until Charles and the girls were out of sight—and earshot. "I could not be more disappointed," she said. "Well, I'm sure I could. A sprained ankle? Violet playing with sharp scissors and ruining her hair? The scrapes on those girls? The running and yelling the moment they arrived. Nothing's changed. Nothing at all."

"I'm glad for that," he said, deciding he wasn't going to take her criticisms lying down. As much as he wanted to pacify her to keep her from following through on her threat, he wasn't going to let anyone run down his daughters without him standing up to defend them. "Because Willow and Violet are great girls. They're active five-year-olds. They fall because they're playing and enjoying themselves. They're curious. They're smart and interesting and have huge hearts. I'm proud of who they are. I wish you could like them as they are instead of wanting them to turn into people they're not."

"What's wrong with wanting them to be appropriate citizens?" Beatrice said. "That's all I ask. Well-behaved, well-mannered girls."

"They are well-behaved and well-mannered." He mentally shook his head, keeping a lid on his temper. He was well used to Beatrice, and this was nothing new. Except now there was the threat of her taking him to court to fight for custody of his children.

The anger welled up again. *I'll have to be dead first.*

"I'm glad you'll have these days with them," he said, trying to keep the ice out of his own tone. "Because I think you'll see, if you're really looking and listening, how wonderful they are."

"I know they're wonderful, Shane. They're half Liza. Of course they're wonderful. But they're a danger to themselves, and you clearly don't watch them or discipline them. They're not being raised right."

Like hell they weren't.

He wished she would look at him and see the man who loved her granddaughters with everything he was. The man who'd loved her daughter. The man her daughter had loved. Had started a family with. The girls had brought Liza so much joy. But Beatrice had always found something to criticize, no matter how young the twins were. He'd never forget Violet and Willow's second birthday party, which he'd thrown at an indoor toddler play space. They'd been in the throes of the terrible twos the moment they'd hit that milestone. Beatrice had been complaining up a storm about the pretty low-level tantrum they'd both thrown over not getting to have their birthday cake yet. *Unacceptable!* Beatrice had snapped at him. *Liza would have had them behaving like those sweet little girls over there*, she'd said, pointing to the quiet, docile little Hayberry twins, who were nothing like his active whirlwinds.

I'm not the enemy, Beatrice, he'd said to her. *I'm the man who loved your daughter so much that sometimes when I look at the girls and I see her in their faces, I just break down inside. I'm not the enemy*, he'd repeated. *And I'm doing the best that I can—which, yes,* is *good enough.*

He'd seen her eyes mist before she'd turned away, and he'd been reminded that there was a heart in that body, despite how determinedly she hid it. He'd known she was reacting out of grief. And he'd stuck to his promise to Liza after he'd lost her to always extend his compassion to her mother. To do his best to meet her at her comfort zone until he was pushed too far out of his.

He was there now.

He bristled, anger rising. "They *are* being raised right. They're loved, happy and wonderful children. If I have to fight you in court, I'm prepared."

Beatrice lifted her chin again. "I'll expect you on Friday at ten a.m. to pick them up. That will give you time to return home at a reasonable hour for their bedtime."

A sudden change of subject while still getting in another dig about propriety. She was impossible.

"Just enjoy them," he said. "Liza would be so proud of her daughters. So proud," he added, tears stinging the backs of his eyes at how very true that was. He blinked them away.

Beatrice gave him the quickest of glances but didn't respond. Instead, she turned and headed back to the house. At least she didn't say something awful like, *I'm not so sure about that.*

Still, this had been every bit the disaster of a drop-off that he'd been expecting.

Chapter Eleven

For the past hour, Ashley had been sitting on a bench in the park, so focused on what was very likely going on at the Shaws' house that she barely gave any thought to the reason she'd come to Jackson Hole. All she could think about was the twins' grandmother pulling Shane aside with her litany of complaints and criticisms.

Her threats to take his girls away from him.

He must be so stressed.

She'd seen—up close—how great a father he was, how devoted and loving and caring, how tuned in to his children he was, and how very happy the girls were with him. She adored those Dawson twins and had seen just how lucky they were to have him as a father. Their sole parent.

She pulled out her phone to check the time. He should be texting any moment now. She kept her phone in her hand and lifted her face to the waning sun. She was sitting on a bench in the park, the majestic mountain ranges in full view, the shops and restaurants of Jackson Hole surrounding the square. The air had turned a bit cooler, but there was no wind and it felt so refreshing on her skin, in her hair. She'd been sitting here since they'd parted, unable to imagine window-shopping, let alone going in any stores.

Not when Shane's entire life felt dependent on the grand-parents' reaction, their assessment of the girls' behavior.

Anger stoked in her belly. How unfair. How dare they? Couldn't Beatrice see how he loved Violet and Willow—how loved they were? Couldn't they see how hard he worked, how he balanced his life as a father? He deserved better than to be threatened.

You care about this man, she acknowledged. *A lot.*

Her phone pinged, and she sat up straight. Shane.

Left the Shaws. Feel like hell. Up for some terrible company?

Aww. Her heart flew out to him.

Absolutely, she texted back. Dinner?

And a drink, was his response. Three emojis of wine bottles following.

She texted back a smiley face and her location. He wrote that he'd be there in ten minutes.

As she put her phone away and waited, she realized that right beside her concern for him was excitement at seeing him. To be with Shane, to sit across a table somewhere and share a meal, share their problems.

Maybe…kiss again.

Yes, she thought, some very good, very sexy memories washing over her.

Maybe tonight, they just needed to forget those problems. Put them aside for just a few hours. Several, even. And…enjoy each other's company, which would *not* be terrible because they wouldn't be focusing on why they were here in this beautiful town. They'd focus on each other. On pleasure. On forgetting just for tonight.

She'd propose it. Perhaps she wouldn't even have to.

Perhaps the evening would naturally lead to it. She had a feeling it might.

At the fifteen-minute mark, she began looking around for Shane. And there he was, walking down the path toward her. She stood, and he held up a hand in a wave. She could see how tense he was in the set of his shoulders, in the set of his jaw, the lack of light in his eyes.

As he approached, she held out her arms and he stepped right into them. She hugged him and he hugged her back, hard, resting his head atop hers. He definitely was tense, but she could feel him relaxing a bit, more a resignation of what was than letting go of anything.

"How bad was it?" she asked.

He stepped back a bit. "Bad. I'm not raising them right, she said."

Ashley shook her head. "That's the wrongest thing I've ever heard. Ever."

He did manage something of a smile then. "I appreciate that." He held out his hand and she took it, and they started walking. "I could use a steak house. The works. Maybe even creamed spinach. And a really good beer."

"I definitely remember passing a steak house on the way here."

"Rodeo Joe's Steaks," he said.

"We're there."

He smiled again and squeezed her hand, and they continued walking. "What would I have done if you weren't here? I'd be sitting on that bench you just vacated, stewing and shaking and going out of my mind."

"Yeah, same here. If you weren't here, I'd still be on that bench, unable to move or think or know what the hell to do." Not that she *did* know.

"It's a good thing we're both here, then." He squeezed her hand again, and she felt such a connection to him, such solidarity.

"I was thinking," she said. "Let's just go where the night takes us. Talk about what we need to and want to. Do what we need to and want to."

"I'm all for that."

"Good," she said.

This might not be an easy night for either of them, but they'd get through it together.

Rodeo Joe's was crowded, but they'd scored a table for two after just a twenty-minute wait at the bar, where Shane had his good beer and Ashley had sipped a vodka and cranberry. Every time he looked at her, her beautiful face and long silky brown hair, and every time he heard her voice or laughter, he'd be transported away from everything going wrong in both their worlds. By the sweetness of their friendship, the comfort of how they supported each other, the excitement of their attraction and the pressure-free question mark that seemed to hang in the air between them, all his tension would ease and he'd just focus on Ashley McCray.

But then a waiter would pass by with a tray of entrées or a man at a nearby table would laugh loudly and the spell would be broken, diverting his thoughts from Ashley back to the force of everything Beatrice had said, and his shoulders would seize up again. At one point when they'd still been in the bar awaiting their table, Ashley had looked at him with concern, stood up from her stool and given him a mini massage. He'd closed his eyes and let her warm, strong hands work their magic. But then their table had been called and the magic hands had unfortunately lifted.

Now they sat across from each other in front of a window with a view of the mountains, the soft lighting and music helping to relax him again. The woman too. Their waiter had come and gone, and Shane found himself focusing on the good meal he was about to have, the easy conversation and the excellent company. He wasn't sure how great he'd be as a dinner partner, but he'd try to stop thinking about the Shaws for at least the next hour.

The waiter returned with their entrées, and they dug in, talking and laughing and offering each other bites of their meals. It was great at first, but then he started thinking of something equally unpleasant.

Ashley would probably go see Harrington tomorrow. He had the feeling she wasn't going to do that tonight, and he was grateful for that. But tomorrow morning was a different story. She'd go do what she'd come for.

Just demand back the money. Don't hope that he looks at you and realizes he screwed up big-time.

That was what Shane was afraid of, that she still had that lingering hope in her heart. That she needed Harrington to say he was sorry, that he made a mistake, could they try again.

His shoulders started tensing again.

"Hey, you look more stressed than you were when you arrived in the park," Ashley said, fork paused midway to her mouth. "You okay?"

Just say it. This is Ashley, who you can talk to. About anything. Don't hold back the truth. "Just thinking about why you're here. Not in this restaurant. I mean here in Jackson Hole. I figure tomorrow morning, you're going to go see what's-his-name."

"At the very least I need to confront him about the money," she said. "But let's not talk about that, Shane."

At the very least? What the hell did that mean? Those two should have *nothing* to discuss other than the wedding bill. In his opinion anyway.

"Look," she said. "We both have a lot on our minds. But we're here tonight in this beautiful, bustling town, and let's just try to enjoy it, put everything aside, just for tonight."

He held up his beer glass. She held up her wine. They clinked. "To tonight."

"To tonight," she repeated, her gaze and smile softer now. She sipped her wine and forked a spear of asparagus. "But I guess I should ask—you'll be leaving for home in the morning? Then you'll drive back to pick up the girls? You'll have to leave home at the crack of dawn."

He stopped chewing and stared at her for a second. He hadn't really thought about it. But he supposed that would be the plan. It wasn't like he'd want to stick around Jackson Hole with all the uncertainty plaguing him. Better another seven-hour drive to get back to his own turf than risk running into the Shaws in town, even if he'd get to eyeball his girls and give them a hug. No, he should leave and drive back when it was time for the world to feel right again: when he'd be able to be with his children.

Except there was the ole monkey wrench now. Ashley herself.

"I was planning on driving back home, yes," he said. "But I don't like the idea of leaving you on your own here, so…" A decision formed as he said the words. "I'll just stick around. Just in case."

"In case what?" she asked.

"In case you need me."

Her expression showed how touched she was. She put down her fork and reached for his hand and held it across the table. "Now we have to eat holding hands," she said. "Sorry, but that's just the way it has to be." She smiled, her beautiful face lighting up.

"I'd have a hard time letting go anyway," he said.

"Same." She looked up at him, almost shyly.

Tonight was going to be interesting, that much he knew.

"If you're planning to stick around," she said slowly, "maybe...we should find a place to stay for a few days."

Oh, yeah, interesting to say the least.

"There are so many hotels, Airbnbs, guest ranches," Ashley pointed out. "Oooh, maybe we can stay at a guest ranch like your cousins have in Bear Ridge."

Shane loved the place, as did the twins. The Dawson Family Guest Ranch was owned by six siblings, second cousins to Shane. They had opened the dude ranch, re-built from ashes and the doom and gloom of family history, and over the past few years had expanded it into one of the most popular in Wyoming. He and Ashley should definitely pick a place like that, where they could go horseback riding, watch comical goats, walk the land, sit by the river, stare endlessly at the mountains, eat good food and just be together.

And whatever else came up...

"Now we know what we're doing after dinner," he said. "Finding our dude ranch."

Her warm smile mixed with the relief on her pretty face shot straight to his heart.

If anyone had told him a week ago that making Ashley

McCray happy would be so important to him, he wouldn't have believed it. But life was full of surprises—the good and the bad—and right this second, he was dealing with the good and was going with it.

No matter where it led or didn't.

Ahhh, Ashley thought as she and Shane arrived at their cabin at the Mountain Valley Guest Ranch and looked around. Heavenly. The medium-sized ranch was just fifteen minutes from the center of town. Their cabin, a hunter green two-bedroom with a steeply pitched roof and a porch with a swing, overlooked a river and had evergreens creating privacy from the neighbors on either side. Small and cozy with a big stone fireplace, a plush dark tan sofa and a big muted soft area rug, the cabin also had a kitchenette and a bathroom with a spa shower—complete with two fluffy robes on hooks behind the door. Oh, yes, this would do nicely. A relaxing place to spend a few days, to think and plan.

With her new best friend, Shane Dawson.

He'd insisted on covering the cost, including any spa treatments she wanted, and she definitely wanted those. Even just the most rudimentary of facials with cucumber slices over her eyes and a mud mask would be a treat. Ranch attractions included horseback riding on acres of trails, a cafeteria with supposedly amazing burgers and shoestring fries, a petting zoo and Be A Rancher For A Day! Workshops where you could help lead the small herd of cattle out to different pastures or milk cows and learn to make cheese. Yes to all of it, Ashley thought, dropping down on the sofa with a very satisfied sigh. She'd always worked solely with the horses at the McCray Ranch; it would be fun to focus on the cows here.

Shane was scanning the brochure of activities they'd received at check-in. "The entertainment is from nine to eleven at the lodge's club—there's a comedian and also a jazz singer, dancing and moonlit walks along the lit path along the river."

"A comedy show? I love it here already," she said.

"Same." He dropped down next to her, and she turned to him and took his hand.

"Thank you for staying in town with me. Just thank you."

He leaned his head back against the cushion and turned to face her. "Thank you for staying with *me*."

But in separate bedrooms, she wanted to add but didn't. Earlier she'd been planning to let the night go where it would. But maybe tonight needed to be about rest and relaxation— not adding more confusion to the mix. If she and Shane got all romantic again, what did that mean about what she wanted? What she intended? She didn't seem to know how she felt about anything except that Shane was becoming very dear to her. He was there from the outset at the biggest disappointment of her life, there to comfort her, there to offer her a ride, a way to process. And he was here now.

And she was so damned drawn to him, so attracted.

Because he *was* here? Because he *was* there for her when she needed someone most? Someone to count on, someone to turn to, someone who would tell her the truth?

Stop, she chastised herself again. *Don't complicate things further. If you think you might be getting back together with Harrington, if that's a possibility, then no more kissing Shane. No more anything with Shane other than friendship.*

But calling a mental halt to whatever might happen between her and Shane didn't sit well with her either. What was going on here? What did she want? And what if she really fell for Shane? Then what? He wasn't necessarily in the market for a relationship.

Had she ever seen him with a woman in the five years he'd been widowed? Had she ever seen any female besides a relative enter his cabin? Had he ever gone anywhere overnight other than to drop off his daughters at relatives' for visits?

From everything she'd seen and heard, the man didn't date.

But he was….attracted to her. That was the only thing she knew.

You're getting ahead of yourself, Ashley, she told herself. *Just try to enjoy yourself while you're here at the dude ranch. In the morning, you'll make a decision about whether you're ready to go see Harrington and confront him. If you need another day, fine. The reservation for the dude ranch is for three nights.*

Too many contradictory thoughts. Stop thinking.

"Let's take a walk along the river and then go to the comedy show. I could use a laugh."

"Me too," she said. Perfect. A walk on a beautiful evening and a show. Just what she needed. "I'll just go freshen up."

She missed him the moment she closed the bathroom door behind her.

Chapter Twelve

The theater in the Mountain Valley Guest Ranch lodge was on the small side, but pretty crowded, as though all the guests had turned up for the comedian. Who didn't like to laugh? Beatrice Shaw, maybe. But most people did, so Shane wasn't surprised that the show attracted so many folks.

There was a stage and around thirty tables, a few waiters weaving between with trays of drinks and baskets of popcorn. He and Ashley were sitting in the front row, over to the left. The drinks were expensive—fifteen dollars, even draft beer—but the venue had a two-drink minimum. At least there was free popcorn.

The comedian, a tall, skinny guy in a Stetson, bolo tie, huge silver belt buckle and cowboy boots, whose stage name was Cowboy Roy, wasn't all that funny. He tried, but his timing was off and his jokes were a little stale. He got a couple of laughs here and there, mostly when he got a bit vulgar.

"Okay," Cowboy Roy said, peering into the audience, clearly looking for something to turn his bad set around. "Enough about me. Who are *you* people? Any newlyweds? Who's on their honeymoon? I hear this place has a special honeymoon cabin with the works—heart-shaped bed, annulment papers just in case..." That didn't even get him a chuckle—big surprise.

Shane glanced over at Ashley to check her reaction; she didn't crack a smile, but then again, it wasn't laughworthy. For the first time, really, Shane homed in on the fact that Ashley's entire life, her future, all the hopes and dreams she'd had for her wedding and marriage, had been taken from her. Shane might think she'd dodged a bullet, but Ashley's heart had been terribly messed with. She'd probably been very excited about her honeymoon—which the Harrises had paid for as their gift—and now, instead of ordering incredible pasta in Italy, a gold wedding ring on her finger, happiness radiating from within, she was here, with him, munching on popcorn and watching a bad comedian joke about honeymoons.

"Huh, no honeymooners," Cowboy Roy continued. "Who's on their third date, then? Third-date rule still a thing? I don't often get past the first date, so I wouldn't know, unfortunately." Shane definitely wasn't surprised to hear that. "Ah, you two," he said, his eyes lighting up as he pointed to Shane and Ashley. "*Definitely* on your third date. I can feel the anticipation, the tension *radiating* off the two of you."

Every head in the place swiveled to him and Ashley.

Oh, God. Oh, no. There was nothing worse than getting singled out by a comedian.

"People, am I right?" Cowboy Roy said, wiggling his eyebrows. "Oh, my, the sexual tension! Sweetheart, tell us, is he getting lucky tonight?"

This was what passed for humor these days? The guy was not funny in the slightest. Where'd they get him from?

Ashley's cheeks were red. "We're not even a couple," she called out, her eyes darting around a bit. Shane wondered if she was worried she might know someone in the audience, someone who knew about her relationship with Harrington. "We're, um, just…"

Cowboy Roy made a "yeah, right" face, and that did get a laugh from the audience. From everyone but him and Ashley. "Just *friends*? Suuuure. You two will be engaged within three months. Mark my words."

Shane stiffened. Ashley turned redder.

"We're not… I'm not…" Ashley stammered, then clamped her lips shut.

"Sometimes the couple is the last to know," Cowboy Roy said with a wink, then turned to a table of four a row ahead. "Ah, double date…"

Shane breathed a sigh of relief that he'd moved on, that they weren't being responsive enough to continue with. Though Ashley had made it clear there was nothing between them.

We're not a couple…

Of course they weren't a couple. They weren't even dating. They were only together in the strictest sense of the word. They'd had a moment, a couple of moments, that was all.

He and Ashley awkwardly ate popcorn and sipped their drinks. The comedian called for a twenty-minute intermission, reminding everyone that they'd have to order their second drink during the second half, and if they left early, they'd be billed for it anyway.

"I can't take another minute of this guy," Shane said.

Ashley rolled her eyes. "Me either. He's the pits!"

Shane laughed. "Now, *that's* funny."

They got up and headed out. As they walked toward the

cabin on the well-lit path, Ashley said, "What do you think about what he said—I mean about us?"

"That we're third-date material?"

She glanced at him and nodded. Her cheeks were slightly flushed.

"I think," he said slowly, "I think that unfunny comedian was right."

"You do?" she asked.

He stopped and turned to face her. "I can't deny I'm very attracted to you. On all levels."

She let out something of a gasp. "All levels," she repeated on a whisper.

"You're a truly lovely person, Ashley McCray. You're beautiful and incredibly sexy, yes, but you're kind and smart and interesting and fun and very nice to five-year-olds."

She flung her arms around him and hugged him. "I needed to hear that. Thank you."

"You're the first woman I've kissed in five years," he whispered. "To be honest, I had no plans to bring romance into my life again. Not that we're dating or involved, like you said. But you just sort of…happened."

She pulled back, her arms still around his neck, a shy smile on her beautiful face. "You sort of happened too."

He leaned forward and kissed her on the lips. "I'm not ready for anything. You're not sure what you're doing. But here we are. Making out."

She grinned. "We're a pair, all right."

He took her hand and they resumed walking. "You said we should take tonight to just…be. So let's just be. What happens happens."

"And what happens at the Mountain Valley Guest Ranch stays at the Mountain Valley Guest Ranch."

He stopped and turned to her and nodded. "It's like we're each taking baby steps that won't really lead anywhere. Maybe that's what we need, what we *should* be doing. Taking the steps to see what's what with absolutely no pressure."

"Yeah," she whispered. "I think that's exactly what we're doing."

She hooked her hand around his arm and they resumed walking. If he just focused on the beautiful April night, the surprisingly warm breeze, the fresh air, Ashley so close beside him, everything was okay in the world. For tonight anyway.

They approached the cabin, and he unlocked the door, the lamp casting a romantic glow over the interior.

"How about that second drink?" she asked. "The welcome packet said every cabin comes with a complimentary bottle of wine."

"Love some," he said. "And you relax. I've got it."

"You've always got everything. What can't you do?" she asked with a smile. "Seriously."

"Well, I'm kind of used to taking care of stuff and giving people food and beverages. I mix a lot of chocolate milk, make a lot of ham-and-Swiss sandwiches for the girls' lunches. Thank God they both love the same stuff right now. Can you imagine if they had wildly different likes and tastes and personalities?"

She laughed. "They are very alike. Just when I think one is the alpha, the other takes over. I love how close they are."

"Yup." He moved to the kitchenette against the wall and found two wineglasses in the cabinets. "Me too. They'll always have each other." He wished he could FaceTime them right now, but it was late, and even if they weren't asleep—and they probably were, given the big day they'd had—Beatrice Shaw would lay into him.

He brought the bottle, a corkscrew and two glasses. They sat together on the sofa in front of the beautiful stone fireplace but didn't bother lighting it because it was too nice for a fire. He opened the bottle and poured.

"To…right now," he said, holding up his glass.

"To right now," she repeated and they clinked.

Ashley sipped her wine, then put the glass on the coffee table, curled her legs up underneath her and rested her head on Shane's shoulder.

This was…nice. Very nice. He could stay just like this for maybe five more minutes—and then he was going to be overwhelmed with the desire to kiss her.

It turned out he wasn't going to have to wait that long. Because suddenly she was moving, straddling him, her hands against his chest. "I don't know anything, Shane. I just know that I want this right now."

"Same. Exactly. And if that's okay, then…"

"It's okay with me," she whispered.

"And me."

Her mouth was on his neck, trailing kisses up to his ear. He closed his eyes to keep control. It was hard enough to keep a grip on himself when he could feel everything she was doing to him. Seeing her beautiful face, her sexy body, would make his self-control shatter.

He pulled off her sweater and opened his eyes to her lush, full breasts hidden behind a lacy black bra. He needed that thing off now. She reached behind her and unhooked it, arching her back. He groaned, his hands, his mouth exploring every inch of her glorious chest. She moved against him, letting out a breathy moan, and he had to still himself to again regain control. He picked her up, Ashley still straddling him, and kissed her as he carried her to one of the bedrooms.

Within thirty seconds, both their jeans and his shirt were off, and the thin cotton of their underwear was all that was keeping them separated. It had to go too. He peeled down her white lace panties; she pulled down his black boxer briefs.

"Very sexy," she whispered, and he felt her lips on his stomach, kissing downward, a hand sliding onto his erection.

He moaned, groaned, arched his back—all while being unable to stop kissing her. He had to be inside her now.

"Oh, hell," he said, opening his eyes.

Ashley, underneath him, opened hers too. "What could possibly be wrong?" she asked, cupping his face.

"Lack of condoms." He bopped his forehead with the palm of his hand.

She grinned. "My cousin Miranda said the same thing the comedian did. That we're the last to know. She handed me three condoms before we left and insisted I put them in my wallet. Which is where they are now." She scooted over the bed and reached for her jeans and her wallet and plucked out all three condoms.

"Hey, you never know. And we can always get more tomorrow." She ripped open one of the little foil packets.

He grinned and then again went very still as she straddled him again and rolled on the condom. Moments later, she slid down on top of him, his hands on her waist, and moved against him.

Slowly at first. And then faster. Faster.

He reached upward to feel her lush breasts and sat up enough against the headboard to suckle her nipples.

"Oh, Shane," she whispered on a breathy moan, and he knew he was close.

They exploded in pleasure together, and she collapsed down on top of him, their hearts beating so fast in what felt like unison.

He stroked her silky hair and closed his eyes. He felt her kiss him on the cheek before she settled against his chest, and they caught their breath together, holding hands.

He didn't have a thought in his head other than how good this felt, how he wished he could stay like forever.

Ashley awoke in the dark on her side, a warm, strong arm over her.

Ahhh, Shane.

She turned slightly to peer at him. The moonlight coming in through the filmy bedroom curtains cast a beautiful dim glow over part of his face. He was so handsome. The dark tousled hair that she'd run her hands through just hours ago. Long, dark eyelashes against his cheeks. The chiseled jawline, which she'd kissed every bit of.

Mmm, sex with Shane Dawson had been amazing. They'd been in such harmony, moving together so fluidly, effortlessly. There had been so much passion, yet she'd felt so safe, cocooned, as though there was only the two of them in the world.

That's probably not real life, she thought. *That's most likely "road trip" sex. Road-trip romance.*

Or was it? Was she right where she was supposed to be? Would she still feel this way even when they were back in "real life"?

Last night he'd told her that she was the first woman he'd kissed in five years. Which meant she was the first woman he'd slept with since becoming a widower. What was he going to want from this? Maybe nothing at all. Maybe, like he'd said, this was about baby steps toward nothing in particular. At most, toward figuring stuff out that they needed to get a handle on as individuals that had nothing to do with them as a couple. They were doing what felt right in the moment.

Ashley turned and looked out the window. She could see the almost-full moon, and the tops of tree branches with their budding leaves. She slipped out from under Shane's arm and left the bed, tiptoeing from the room, quietly closing the door behind her. She went into the other bedroom, where she'd put her suitcase, and quickly put on a long sweatshirt and yoga pants, then pulled her hair back in a ponytail.

In the living room, she went over to the sliding glass doors that opened out onto the small patio. It was way too chilly to go outside, even though she could use a blast of cool air on her skin, on her brain.

Miranda. She needed to talk to her cousin. She'd help her make sense of what she was feeling without any judgment. And best of all, she'd be awake at—Ashley glanced up at the round clock with little cows for numbers on the kitchen wall—12:17 a.m. Even if baby Roxy was mostly sleeping through the night now, Miranda was a night owl. She sent her a quick text and asked if she was awake and up for FaceTime.

Her video-call app pinged five seconds later.

Ashley smiled. She owed Miranda a lot more than just good donuts for all this. "Hi," she said to her cousin.

"Oooh, something happened—something good," Miranda said, a twinkle in her eyes. "I can see it in your face."

Ashley moved over to a chair farthest from the bedroom she'd just left and glanced at the door to make sure it was still closed. It was, and she didn't hear a peep from inside. "Something did," she whispered. "And it was amazing." She couldn't stop her goofy smile.

"Oh! Well, I am not surprised. I knew you two were going to be together. Just a matter of time. And comfort."

"I don't know how comfortable I am," Ashley said. "I mean, what am I doing? I'm in Jackson Hole for a reason. And I'm sleeping with another man?"

"First of all, you're in Jackson Hole to demand your family's money back from that jerk who stood you up at the altar. And Shane isn't *another* man. There's no other man, Ashley."

She bit her lip. That was true. She wasn't engaged. She wasn't anything with Harrington at the moment. This was why she knew calling Miranda was a good idea. Her cousin would say it straight, even if it did ping her heart. And she knew Miranda thought Harrington Harris needed to be kicked to the curb the way he'd done to Ashley.

"He broke up with you in the worst way, honey. You're not cheating on Harrington, if that's even a thought in your head."

"I know," Ashley said. "But if I harbor any hopes of giving the relationship another chance without all the pressure of a wedding…"

"Well, then ask yourself why you slept with Shane. Test how you feel. About Harrington. About Shane. About everything. Maybe you keep clinging to the idea of another chance with Harrington because you're scared of how you feel about Shane. And I understand that, Ashley."

Huh. She hadn't considered that. Ashley wasn't a dummy—

she knew that Harrington had done her wrong. *I don't love you after all...* Was she sticking with this idea of him in her life because it felt safer than admitting she now had feelings for someone else? Scary feelings?

She let out a big sigh, because it sounded like the truth.

Miranda gave her a gentle smile, full of compassion. "You don't have to know everything. But if you want my opinion, and I think you do because you texted me at midnight, you need to move on from what's-his-name. He's past. Maybe Shane isn't the future—who knows? But he *is* the present, and he's helping you figure things out. He's a great guy, he's safety personified, and he's there for you. And from the look on your face when you popped on-screen, he's great in bed," she added with a devilish grin.

Oh, yeah, he was.

Ashley tried to keep the moony look off her face that the comment had brought on. "I knew I could count on you to set me straight. You're right—I don't know how I feel about anything and I don't have to know. Thank you for talking me through. I owe you."

"All you owe me is a visit sometime soon again. Love you, hon."

"Love you too," she said, and then the screen went dark.

She sat there for a while, looking out at the dark patio, at the moon. Thinking about Shane. Thinking about all Miranda had said.

He's safety personified...

No, he wasn't. Not at all. Shane wasn't safe. He had his own heart, mind and soul, his own reason for being in Jackson Hole and sticking around. His own worries and stressors. Like Miranda had said, she couldn't know if there was any future for them. Maybe all they had was the present.

And if that was the case, she needed to protect herself, and most especially protect her still-healing heart.

Don't fall in love, she told herself. *Whatever you do, do not fall in love with Shane Dawson.*

Their agreed-upon motto, *what happens on the road trip stays on the road trip*, was feeling more and more like utter nonsense. When she did go home, she'd take every memory with her and not forget a moment of it. Especially not after what went on in that bedroom just hours ago.

And Shane would be right there with her at the McCray Ranch.

Tread carefully from here on in, she told herself.

All she wanted right now was to go back into that bedroom and slip into bed beside Shane. She didn't, though. She got up and went into the other room, closing the door behind her.

She had no idea what this meant. Maybe she just needed a little space right now. To think about sleeping with Shane. How she felt about it. Everything Miranda had said.

Maybe she *was* just scared. Of just how deep her feelings for Shane Dawson went.

Chapter Thirteen

Shane woke up in the morning with an instant smile on his face. He kept his eyes closed, wanting to snuggle with Ashley, but when he reached out his hand, all he felt was…bed.

He opened his eyes. He was alone.

Disappointment socked him in the gut until he realized she just might be in the bathroom or the kitchen, making coffee. Maybe she was sitting out on the patio. He listened for signs of her up and moving around, but there was just silence in the cabin.

Shane got up, then rummaged through his suitcase for jeans and a T-shirt and got dressed. He headed out. Ashley wasn't in the living room, kitchen or on the back patio. He walked over to the second bedroom and quietly pulled open the door.

She was in bed, fast asleep.

The disappointment hit him hard again at the proof that at some point in the night, she'd woken up and left him.

He backed out and closed the door, going into the kitchen to start coffee. This was probably a good thing, he thought, choosing a macadamia nut blend K-Cup. *You don't know what you want from this. She doesn't know either.*

What he did know was that last night had been amazing. That he felt relaxed and sated. That he'd missed sex more than he'd realized.

That being with Ashley had felt right and good. They'd come together naturally, out of friendship, caring, attraction, desire. They weren't dating, there were no expectations, no third-date rule. They'd made love because their relationship, whatever it was, had led them there itself.

He liked that.

He drained his coffee and took a quick, hot shower, wishing he had company. When he came out, he saw Ashley on the patio, drinking her own coffee. She turned just then and he held up a hand, and her smile lit up her whole face.

She might have left him in the middle of the night for whatever reason, but that there was something between them, something special, wasn't in doubt.

Let it be, he told himself. *It'll work itself out.*

She came in then, and just as she said she was going to hop in the shower, his phone rang.

He went back into the bedroom and grabbed it. Huh. Beatrice. Calling to complain about the twins' behavior?

"Hello, Beatrice. Everything okay?" he asked, knowing full well it wasn't. She wouldn't be calling otherwise.

"Well, I'm…not sure. Charles and I can't find Violet. We're sure she's somewhere on the property, but we can't find her and she's not responding to us calling her name."

He frowned. "Do you think she's hiding? Did something happen?"

Silence for a moment. Then she said, "I simply told the twins at breakfast that I would be taking Violet to my hairstylist later this morning for an emergency cut to make her hair look more attractive. She seemed upset and said she liked her hair how it was. I told her that was nonsense, that her hair didn't look nice, and she burst into tears and ran off."

Oh, God. "Beatrice..." *How could you? Why can't you see the damage you do?*

"I didn't realize I'd upset her so much. Her hair looks terrible. Anyone can see that. She kept saying 'It looks like Miranda's!' Well, I can't even remember who this person is, for heaven's sake. What matters is that her hair looks awful and needs to be fixed."

He shook his head. Did she hear herself? Did she truly think she was in the right here? "Well, Violet doesn't think so. Does Willow have any idea where her sister is?"

"If she does, she's not saying. She's called out for her a few times, but Violet isn't responding. I'm hoping she's hiding in the house or in the yard. I didn't know if you were still in town or if you'd driven home last night. Maybe you could come find her if you're still around."

If she was asking for his help, she had to have checked everywhere for Violet and was truly nervous that she couldn't find his daughter.

He couldn't imagine Violet having gone far, no matter how upset she was. She was probably in some nook or cranny, either inside or out. "I'm still in town. I'll be there in twenty minutes. Try not to worry, Beatrice. We'll find her."

His words were kinder than she deserved, he thought.

But he could hear the relief in her silence, strangely enough. "Excellent," she said.

Excellent. She never lost her pretentious formality. Fuming, he jammed his phone in his back pocket and paced the cabin, waiting for Ashley to come out of the bathroom.

She did five seconds later. She took one look at his face and her eyes widened. "Oh, no, what's wrong?"

Shane explained about the phone call.

"Oh, poor Violet," Ashley said. "She must have picked a really good hiding place. If she's not coming out, it's probably somewhere she feels safe for the time being. I'd guess that she's someplace either in the house or outside that she's found before."

He immediately thought of finding Ashley in the stables loft after she'd run from the wedding. "I need to think of what her version of the loft would be."

She nodded. "A place her grandparents may even have looked but didn't spot her. That's why I like the loft so much. You can hide in the recesses and go perfectly still and remain unseen, even if people come looking for you. Think of crawl spaces, even in the house. Or she might be way up in a tree outside or tucked far in a spot that a little five-year-old can't be seen."

"Will you come with me?" he asked, surprising himself. But she clearly knew the hiding instinct, knew good spots, and perhaps most importantly, she knew Violet. Ashley would probably find her faster than he or the Shaws would. He couldn't imagine Violet ignoring Ashley if she called for her.

"Bringing me along might not help your case," she said. "I mean, they're your late wife's parents. I'm your boss's daughter, yes, and you gave me a ride to Jackson Hole, but I'm a woman, and it'll be clear to them that we were together when they called you."

He considered that. "I think you're more helpful in this situation than potentially hurtful."

"If you're sure."

"I am. I think Violet and Willow will like it that you're

there too. You may even draw Violet out just from her hearing your voice."

"Give me ten minutes to get dressed and dry my hair," she said.

He nodded. And before she disappeared behind her bedroom door, he called out, "Thank you, Ashley. Really. Thank you."

She poked her head out, drying it with the towel that had been wrapped around it. "Of course."

It seemed more like two minutes when Ashley was grabbing her jacket and heading out the door with him.

"I'm sure Violet's okay," Ashley said as they got inside his SUV. "She has a case of hurt feelings and doesn't want to get her hair cut. But I have no doubt she's safe and nearby. She could even be two feet from where Beatrice stood to call you."

Buckled up, he reached over with his right hand to squeeze her left one. "See, this is another reason why I need you with me for this. You're making me feel a hell of a lot better."

She squeezed back, and he started driving. "Look, just to clear the air so it's not lingering…"

Ah. Last night. Or more accurately, the middle of last night when she left his room and went into her own.

"That's fine, Ashley. You don't need to explain."

She didn't, really. And he wasn't sure he wanted her to even try. He had a feeling that he wouldn't like anything she'd say.

He'd woken up alone and had been surprised to discover he was disappointed. Surprised because he thought he was well used to being on his own. But suddenly she'd created an absence. And maybe he wasn't really ready to think too deeply about any of this.

"It was kind of a big deal," she said. "I mean, that we…"

He glanced at her and smiled. "Yes. It was."

"I woke up at like midnight and was bursting with it, not sure how to feel, where to fit it. So I FaceTimed with Miranda, actually. And then afterward, I guess I felt funny about getting back into bed with you. So I went into the other bedroom."

"Funny why?" he asked.

She gave a little shrug. "I think because I wasn't sure that I belonged back beside you," she added more tentatively.

"Hey," he said gently. "I understand. I have the same doubts. I missed you when I woke up. I absolutely did. But we're both in a confusing place, and we both have to do what feels right in the moment. So it's okay, Ashley."

"Why are you so understanding?" she asked with a shy smile. "You just seem to…get me."

"And you get me."

"Is it because we've known each other for years? I don't think so because we never really interacted all that much. I mean, before this past year when you started butting into my relationship." She laughed. "'He doesn't deserve you, Ashley,'" she said in her best imitation of him, adding his trademark head shake.

He laughed too. "Well, he doesn't, dammit."

Now it was her turn to squeeze his hand. And then she turned her attention out the window, he supposed to let everything they'd just said settle.

That was fine. Right now, he was more focused on his little girl, upset and probably trying to cry very quietly, wherever she was hiding. What mattered was finding Violet, soothing her wounded spirit and trying to help make things right between her and her nana. He might not like

Beatrice Shaw—and right now, the woman was a huge threat to him—but she was his daughters' grandmother and a very strong connection to their mother. He'd preserve that relationship for their sake.

Not to the point of losing his daughters, though. For that, he'd fight Beatrice Shaw with everything he had.

From the look on Beatrice Shaw's face at the sight of Ashley on her doorstep, it was crystal clear that the woman did not like that she was there. There were assumptions and judgments in her eyes, and she barely glanced at Ashley after opening the door wider to let her and Shane inside. But even in the brief glance, Ashley knew the woman had taken in her sweater and jeans and short red leather jacket, the lack of makeup and loose long hair. Beatrice was dolled up even for just past 8:00 a.m. in a twinset and slacks, her hair coiffed, lipstick and jewelry on.

Willow hurried over to them as best she could in her boot and hugged them both. Ashley could feel her grandmother's eyes boring into the sight they made, her little granddaughter hugging her "father's girlfriend."

Not that she was. But it seemed obvious that Beatrice thought so.

"Beatrice, Charles, I'm sure you remember meeting Ashley a time or two when you visited the McCray Ranch," Shane said.

Ashley wasn't so sure they did. They'd barely paid her any attention then. Or her parents.

"Yes, of course," Charles said graciously, reaching out two hands to hold Ashley's briefly.

Beatrice narrowed her gaze on Ashley, then slid it to Shane. "I didn't realize you were together. Didn't someone say something about a canceled wedding? It's a bit confusing."

Ashley felt her cheeks pinken. *Actually, lady, we are together, whether you like it or not.* She'd only said it in her head, but despite the woman's grief over losing her daughter, Ashley felt like Beatrice deserved some plain talk. It wasn't Ashley's place and she'd keep her mouth shut. But still.

And really, she and Shane weren't *together-together.* They were something but neither knew what.

Shane cleared his throat. "Let's talk about where Violet might be." He turned to Willow. "Sweetheart, any ideas? Does Violet have a favorite place in the house that's easy to hide in? Or maybe outside in the yard?"

Willow shrugged her narrow shoulders. "I can't think of any place."

Shane gently cupped his daughter's chin. "Okay. Don't you worry, hon. We'll find her, okay?"

"I know you will, Daddy." She threw her arms around him and squeezed, and Ashley's heart pinged at her sweet trust. She glanced at Beatrice just in time to catch the woman actually seeming touched, but then Beatrice's gaze shot to Ashley and turned icy again.

"What was she wearing the last time you saw her?" Shane asked. "Violet hates being cold, so if she wasn't wearing a sweatshirt or fleece hoodie, she's probably not outside—she would have come in by now."

Willow bit her lip. "She was just wearing her favorite T-shirt, the red one that says Cowgirl on it."

"Oh, is that her favorite?" Beatrice asked—a bit nervously.

Shane whirled to her. "Did you say something to her about her shirt too?"

"Well, just that she should change into one of the outfits in her closet before we left for the hair salon," Beatrice said, defensiveness in her tone.

"One of the outfits you bought for her," Shane said flatly.

Her chin lifted slightly. "Yes. Clients at Jackson Hole Hair dress to the nines."

"Beatrice, Violet is five. *Five.*"

"We weren't going to the playground, Shane," Beatrice countered. "We were going into town to my high-end salon. There's nothing wrong with dressing appropriately for an outing to somewhere special. And there's certainly nothing wrong with teaching that to a little lady."

Ashley was mentally shaking her head so fast she got a little dizzy. But again, it wasn't her place to say anything, and contradicting Beatrice at this moment wouldn't help Shane or Violet, particularly with Willow listening in. Shane was doing fine without her help.

"Let me look around," Shane said. "I may notice Violet-sized nooks and crannies where she might be. Did you check all the closets?"

Charles lifted a hand. "I did. I don't think any of them are possibilities unless she's really wedged in behind something and I missed her."

"Do you mind if I check all the closets again while Shane looks in all the other spots?" Ashley asked. "Closets were where I hid as a kid when I was upset about something."

"That's fine," Beatrice said. Exasperation was all over her face. The thought of a "stranger" looking through her closets clearly didn't sit well. "What's important is that we find Violet."

"Can you give me the lay of the land?" Ashley asked. "Bedrooms are upstairs?"

Beatrice nodded. "Yes. There are four. Violet and Willow have a room that they share at the end of the hall. They tell me every time they visit that they want to stay together. That room was their mother's before she married Shane, so I suppose it's special to them. Then there are two guest rooms, and our bedroom is the first one off the landing."

Ashley nodded. "I'll head up now." She gave Shane a nod and started up the grand staircase that curved. She saw Shane head into the family room, and then she glanced down in time to see Beatrice throwing up her hands, looking very upset, and Charles walking over to embrace her.

Ashley knew where Violet was. She'd bet anything on it.

She walked down the hallway, shining hardwood with a muted runner. Family photos lined the walls in all shapes and sizes. Ashley was surprised in a good way to see them. Beatrice had struck her as the type to prefer expensive art over family mementos. There were so many, Beatrice and Charles smiling in front of vacation locales, lakes, petting zoos, amusement parks and cities, many with their daughter, Liza, at various ages, and many with the Shaws and the twins. Ashley stopped toward the end of the hall, where a large photo of Liza and Shane, each holding a newborn, had been taken in front of Shane's foreman's cabin. Her hand flew to her heart. What a beautiful photo. The happiness on the new parents' faces was something else. How lovely that whenever the twins visited, whenever they came and went from their room, this greeted them.

The door was ajar, and Ashley stood outside and listened. Quiet. She was 99 percent sure she'd find Violet in the closet, not because it was her and her twin's room, but because it had once been their mother's. And now that she'd seen the photographs, especially the big one with the Dawson family, her surety was 100 percent.

She went into the room and looked around. Very girlie in white and pale yellow, but nothing in the room said Violet and Willow, had their personality, their stamp. There was some of the twins' artwork in frames on the walls, and between the windows a framed "self-portrait" of Liza Shaw, age eight. Ashley's hand went to her heart again. Liza had given herself a purple face and pink hair and green ears and a striped shirt. There were a few dogs beside her—at least Ashley thought they were dogs. They were also multicolored and missing a leg here and there.

Ashley walked over to the closet. She gently pulled open one of the double doors and peered inside. It was a walk-in with lots of hanging clothes and, toward the back, a second row of long coats. Ashley stepped inside. She peered very closely at the floor toward the back. And there, she noticed a flash of green that moved. Like a socked foot. It had darted behind a long red puffer coat.

Ashley had no doubt that coat had belonged to the twins' mother. And that Violet was hiding behind it. Maybe even sitting inside it since it just about reached the closet floor. She went farther in and sat down in front of the red coat.

"Hey, Violet. It's Ashley. I have a feeling you're inside that zipped puffer coat."

Silence. And then a sad little voice said, "My nana is making me get my hair cut to fix it. But I like it. It looks like Miranda's. And Miranda said she likes my hair. You heard her say it, right?"

For the third time in two minutes, Ashley's hand went to her heart.

"Yup, I did. Is that why you're hiding up here? Because you don't want to get your hair cut?"

Violet didn't respond at first. Ashley heard a sniffle. And finally, "I don't think my nana likes me." She heard crying, then sobbing, then movement of the bottom of the coat, and Violet's head peeked out from under it, her green eyes red rimmed, tears falling down her face. She crawled out from under the coat and flew at Ashley.

Ashley wrapped the little girl in her arms and held her, stroking her hair. "Violet, honey, I know your nana loves you very much."

"She doesn't like my hair or my favorite shirt," Violet said through her tears.

"Well, I think your nana has a different style. But she loves the person you are. Inside and out. She always has. I remember one time when your grandparents came to the ranch to visit your parents. You and Willow were just a month old. And your mother was wearing red jeans, a black leather jacket and white studded cowboy boots. And a white studded cowboy hat. Your nana said, 'Oh, Liza, really! What on earth are you wearing?' And do you know what your mommy said back?"

Violet peered at Ashley. "What?" she asked, her eyes wide, the tears drying up.

"Your mommy said, 'You know you love me anyway.' And do you want to know what your nana said back to that?"

Violet nodded. "What did she say?"

"Your nana said—"

Suddenly, the closet door opened and there stood Beatrice Shaw, tears misting her eyes.

Both Violet and Ashley stared up at her, Ashley's heart suddenly pounding.

Beatrice sucked in a breath. "I'll tell you what I said. I said, 'That's right, Liza Lee Shaw Dawson. I do. I love you more than anything on earth except maybe those two babies. I love you all so much my heart feels like it might burst.'"

Violet's mouth dropped open. "Is that what you said?"

Beatrice nodded and ran a quick hand under her eyes to dab at her tears.

"That's exactly what she said," Ashley confirmed. "I remember thinking it was one of the nicest things I'd ever heard anyone say."

"That *is* nice," Violet said, looking shyly up at her nana.

For a moment, Beatrice seemed lost in a memory. "Oh, how your mother loved those white cowboy boots. She'd had them since she was a teenager and they were so beat-up." She smiled shakily.

"I want to get white cowboy boots," Violet said. "Willow will want them too."

"With studs along the toe area," Beatrice added, dabbing under misty eyes.

Ashley could see Violet picturing the boots, her face brightening.

Beatrice knelt down. "Violet, honey, hair grows and yours will too. I won't make you get it fixed if you don't want to."

"You won't?" Violet asked.

"I won't. That's a promise. Your mother was headstrong like you and your sister. Do you know what *headstrong* means?"

Violet shook her head. "You call me and Willow that a lot, but I don't know."

Beatrice touched Violet's chin with gentle fingers. "It means you have your own strong ideas about who you are and what you like. And I should be more respectful of that."

Oh, my heart, Ashley thought. This was going so much better than she could have hoped.

"Do I have to change my shirt?" Violet asked, looking down at the long-sleeved red T-shirt with the sparkly letters spelling *Cowgirl* in rhinestones.

"No," Beatrice said with a smile. "And I have a fun idea for this morning. Since Willow's ankle needs to rest up, why don't we go to the paint-your-own-pottery shop? You two enjoyed that last time you visited."

Violet brightened. "I love that place! There was a dog with long ears I wanted to paint last time but I picked something else. I wonder if they'll still have it."

"Well, we'll go see, won't we," Beatrice said, holding out her hand.

Violet ran over and wrapped her arms around her grandmother's hips.

"Oh, my," Beatrice said, her gaze darting to Ashley for a moment, then back to her granddaughter. "And after pottery, maybe we can go shopping—for white cowboy boots with studs on the toes."

Violet's eyes widened, and she gasped. "Really?"

"Really," Beatrice said, again her eyes teary but a gentle smile on her face.

"I love you, Nana," Violet said.

"I love you too," Beatrice said. "I do indeed." She gave Violet a strong hug and then pulled back. "Ready to go tell everyone about our new plan for the day?"

Violet ran ahead.

"Little ladies walk nicely!" Beatrice called after her.

Ashley mentally sighed. Just when she thought Beatrice had learned something important, something precious about her grandchild, she was back to her old self. Still, the woman got serious points for offering to take the twins shopping for cowboy boots.

And since Ashley had heard a little thud as Violet leaped off the bottom step and called out, "Hi, I'm right here!" she probably hadn't heard her grandmother's request.

Ashley ducked her way out of the closet.

Beatrice stepped back to give her room to come out. "Thank you. You were an enormous help."

"You're very welcome," Ashley said. Even when being nice, the woman was so damned intimidating. But Ashley could see the questions in Beatrice's eyes—everything from, *So, how well did you know my daughter? Were you friendly? I know she wasn't living at the ranch long before...* To, *What is going on with you and Shane? Are you dating?* To, *Didn't I hear you were left at the altar just days ago?*

Beatrice turned slightly. "Well, let's head downstairs and join the others."

Ashley followed her, the woman not saying another word. That Beatrice had questions wasn't in doubt, but Ashley doubted she really wanted answers—or that she'd be happy with them, no matter what Ashley said.

As they reached the bottom steps, Ashley could hear Violet in the living room. "I don't have to change my shirt either! And Nana and Pops are taking us to paint-your-own pottery. Maybe they have that long-eared dog again, Willow. And guess what else?"

"What?" Willow asked with bated breath.

"Nana's taking us shopping for white cowboy boots with

studs at the toes like Mommy had!" Violet said. "Mommy loved hers and had them since she was a teenager."

Ashley glanced at Shane, who now seemed lost in a memory himself—and very surprised that the subject of the boots had come up. There was a question in his eyes— she'd fill him in when she could.

The girls were chattering excitedly. Shane walked over to Ashley.

"I don't know what you did, but thank you," Shane whispered to Ashley.

Beatrice stopped in the living room archway and glanced at both of them for a moment. "Well, I see Charles went outside to look for Violet, so I'll just go tell him the good news. If you'll excuse me." With that, she moved over to the sliding glass doors to the deck and stepped out.

With the twins deep in excited conversation and not paying attention to anyone but each other, Shane pulled Ashley into a quick hug. "Just when I'm not sure if I can trust my instincts or not, you prove me A-OK," he said. "I knew bringing you was a good idea. So what happened? Where'd you find her? And Beatrice was there too? And how on earth did the boots come up in conversation?"

Ashley smiled and whispered a very condensed version of what had gone on upstairs in the closet. "I'll fill you in on the details once we're back in your SUV."

He gave his head a shake, wonder lighting his eyes. "I'd kiss the daylights out of you, but this is definitely not the time or the place."

"Maybe the time, but not the place."

He laughed and squeezed her hand, and they turned to where the twins were still chattering away, now about the boots. Both their faces glowed with happiness. Ashley's heart gave its usual clang where the Dawson girls were concerned. She glanced at Shane as he watched his daughters talking a mile a minute, the relief, the love in his expression, a thing to behold.

And she'd helped. That had felt so good.

Chapter Fourteen

It had been much easier for Shane to say goodbye the second time now that there was some proof that Beatrice wasn't made of stone, that she was capable of changing her mind for the right reasons, that she was able to compromise. The hair and shirt, fine. The running and leaping, no. Okay— he'd take what he could get. He'd smiled as Ashley had told him about the criticism going unheard, Violet already at the bottom of the staircase and calling out that she was back.

Yes, she was. His little girl's spirit was intact. That was what he cared about.

It was what Beatrice should care about too, and he wasn't entirely sure she understood that. She'd been moved by the memory of poking at her daughter's outfit, by Liza's comeback, by her own, and she'd finally connected Liza's free-spirited ways with her children's, which had meant something to her in that moment. To the point that she'd offered to take the twins shopping for boots just like the ones Beatrice had despised the sight of for years. *That* was something, almost a little miracle.

All Shane knew as he drove into town was that he was less worried, less stressed, less scared deep down that the Shaws would petition for custody.

Thanks to Ashley. Had he been there on his own, would

he have come up with that exact memory, with that story? She was gifted in that way, and he was grateful.

They stopped for coffee at a huge bakery-café with a lot of thrift-shop seating—old velvet sofas and benches, over-stuffed chairs. Many people were on laptops with head-phones in. At least twenty people waited to order at the counter. Shane and Ashley got in line.

Could he kiss those daylights out of her now that they were away from the Shaws' home? He sure wanted to, but he was also sure no one in the café wanted to watch him and Ashley make out.

He felt so close to her right now. He yearned to kiss her, hold her, touch her, be one with her again. Like he'd been in bed with her last night. One. Their bodies joined.

And he knew it was much more than that.

Somehow, Ashley McCray was becoming indispensable. She was like a talisman for him and his children.

He linked his arm around hers since it was the most he could hope for at the moment, the connection going straight to all his nerve endings. The smile she sent him lit up his heart.

He was going to have to admit to himself that he and Ashley were more than just partners on a road trip. That there was something so truly special going on between them—something that made him feel like he'd woken up from a long, dry slumber.

She eyed him, tilting her head. "Penny for your thoughts, as my dad always says? You're clearly a million miles away."

Nope, I'm right here. Thinking about you.

"I was…wondering if you were going to ask if they have carrot cake muffins," he said. "Or carrot cake scones," he added, suddenly feeling a little shy in the region of his heart.

She laughed. "Trust me, if they have either or both, I'm in."

He breathed a sigh of relief that they were talking about confections and not themselves, that he hadn't blurted out that he'd been thinking about how much she meant to him. That he had big feelings. He might have Ashley on the heart and soul, but he wasn't quite ready to talk about it.

"I want an iced coffee and something chocolaty," he said. "Maybe a good old-fashioned brownie. Think I can actually find just a plain, amazing brownie?"

"Probably not," she said on a laugh. "It'll have all sorts of stuff in it, maybe oats or even kale chips. But I can see in that display they have a very good lineup of fun bars. Chocolate chip coconut? Oooh."

He tried to peer around the very tall man in front of him, but he kept shifting on his feet and Shane didn't have a good view of the counter. He glanced left out the front window, his attention taken by a huge Great Dane in a pink leather collar walking beside its owner, a petite woman. He was about to point out the dog to Ashley, but then he did a double take.

Behind the woman and the huge dog.

No, it couldn't be. He squinted to peer more closely.

Oh, hell. It *was*.

Harrington Harris IV. Holding the hand of a woman with long blond hair.

Oh, no. No, no, no.

The two of them looked almost like twins. Both blond, fit and tall, super healthy looking, super rich looking. They were definitely not related, however, because they paused just before the door and kissed like they couldn't wait another second.

Repeat: oh, no. *Please keep walking after your stupid kiss. Please don't come in. Keep going. Follow the big dog.*

He took a sidelong glance at Ashley, who was still focused on the display since she had a better view of it to the right. She definitely hadn't been looking out the window—she hadn't seen Harrington. Or the kiss.

The door opened.

Shane sent up a silent prayer. Surely this morning's fortune would bring more luck and it wouldn't be the blond couple who entered. Right now, he didn't see them. Had they passed by when his attention had been on Ashley for those few seconds? Or were they about to walk in behind the family that had just entered?

Dammit.

In walked Ashley's former fiancé, his arm slung around the woman, chuckling away at something.

Hell.

Shane watched Harrington notice Ashley, his expression turning to shock as he stopped short. A guy walking behind him from the cream-and-sugar credenza with a mug of coffee crashed right into Harrington, his coffee sloshing on the floor.

"Jeez, dude, what gives?" the guy muttered.

Harrington quickly turned. "What? Oh, sorry," he said distractedly, reaching into his pocket and pulling out a ten, which he handed the guy—who gave a confused sort-of smile, took the ten and disappeared into the crowd with his sloshed coffee.

At the sound of Harrington's voice, Ashley's head swiveled in that direction.

She gasped.

They were now both staring at each other.

The blonde woman with Harrington was looking at him as if he were having a medical emergency. "Um, Harrington? Baby, what's wrong?"

Shane glanced at Ashley. The look on her face...

"Ashley?" Harrington said in clear disbelief. "What are you doing here?" He then noticed Shane and confusion crossed his features. He was staring at Shane now, clearly trying to place him. *Yeah, try real hard, jerkface.* "You're the foreman, right?"

Shane sighed. He didn't bother responding.

"Baby?" the blonde woman said, looking from Harrington to Ashley. "Who are these people?"

Harrington quickly patted the woman's hand but didn't answer her. "Um, Ashley, can we talk in private?"

Ashley glanced at Shane—and swallowed. "I'll just be a minute, I'm sure."

Shane nodded and attempted to keep the death glare off his face.

Harrington whispered something to the blonde woman, who got in line. Then Harrington walked to the back of the café. Ashley followed. Slowly.

She turned back and looked at Shane again with trepidation in her eyes.

Shane tried to stop glancing over his shoulder to see them, but it was no use. He didn't want to leave Ashley alone with Harrington, even if "alone" didn't mean much in the crowded shop. Either way, Shane felt better simply keeping them in view. They were now sitting across from each other on overstuffed chairs against the wall.

They both looked equally uncomfortable. Horrified, Shane would say.

But that didn't mean that Harrington wasn't about to be

reminded that this was the woman he'd dated for a year, proposed to, was engaged to…the woman he must have had strong feelings for, maybe even loved, if he were capable of loving anyone but himself.

Anything could happen.

And Shane wasn't having it.

If he could march over to them and pull Ashley away, he would. Bring her to safety—away from that dirtbag.

Bring her to *himself.*

It took everything in him to stay where he was.

Ashley stared at the man she'd loved for a year and thought she would marry. He was familiar, of course, the same old Harrington in his Nantucket red faded chinos and white linen shirt, sleeves rolled up, the very expensive watch on his wrist. The slightly long, wavy blond hair and the warm blue eyes.

But something was dramatically different inside her as she looked at him. She didn't feel what she'd expected to when they finally came to face-to-face.

She certainly didn't feel *love.*

To her surprise, she found she no longer cared at all if he took one look at her and realized he'd made the biggest mistake of his life.

She just felt…numb.

Everything Shane had said to her over the past year regarding Harrington suddenly rang so true. *He doesn't deserve you…*

Why had she put up with it? Why had she allowed the man who supposedly loved her to treat her like that? Sure, she hadn't let *everything* slide. Sometimes she'd get upset and tell Harrington to leave or give him the cold shoulder for a couple of days and demand an apology for this or that. But she'd always accepted the apology—which he'd probably never meant.

She'd always gone back for more, intoxicated by *something*. Was it his glamour? His good looks? His wealth? Not that she was a gold digger—far from it—but his aura of sophistication was so different from anything she'd ever experienced. She'd been surprised and flattered that, out of all the women in the world, he'd chosen her, fallen for her. Particularly because she had seen those big glimpses of his heart. She'd fallen hard for him for good reason, even if part of the attraction had been because she'd been dazzled by the trappings. The superficial. The man who could have anyone had fallen for *her*.

Until he realized he didn't love her, of course. Noted by text.

"Why are you here?" he asked, head tilted slightly.

She could feel the scowl pulling at her mouth. "That's what you have to say to me? Not 'I'm sorry'?"

"I figured we were past that, Ashley."

Jerk! Asshat! Scumbucket!

"You left me at the altar, Harrington. In front of all my family and friends. You made everything about our relationship a lie. We're past 'I'm sorry'?"

He shook his head. "Please don't get dramatic. *God*," he added, stretching the word into a very long syllable. "I *am* sorry for everything. But I'm not sorry I didn't marry you."

Nice. Very nice. What a way to put it.

"Because you're involved with the blonde?" she asked, glancing back where the extremely attractive woman was now sitting at a table, sipping an iced coffee and sending nervous glances their way. Ashley's gaze landed on Shane, also sitting at a table, not sipping anything. The hard set of his jaw, the intensity of his expression, told her he was worried about this conversation and how it would end.

"I met her the week before the wedding," Harrington went on. "Not two hours later, two hours in her company, I realized that I loved Gwenyth. That I understood what everyone was always talking about—love at first sight, a chemistry that just grabs you by the heart and soul. You just *know.*"

She gaped at him. A week before their wedding date, he'd fallen in love with someone else. A montage of that week rolled in her head—he'd suddenly had to go away on "business" despite not having a job. Something to do with investments, he'd said. He'd had to cancel their rehearsal dinner the night before the ceremony because he couldn't get back till late that same night, but he'd said, *Ashley, I don't need to rehearse to walk down the aisle to you.*

At the time, she'd thought that was so beautiful, so romantic. The man she was marrying loved her deeply, she'd believed.

What a load of bunk! What a lie.

What a fool she'd been. An utter fool.

She'd thought he was in California, dealing with the "investments," when he'd been right in town, in bed with Gwenyth. His real soulmate, apparently.

"I'd never experienced such a powerful feeling before," he continued. "I didn't lie about being in California. I went away with Gwenyth to figure things out. I came back the night before the wedding because it felt like the right thing to do, to face you in the morning. But I couldn't. So I just took off for Jackson Hole with Gwenyth and sent you that text from a gas station."

A gas station. How fitting. Bile inched up in her gut. She felt sick.

"I didn't mean to meet someone," he added. "But I ended up finding my real one true love."

"How special for you," she said, bitterly. But she did feel bitter. Was she supposed to be happy for him? "You owe my parents forty-seven thousand dollars. I subtracted the value of the engagement ring, which I'll sell. You also owe my maid of honor and bridesmaids one thousand seven hundred and sixteen dollars for the dresses and shoes they wasted good money on." She'd left it to the dresses and shoes only, since her parents had paid for the bridesmaids' hair and makeup and had given each woman a gold bangle as a gift. "I want two checks right now. One to my father and one to me so I can reimburse the bridal party. Or you can wire the money. Right now."

He stared at her for a moment, then pulled out his phone and pressed in some numbers. "Clark, HHJ here."

Oh, brother. She'd always hated when he'd referred to himself that way. Harrington Harris Junior. Clark was his wealth management agent and personal accountant. Harrington had often whipped out his phone to call or text the guy during their relationship.

"Can you arrange for two bank checks—one to Anthony McCray in the amount of forty-seven thousand dollars and one to Ashley McCray for one thousand seven hundred sixteen, for pickup at the Bear Ridge Bank and Trust?" he chirped into the phone as though he was ordering room service. "Yes. Perfect." He pocketed the phone and turned his attention back to Ashley. "Done."

She lifted her chin. There. She'd done it. This was what she'd really come for, the no-matter-what reason. To get her family's money back, to get her bridal party's money back too. "Well. Good. Thank you. My parents will appreciate that."

"For what it's worth," he said, "and I know it's not much, I *am* sorry, Ashley. I do wish you the best."

She couldn't say the same. So she said nothing. Harrington stood up and headed to where Gwenyth was waiting. Then the happy couple both quickly left.

Ashley didn't move. Didn't turn. Didn't stand.

Numb. Every bit of her—numb.

She could feel a shadow behind her. Then next to her. She glanced up. Shane. Looking at her with concern.

But instead of flinging herself in his arms the way she wanted to, she just sat there, her body feeling like lead.

Not sure exactly where she'd go from here.

She felt so stupid, so played, so betrayed. Harrington himself almost didn't even factor in. She didn't mourn the loss of him in her life. She mourned *herself*—the person she'd been in the days before her wedding, when she'd been practicing writing *Ashley Harris* over and over in her journal like a sixteen-year-old, when she'd been making lists of baby names, even though that would be years off, when she'd been searching online for recipes of his favorite meals so that she could practice making them…when she'd been so certain she was loved, and all the while, he'd been sleeping with someone else. Deeply involved emotionally with someone else.

And she'd had no clue. That was what had her so upset.

That she hadn't known—about something involving her and her entire life, her future, her hopes and dreams. How could she not have known?

"Ashley?" Shane asked, a warm hand on her shoulder. "How'd it go? Are you okay?"

She sucked in a breath. And didn't answer. Couldn't answer. Couldn't find her voice.

Shane sat down in the chair Harrington had vacated. "Ash, listen, if you just need to go back to the cabin at the dude ranch and lock yourself in your bedroom, that's okay."

Yes. That was what she needed right now. It dimly occurred to her that, of course, Shane Dawson knew that. He always knew what she needed.

But maybe even a very good man like Shane Dawson wasn't what he seemed. She didn't know his private mind and heart, just as she hadn't known Harrington's. Shane had a lot going on. They'd made love, which had to have complicated things for him emotionally where she was concerned.

She couldn't put any stock in even her friendship with Shane.

Great. Now she was being cynical and distrusting, even of the man who'd been nothing but honest and kind and helpful. A lifeline.

"The cabin, yes," she finally said. "That is exactly where I want to be." She looked over at him, her handsome Shane, and her heart did lift a tiny bit. He was her rock. But right now, nothing could break through the numb, the doom and gloom, everything her former fiancé had said so blithely.

She was an idiot. A big stupid idiot.

That actually *did* break the numbness inside her. Because it reminded her of the Dawson twins and their favorite insult that they were probably trying very hard not to use while at their grandparents'.

And suddenly her eyes got misty and she needed to be in that bedroom at the cabin, behind closed doors, under the covers.

Alone.

Chapter Fifteen

Shane had taken one look at Ashley, slumped and dejected in that overstuffed chair at the café, and had taken her hand and led her out of the place with an "I've got you."

And he did. He'd gotten her settled in his SUV and didn't say a word, didn't ask anything of her, even another *You okay?* He could tell that she wasn't. She needed time and rest and someone to take care of her, and he had two days to offer her just that, to be her personal concierge.

At the cabin, she'd gone straight to her bedroom and closed the door, then had come back out a minute later.

She'd told him everything Harrington had said. About falling for the other woman. About lying about a business trip. About the real reason for canceling the rehearsal dinner.

Ah, he'd thought, wishing he could go to her and pull her into his arms, but the pain and anger on her face were like a force field radiating "keep off" vibes, so he stayed put.

But still, he ached for her. She'd been betrayed and had been feeling every bit of it.

"How could I not know?" she'd asked, her face so pale, her eyes devoid of their usual spark. "How could you not know you're being deceived? Does that mean I can't trust myself? My feelings? Others? What the hell?"

He'd understood then that it wasn't so much Harrington or even a broken heart that had her so despondent. Well, of course she had a broken heart in the sense that she'd been hurt and humiliated. But it was her *spirit* that was broken. Her faith—in people and love and everything she'd believed in. Solid ground had turned to sawdust for her.

All he could do was be there for her, let her take her time.

When the world had fallen apart for him, he'd certainly taken his.

Now he looked toward the bedroom door, leaning an ear to hear any signs of movement. Not a peep in the past three hours. A half hour ago, he'd ordered cabin service from the dude ranch's cafeteria, which should arrive any minute. He got a few different things, figuring if he got a good selection, Ashley would find something to like—a cheeseburger with steak fries, a turkey BLT and the chili, which they were apparently known for far and wide. He'd also gotten a Caesar salad since he knew she loved those. And two kinds of desserts.

He had a feeling she'd have little appetite. That was fine and what reheating in ovens and microwaves was for.

He was making himself a cup of coffee at the kitchenette when his phone buzzed; he'd put it on Silent so as not to disturb Ashley.

Anthony McCray.

"Shane, I just got a call from the bank that there's a cashier's check for an enormous sum waiting for me to deposit. And one for Ashley. Both from Harrington. She saw him? How'd it go? Are they together right now?"

Shane didn't know how much to say to her father but opted for a short form of the truth. "They actually ran into each other by chance today. They spoke briefly, five minutes maybe, and then Harrington left. She's taking some time to herself right now. We're staying at a cabin I booked at a dude ranch in Jackson Hole. I'm not sure if she's up for talking just yet, but I can check."

"Aww, poor gal. I'll let her be for now. Thank you for being there, Shane."

"Of course," he said, and they disconnected.

The doorbell rang with their room service. Shane set the bags on the coffee table, then went to knock on Ashley's door.

"Hey," he called. "I ordered a bunch of stuff for lunch. Hungry?"

Silence.

He waited a beat and was about to walk away when the door opened. Ashley, looking tired but more like herself—absolutely beautiful, that sparkle half-back in her eyes—walked up to him and put her arms around him.

"What's this for?" he asked, surprised as could be.

"Just for being you. And I am hungry. I'm surprised, but then again, I came to good realizations while I was under the covers in there, and I'm feeling more okay. Not completely, of course, but a little better."

"I'd love to hear about those realizations," he said, heading to the kitchenette to grab some plates and silverware, which he brought to the coffee table.

They sat down and opened containers. Ashley took half the BLT and a bunch of steak fries. He chose the cheeseburger.

"Ah, this looks so good," she said, then took a bite. She sipped from the bottle of iced tea he'd also ordered. "What I realized is that I'm done with being a confused dummy. Took a few hours under those covers, but I finally got to *anger.* Since the canceled wedding, I've been hurt and upset and unsure, but I wasn't really angry. The past few hours, I felt the full force of it. He betrayed me. Lied to me. Carried on an affair the week before our wedding day—"

He shook his head. For the past several days, Shane had wondered what had really led the jerkface to cancel the wedding, but he hadn't landed on "met someone else."

She swiped a fry in ketchup and popped it into her mouth. "And you know what? Not that I'm letting him off the hook for how he treated me, but I realized something. Even though half of me wishes all sorts of bad things for him, the other half is like, good for him. It's what everyone wants. To find the person you really belong with, the person who makes your heart sing, all that, you know?"

He knew. *Ashley* made his heart sing.

"I wasn't that for him," she continued, "and as I'm sure you'll say, he wasn't that for me. I compromised, let things go, accepted what I shouldn't have. Maybe my soulmate is out there, waiting for me. Who knows, maybe I've already met him at the worst possible time." She shyly smiled and seemed to be holding her breath.

"That's how I feel," he said softly. And it was true.

She let out the breath. "Oh, Shane," she whispered, scooting over and pressing herself against him.

He wrapped her in a hug and put his head against hers. "We feel what we feel, right? Yes, it's bad timing for a few reasons. I didn't think I'd ever be interested in anyone else, Ashley. But here you are. Slammed right into my heart."

"Same," she said, pushing up with her arms against his chest to look at him. "I'm certainly not ready for a new relationship, but I seem to be in one."

"What happens on the road trip doesn't have to *stay on*

the road trip," he said. "We can bring it all home with us if we want."

Her smile lit up her beautiful face, and it took a real effort to keep from kissing her. She'd need a few days to recover from everything that had happened with the jerkface, even if she didn't realize it. And that was fine. Because he needed a few days too—to let himself accept that he had feelings for another woman. That maybe the twins would have a stepmother after all. A mother in their lives to love them, care about them, share in the triumphs and tribulations of raising them. The twins seemed to have them married off in the future anyway. They hadn't brought up the *M* word since that first and only time, but the idea of it was in their heads, in their hearts.

It wasn't necessarily in his. Marriage was a huge step. And he and Ashley weren't even dating. But the label didn't matter. Only what they felt did. "We can both take it as slow as we need," he said. "We don't have to call this anything."

She nodded, the sparkle well back in her hazel eyes. "We'll just take it day by day and know the most important thing— that we have each other's backs, that we're there for each other."

He squeezed her hand. She kissed him on the cheek.

"How is it possible that I felt so betrayed and awful three hours ago and so lucky right now?" she asked.

"That's life for you. Ups and downs. Downs and ups. Sometimes in the same minute."

She leaned her head on his shoulder, linked her arms through his, and they sat like that for a long while.

The next two days were everything Ashley needed. She and Shane spent a lot of time together and made sure to take some time apart too. Ashley went on long walks by herself around the dude ranch, popping in to the petting zoo to see her favorite goats, who always made her laugh as they hopped on and off logs. She'd stop into the cafeteria for iced coffee and to try to get the recipe for the excellent chili out of the longtime cook, who refused to share his secret ingredients. Alone with her thoughts, she had time and space to think and understand and process.

Including how much she felt for Shane Dawson.

They'd shared meals—and a bed—watched TV and movies, borrowed books from the ranch library and curled up on chairs with views of the mountains to read. They took walks together, holding hands, they rode out on the trails, they hiked and had picnic lunches. They talked and laughed and ate and sometimes were quiet, companionably so.

Two days of just what the doctor ordered.

She'd video-called her parents after Shane had let her know her dad had called. She'd assured them she was okay, that she'd be home tomorrow.

Tomorrow. Already?

She wasn't quite ready to leave the dude ranch, but she missed her parents and her horses.

And she did want to see how things would feel with Shane once they were back home. They lived on the same property, only a stone's throw away. They'd see each other all the time, planned or unplanned. They'd both return to their regular, scheduled lives. And Shane was very busy. Not only with his work as the foreman at the McCray Ranch but with his daughters.

Would a new relationship even fit in for him?

She'd discussed this all with Miranda on the phone during her long walks around the dude ranch. Her cousin thought she and Shane had something very special and that Ashley was doing exactly what she should be. No labels, no rushing, no declaring. Just feeling. Just enjoying each other's company.

But now, as Ashley packed up her clothes and made a pile of things she needed to return to the lodge, like the library books and a steamer she'd borrowed to get the wrinkles out of the dress she'd worn to the country-and-western dance last night, she realized she was more than a little nervous about being involved with Shane.

Scared, really.

Scared that what she'd felt for him was way more intense than anything she'd ever felt for Harrington. It had to do with their chemistry and closeness, real friendship, even her relationship with his daughters. She loved those girls, and now she'd be much more intertwined in their lives. Her role in what had gone on in the Shaws' house, in the closet with Violet and Beatrice, had made her feel even closer to all of them. Even to Beatrice herself. She was enmeshed in Shane's life in a way that she'd never been with her former fiancé. She'd never felt a part of Harrington's family. But would that feeling last when they were back to their usual lives?

There would be a lot to adapt to once they got home and settled back.

She glanced at the clock on the bedside table. Almost five. Shane was helping the owner figure out a problem he was having with the books—foremen talk. Ashley figured she'd take the pile of stuff she had to return to the lodge. She'd stop for iced coffee on the way back and once again try to get that secret recipe out of the cook. The chili was that good. And then she and Shane would take a walk on the ranch and then have a special last dinner in town.

A special last night in the cabin too, she thought with a smile as she headed out with her tote bag of things to return.

Ashley pulled open the door to the lodge and headed to the Welcome desk, staffed by Maya, who was usually all smiles and full of fun information about the ranch and the activities. The two had managed to get chummy the past couple of days since Ashley had stopped in often to ask for tips about where to explore or to just say hi. They hadn't gotten too personal, but they'd both shared that they'd gone through recent breakups. Maya had seemed fine, but right now, she looked really glum. And if Ashley wasn't mistaken, she'd been crying.

As she reached the desk, Maya quickly dabbed under her eyes as if wiping away tears. She put on a smile that was definitely forced.

"Maya? Everything okay?"

Maya glanced around. There were some guests milling around by the brochures and a few sitting in the chairs on the far side of the room, but otherwise, no one was waiting for Maya's attention. "Guy problems." She sighed. "I just lost my best friend. The best friend I've ever had." Now tears filled her eyes.

"Aww, what happened?" Ashley asked.

"So you know how I mentioned that a couple of months ago, my boyfriend of three years, who I thought was going to propose, dumped me the night before Valentine's Day? What I didn't get into was the fact that he'd met someone else and he wanted to 'explore' it. So instead of a ring, I got my heart handed to me. I was a wreck for weeks."

"I'm so sorry," Ashley said. "Sounds really hard." And familiar.

"It was. But my best friend—a guy—helped me through. And one thing led to another, and all of a sudden we were a couple. Jonas was just so good to me, so attentive, when I really needed someone. He's the best."

Ashley knew all about that too—from her own life. She was suddenly listening very hard.

"But then *I* met someone else," Maya said. "A new cowboy on the ranch. Oh, my God, Ashley. I've never been so attracted to a man in my life. We just get each other. Understand each other. The connection between us is just unreal. But Jonas and I had become a couple and…I realized it was more a rebound thing. He offered more than friendship suddenly and I saw him in a new light—or thought I did. But now that I've met Daniel, I realize I'm not in love with Jonas and never was."

"Oh, wow," Ashley said. "And you told Jonas?"

"He was so hurt. And furious. He told me we're not friends anymore. That I was a user. He accused me of taking advantage of him for a rebound romance." Her eyes filled with tears. "I do love him—but as my best friend. And now he won't even talk to me. I don't know if he ever will."

"Maybe he just needs time," Ashley offered. "He's hurting and upset, like you said. Give him some time, Maya."

Maya nodded, biting her lip. "I really miss him. His friendship means so much to me, and I screwed up. I should never have gotten involved with him. I was close to his sister also, but she told me off and told me we're through too." Her eyes welled with tears again.

"I'm really sorry, hon," Ashley said. "I think you need to give them both time. In the meantime, be kind to yourself."

A family came in then and headed for the desk, standing behind Ashley.

Ever the professional, Maya smiled at the group. "Be right with you, folks." She leaned closer to Ashley and whispered, "Thanks for talking me through it. I do feel better. It's just a tough situation."

Ashley nodded and gave her hand a squeeze. "I'll come say goodbye at checkout tomorrow." She put the books in the book chute on the side of the desk and handed back the steamer.

Maya checked off its return. "Definitely don't leave without saying goodbye."

As she headed out of the lodge, Ashley's stomach was turning every which way. She dropped down on the bench outside, the fresh April air doing little to reinvigorate her.

Was her relationship with Shane about rebounding? He'd become her best friend on this road trip. And much, much more. Their relationship had deepened in ways she never could have dreamed. That was all very real, though.

But it likely had felt real between Maya and her best friend too. Jonas. Until she met someone who made her realize that her broken and needy heart had innocently mistaken their relationship for more than it was.

Could that be the case with her and Shane? If she hurt him…after what he'd been through… She was his first kiss after being widowed. His first sexual experience after. His first foray into caring about someone again.

Not to mention, if she hurt him, she'd hurt his daughters.

Ashley shivered and bolted up, suddenly needing to move. But not wanting to think. Surely she'd know if something wasn't really there between her and Shane, wouldn't she?

She certainly hadn't known that about her and Harrington. But then again, she felt so much for Shane Dawson.

She *loved* him.

Oh, God, she did. She loved him. Loved his enormous heart. His warmth. His integrity. Loved everything he was. At the start of the road trip, he'd asked for ten reasons why she loved—past tense—Harrington. She could list *hundreds* of reasons very quickly about why she loved Shane.

So it must be real. It wasn't rebound. She wouldn't hurt him or his twins.

But then again, she *hadn't* known Harrington didn't love her. He might not have either until he met Gwenyth. And what about Maya? She was so sweet. Ashley was sure she hadn't meant to hurt her friend Jonas. She just hadn't known that what they had wasn't love…not until it was too late, and she'd already hurt her friend.

It all seemed so complicated now. But was she supposed to step away from Shane just in case he was her rebound relationship? That was nuts. She *did* love him.

Maybe she should talk about it with him. Just tell him about what Maya was going through and see if it provoked anything in him about the parallels. Maybe it wouldn't. Maybe she was just being cautious. Which she should be.

If only love came with guarantees.

Chapter Sixteen

For their last night in Jackson Hole, Shane made reservations at a popular barbecue restaurant known for being more fun than romantic, but he and Ashley both wanted to try it before leaving, especially because Ashley mentioned she would never return to Jackson Hole as long as she lived.

He'd paused at that, a little surprised, maybe a little stung, that she still associated the place with her former fiancé more than with him. But as he'd told himself a few times the past couple of days, these things would take time. One day, surely, the memories would shift. The feelings they'd shared on the road to Jackson Hole, and during their time here, would take over, and the painful parts of the journey would recede.

They'd both dressed up more than the restaurant called for with its bright lights and colorful decor, and he could barely take his eyes off Ashley in her sexy black dress, her silky hair loose around her shoulders, her mouth a glossy red. He was in head-to-toe black, wearing a button-down shirt with the sleeves rolled up and black pants. The restaurant had a dance floor in the bar area, and perhaps after dinner they'd sway together to a few songs before heading back to the cabin for what would be their last night at the dude ranch.

But as he and Ashley were led to their table, he couldn't help but notice that she seemed subdued.

Once they had their drinks and menus, he reached for her hand.

"I'm just gonna ask," he said. "You've been quiet. What's on your mind?" He could guess, but he'd rather not. Speculating never got anybody anywhere.

"This is one of my favorite things about you," she said. "You say what needs to be said. Ask what needs to be asked."

"Uh-oh, though. That means something's wrong."

She told him about returning some things to the lodge and talking to the desk attendant, Maya, who she'd gotten friendly with the past few days.

He bristled but tried not to let it show. "So you think that'll happen with us? That I'm your rebound guy?"

It was possible, of course. Probable, even. She'd been left at the altar days ago, and things between her and the guy helping her through, her rock, had turned romantic. Anybody would call that a rebound. It was one of the oldest stories in the book.

But what was between them was so strong. Their connection was based on deep friendship and wild attraction and explosive chemistry—all very powerful stuff. That was more than just a rebound…wasn't it?

She bit her lip. "I don't think being with you is about rebounding. How could what you are to me be reduced to that?"

Okay, that he liked. She agreed with his assessment of them.

"But," she added, taking a sip of her drink, "Maya didn't think so either. She thought she and her best friend had blossomed into something she never expected. And now he won't talk to her. *You've* become my best friend, Shane. I can't lose that."

"We're not just one thing, though," he said. "You've become my best friend too, Ashley." She certainly had. Talk about unexpected.

"Maybe I shouldn't even have brought it up. Maya's not me. You're not Jonas." She took another sip of her drink, clearly conflicted.

He sat back, his spirit a bit sunk. "You should always bring up everything. It's important to talk things through. Even when we both don't have any answers."

"I want answers, though."

He took a slug of his beer. "I just know that everything in life is a risk. There's no way around it."

She sighed. "I want a guarantee. There, I said it. I want to know for sure that neither of us will hurt each other."

Yeah, me too.

"I'm a widower, Ashley," he blurted out. "My five-year-old daughters haven't had a mother since they were three months old. There *are* no guarantees."

The look on her face. Maybe it wasn't the uplifting thing to say. But it was the truest thing he knew.

He reached across the table to take both her hands. "What's the alternative to us being together? You think I'd give you up just because I fear losing you—to anything? No way."

"But it's not that simple."

"Yup, it is. I want to be with you. That's what I know most of all. Do I have worries? Of course. But you're more important to me. I'd rather have you in my life than not, Ashley. That's what it comes down to."

She reached out her hand to touch his face for just a second. "I want you in my life too. I *need* you in my life." She paused, clearly thinking hard about something. Finally she said, "What if…when we get home, things aren't the same? What if this was a road-trip romance and it just doesn't carry over to real life? If things become strained between us, it'll affect Violet and Willow. Maybe I'm getting way ahead of myself, but those girls mean a lot to me."

This was one of the reasons why he felt so strongly about Ashley McCray—she cared so much about others. His daughters, in particular. "I never want them to hurt, Ashley. But if there's one thing I *absolutely* know, it's that I can't protect them from life itself."

"I know, but—"

The sound of racing footsteps had him glancing over to his right just as he heard a very familiar voice.

"Daddy!"

Suddenly, as if talking about his daughters conjured them, Violet was running toward him in, yes, white studded cowboy boots, Willow trailing in her black boot on one foot, a white cowboy boot that matched her sister's on the other.

Aww. Beatrice had made good on her offer. And the symbolism was very moving.

But—a big but—the Shaws were coming toward the table, Charles with his usual good-natured expression and Beatrice Shaw with her more typical murderous expression, staring at him.

"No running, girls," she hissed with a very forced smile. "This is a restaurant."

The Shaws stopped a few feet from the table. Beatrice was glancing around as if making sure she didn't know anyone dining around them.

"What a great surprise!" Shane said, giving both girls a

hug. It was. Unexpected, yes. But a very nice surprise. He'd missed the twins so much. And seeing their faces right now lifted up his heart like nothing else could. His girls were here beside him—all was right in the world.

They both hugged Ashley, chatting a mile a minute about their day and how much fun they'd had, both lifting up a foot to show their boots. Apparently, the Shaws had given them a last day for the record books. Pony rides. A picnic lunch and then a visit to the toy store in town, where they each got to pick out three special things.

He was about to say, *Wow, that is some amazing day you two had*, but Beatrice was glaring at him. And avoiding looking at Ashley.

"Girls, our table is ready and the host is waiting," Beatrice said, her tone strained.

"You're picking us up tomorrow, right?" Willow whispered in his ear, hand cupped.

"Right? Right?" Violet also whispered, hand cupped.

"Girls, we don't whisper in front of others," Beatrice said in that same strained tone.

Violet and Willow looked at their grandmother with little nods, then back at him.

"Yup," he assured them. "Ten a.m. sharp."

"And, Ashley, you're driving back too, right?" Willow asked.

"Sure am," Ashley confirmed.

Both girls clapped and hurried over to their grandmother. Who was still staring at Shane and looking...pissed off.

Because he appeared to be on a date?

Charles waved, and the four disappeared around a bend into the large dining area.

"That was awkward," Ashley said. "Beatrice didn't even say hello—to either of us."

"She's upset about something. But she always is. And the running and whispering didn't help, I'm sure." He shook his head on a sigh, wishing things could be different with his former mother-in-law. But he had a sinking feeling this was how it would always be.

"I thought you all turned a corner," Ashley said. "With what happened with Violet and her hair and bringing in that sweet memory of their mother. The girls were wearing their white cowboy boots, for heaven's sake."

Nothing positive lasted long with Beatrice, unfortunately. "One step forward, two steps back with Beatrice Shaw. It's always been that way. Just when I think I finally have her approval, she lets me know just how disappointing a father I am to her grandchildren."

"But you're an amazing father!" Ashley practically shouted. She leaned closer, lowering her voice. "You are. Anyone with eyes and ears and a heart should be able to see that plain as day."

He almost laughed at the idea of Beatrice Shaw being some kind of mythical creature without those attributes. A gargoyle, say. It helped.

"Does it get to you?" she asked. "Her opinions of you?"

He sat back. He both hated talking about this and needed to. "It did at first. Especially in those very harrowing weeks and months right after we lost Liza. But I quickly saw there was no pleasing the woman. And I stopped trying. I just did what I felt was right. I'm their father. Their sole parent. Beatrice Shaw isn't the boss of me."

Ashley squeezed his hand. "Yeah. She's not."

But she did have power—and could wield it in the courts.

She could try to make a case for taking custody from him. He couldn't see her complaints actually getting anywhere with a judge, but it was possible. Violet and Willow did have hot dogs for dinner once a week. They did have candy every single day. They did call people stupid dumb idiots. They didn't always remember to brush their teeth before bed, and sometimes he was so tired he'd forget to make sure they did. Violet did get her hands on sharp scissors. Willow did sprain her ankle. They ran in restaurants. They whispered in front of people. Maybe those kinds of things would add up to a judge thinking he was deficient—especially given the Shaws' input.

"You know what helps, Ashley?" He leaned forward and took both her hands again. "I was alone before. Now I'm not. Or at least, I don't feel alone with you in my life."

Her eyes got misty. "I don't feel alone either."

"So maybe that's all we need to know right now—about us, I mean."

She smiled softly and nodded, and he could see she was a bit more at peace about their earlier topic of conversation.

"So let's order from this great-looking menu and enjoy our dinner," he said, opening his. "My girls are in this restaurant, and it's nice knowing exactly where they are and what they're doing. I haven't had that the past few days."

"Aww," she said. "They're always on your mind, aren't they? As they should be."

He nodded. Of course they were.

The waiter came by then and took their orders.

A chill did run up his spine when he thought of the look Beatrice had given him. He supposed from her point of view, it was just emotionally complicated. She might worry a woman in his life would change the dynamic between him and the Shaws, the visitation schedule. She might worry that if he and Ashley broke up, the twins would be hurt because it was clear they liked her so much. He had avoided dating so as not to bring his love life into their worlds. It had been an easy way to protect the three of them because he hadn't wanted to date.

But now what? If he and Ashley did break up a few weeks from now, the twins would be upset. They adored her. If it really upset them, it might even impact how they did at school—maybe they'd have trouble concentrating on their lessons or they'd get into more fights. Would that give the Shaws more ammunition to go for custody?

But a preemptive move when things were so good between them? There was no way he'd end things with Ashley now because of what *might* happen in the future. Even the near future.

Hadn't he just said ten minutes ago that he wouldn't give her up because he feared losing her—to anything?

He wasn't going to spend his last night with this wonderful woman with all this weighing on his mind. He had to let it go for tonight.

He was just having a damned hard time getting there.

As they were leaving the restaurant, Ashley noticed Shane taking a peek around the bend where the dining room continued on. From the looks of that section, families were seated there, couples on dates in the other. The family section sure was loud. But Ashley liked the happy cacophony. It was full of life and love. The couples section was too, she supposed, but in a different way. She'd had a long go of being a couple and definitely saw herself in the family section.

"Are the twins and their grandparents still here?" she asked him.

"I don't see them," he said, and they continued heading toward the exit. "Violet and Willow are pretty quick eaters, and I can't imagine Beatrice wanted to prolong being here with us in the next area. I keep expecting my phone to ring and to see her name flash on the screen so she could deliver a fresh litany of complaints. And maybe the third degree about my love life."

"That's really none of her beeswax," Ashley said.

"No, it's not. But she'll make it hers. 'Are my precious granddaughters being subjected to your sex life?' She's planning to come at me. If not tonight on the phone, tomorrow morning in person when I pick up the girls. I have no doubt."

They passed the entrance to the bar, where the DJ was playing vintage Bee Gees. Had they not run into the Shaws, Ashley would have pulled Shane onto the dance floor when a slow song came on. That would have been a nice good-bye to Jackson Hole, swaying with him, chest to chest, lips to lips. But running into the Shaws had thrown some cold water on their night, and she could tell Shane wanted to get back to the cabin and decompress in private. She did too.

Shane held the door open, the evening April air cool but holding the promise of the warmth of spring. "I had big plans for us to go dancing and make the most of this last night. But between *our* conversation and what's coming from Beatrice, I wouldn't mind sitting on the patio at the cabin and just staring up at the stars with you."

"I think that sounds perfect," she whispered.

Ten minutes later they were heading up the long drive of the dude ranch, where she'd had both a wonderful and painful time. For tonight, since she had no idea what would happen when they got home, she wanted the next several hours to be special.

They'd start by watching the stars, and then Ashley made a mental list of just how she could distract Shane from the threat of his phone ringing. Given that he'd be at the Shaws' house tomorrow morning, Ashley doubted his phone would ring tonight.

Once in the cabin, they grabbed waters from the fridge and went outside on the patio, each taking a side-by-side chaise. Ashley grabbed the big chenille blanket folded in the basket under their chairs and pulled it across them. She noticed Shane had set his phone on the small table beside his chaise.

"Ahh," he said, stretching out and turning to look at her. "Very nice. We've got the moon and the stars and this cozy blanket to keep us warm."

"It's truly heavenly," she said.

For the next few minutes, they both just stared up at the sky. Minutes turned into a half hour. No call. Shane seemed to relax. Ashley felt him reaching around for her under the blanket and then take her hand and hold it.

"I like this," she said, turning to smile at him.

"Me too. Getting chilly?" he asked. "We can go inside and put on some music, have that slow dance after all."

"Sounds perfect," she said on more of a whisper than she'd planned, but he'd managed to touch her, as usual.

Inside, he left on just one lamp and then tapped at his phone, and suddenly Frank Sinatra filled the room, a sweet, slow, romantic oldie. She walked over to him and slid her arms around his neck, resting her head against his chest. His hands were at her waist. Then he slid them around her neck too. They moved slowly on the living room rug, swaying to the music, the song and Shane's heartbeat in her ears, her heart happy and full.

"Let's forget everything but this," she said, pulling back a bit and looking up at him. "How this feels. Because it feels really, really good."

"Agree on all counts." He leaned in for a kiss. Her nerve endings were on fire, her toes slightly curling, a warmth spreading inside her.

She kissed him back, with all the passion she had, and she heard a low groan escape him. Smiling, she took his hand and led him to his bedroom, his playlist still audible from where he'd left his phone in the living room.

She ran her hands under his shirt, then slowly unbuttoned it and slipped it off him, slightly gasping at his chest, which never ceased to delight her. So muscled and hard with a faint line of dark hair running down the center. She kissed that hair line until she was squatting before him and undid his belt, then the button and zipper. Off his pants went until he was standing in just those super-sexy black boxer briefs.

She stayed where she was and slipped a hand inside, his head dropping back with a moan, his muscles tensing. She wrapped her palm around his erection and slid it up and down, up and down, until he growled that he was dangerously close to losing control. She slowly let go and inched down the boxer briefs, trailing her tongue along his erection as she went. His entire body went rigid, and then he picked her up like she weighed nothing and carried her to bed.

He undressed her quickly, practically tearing off her bra, his hands and mouth exploring her breasts as he worked off her panties with one hooked finger, the hands and mouth following. Ashley let out a low scream and arched her back, barely able to contain her pleasure.

She heard a foil packet being ripped open, and she smiled.

And then she felt him inside her, filling her, thrusting inside her slowly, then faster, faster, his hands in her hair, his mouth fused to hers. Then he was kissing her neck, and she heard him whispering her name before she exploded in pure pleasure. He did too just moments later.

And then she wasn't aware of anything except their rapidly beating hearts, making Ella Fitzgerald barely audible from the living room, and the waves of love coming from deep within.

Chapter Seventeen

Everything came down to today.

Shane would pick up his girls—and find out if their grandmother planned to make good on her threats to petition for custody.

Shane would arrive back at the McCray Ranch tonight, drop off Ashley at her cabin, and things could possibly not be the same the next time he saw her.

At least he was as physically relaxed as he could be, given last night. He and Ashley had made love twice, a second time in the middle of the night, and they'd fallen back asleep with her head on his chest. That had ensured that much of his tension had been worked away. Their relationship—as far as a future was concerned—was a bit up in the air. But he'd learned to take things one day at a time years ago. And he'd do that with Ashley.

But now, as he pulled into the Shaws' driveway, Ashley in the passenger seat, his shoulders bunched back up. Ashley herself and their romance factored into what might happen in that house.

"Here goes everything," he said as they both hopped out of the SUV.

"Fingers crossed."

He crossed his too and rang the doorbell.

Charles opened the door, looking somewhat stressed. "The gals are in the living room. They're packed and ready to go, but Beatrice is just having a word with them."

A word. Criticizing them for this and that, he was sure.

Charles led the way into the living room. "Girls, your dad's here."

The twins were sitting on the love seat, side by side, hands folded in their laps, which was unusual and clearly a Beatrice directive. They were each in a play dress, their hair in pigtails, which they hated. They'd been clearly getting a "talking-to."

"Yay!" Violet shouted, both girls leaping up.

Beatrice gave Violet a sharp look. "Young lady, we just discussed this. We don't shout. We don't jump up when someone else was in the middle of speaking to you. Please sit back down."

"But Daddy's here," Willow said, both girls sitting back down, frowns pulling at their sweet faces.

They looked down at the table, then up at each other, then back down. Were they supposed to be robots? Were they not supposed to be excited to see their father and leap into his arms? He sure wanted that.

Enough was enough.

"Beatrice, honestly, is all this really necessary?" he asked, exasperated. For a few years now he'd tried very hard to hold his tongue and let "their house, their rules" keep him from contradicting her when it came to how she disciplined the twins in her home. His sympathy and compassion for her also played a big part in that.

But what the hell, already? She could dictate her relationship with them but not *his* relationship. He was more than happy to have them hug him whenever they wanted. *Leave them alone.*

"Violet went flying down the stairs again this morning and leaped off, landing on her knees," Beatrice said. "She caused a painting to actually fall off the wall in the hallway."

"And this is the end of the world why?" he asked, at the end of his patience with her. "Why can't you let them be five-year-olds who run and jump?"

Beatrice scowled at him and marched over, pointing a finger in his face. "They will learn to be respectful young ladies. They're too wild and undisciplined!"

"I disagree," he said. "And another thing. Until you can love them for who they are instead of what you want them to be, I think a break from visits is a good idea."

Beatrice gasped.

Charles gasped.

The twins' mouths dropped open.

"You want them to be little ladies?" he continued. "Well, they're not. They're five. They are who they are and they're great. Every day is a learning and growing adventure. They're wonderful girls, loving sisters, with curious minds and happy hearts. I won't have you try to break their spirits. I don't think you could, honestly. But I'm done letting you try to squash them."

"How dare you," she snapped—but there was a slight change in her face. Less stony, more tentative. "You leave me no choice but to call my lawyer."

"I'll be doing the same," he snapped back.

"Isn't that interesting," Violet said suddenly, her face crumpling.

"No," Willow responded. "It's not!" And both twins hurried over to Ashley and buried their faces in her stomach. She knelt down and wrapped them in a hug, soothing them with whispers.

Shane doubted the twins even knew what a lawyer was, and they certainly didn't know the context here, but they sure had heard enough tension and anger in the back-and-forth to feel nervous. To need to be soothed.

Dammit. "I'm not proud that we just did this in front of them, Beatrice. But you've pushed us all too far."

Beatrice turned to her husband. "Charles, say something."

The man looked at his wife. "Honestly, dear, I don't know what to say. Neither of you is wrong. You're not wrong. Shane's not wrong. There, I said it. And it's true."

Beatrice's mouth dropped open. Although she was the one who was more authoritative, Shane had always gotten the sense that Charles's voice and opinions were very important to her.

Good for you, Charles, Shane thought. He too had clearly had it with letting Nana run the show.

Violet pulled away from Ashley and walked over to her grandmother. "Nana, I know why you don't like when I run down the stairs and jump off the third step." She spoke in her usual voice—not shyly, not quietly.

Shane stared at his little girl. She had spunk, that was for sure. Her twin was watching, listening hard.

"You're afraid I'll die like Mommy did," Violet said. "And Willow. She already hurt her ankle."

Shane gasped. So did Ashley. And Charles Shaw.

Shane had expected his daughter might say any number of things, but he hadn't figured on *that*.

Beatrice's lower lip was trembling. She turned away for a moment.

Five sets of eyes were staring at her. Shane had no idea what would happen next, how she'd react, what she'd say. His heart went out to Beatrice in that moment. Because he knew Violet was right. One hundred percent.

His girls had heard enough, though. None of what he and their grandmother had said had been meant for their ears. He'd been trying to shield them from all that, but maybe they did need to hear him defending them, standing up for them, as he had.

Yes, he thought. She'd pushed him too far.

Beatrice knelt down in front of Violet, her expression unreadable. "You come here too, Willow," she said.

As Willow slowly walked over, Beatrice opened up her arms. Both girls hesitantly went to her.

"You know what I think, Violet?" Beatrice said, her eyes misting now. "I think you're right."

"You do?" Violet said, her own eyes wide.

"You yell at us all the time so we won't get hurt like Mommy did?" Willow asked.

Beatrice touched each of the girls' chins. "I think so. I think I'm very scared of that. And if you didn't run or jump or climb trees or touch scissors, you wouldn't risk getting hurt. But that's silly, isn't it? Your mother wasn't doing anything reckless when she got into that accident."

"Nana, what does *reckless* mean?" Violet asked.

"It means risky," Beatrice said. "Like driving too fast. Especially in the rain. But your mother wasn't driving fast—in fact, she was driving extra slowly. She simply got into an accident and hit that guardrail. It wasn't anyone's fault, certainly not her own. That's what an accident is."

Oh, Beatrice.

She took in a deep breath. "I've been hard on you girls because I want to keep you safe. And I want you to be like your mother was before she became a teenager and developed not only a mind of her own, but a voice of her own. Oh, she wouldn't listen to a word I said!" She smiled shakily.

Violet's and Willow's eyes were huge. "Did she get in trouble all the time like we do?"

"Yes. I constantly tried to get her to be well-behaved and quiet, to wear pretty dresses and headbands in sleek hair. Instead, she wore ripped flannel shirts, jeans she drew on, huge black boots, and cut her hair into all kinds of weird cuts."

The twins laughed. "Like mine?" Violet asked, touching her bangs.

"Just like yours," Beatrice said with a smile. "But that's the thing. Your hair's not weird if you like it. It's you. And like your father said, you two are wonderful girls. I'm very proud of who you are."

Shane thought he might fall over, he was so surprised. He glanced at Ashley, whose hand was on her heart. She looked half astonished and half like she might cry.

The girls beamed. "Even though we mess up all the time when we're here?"

"You don't mess up," Beatrice said. "I'm the one who messed up. You two are just right."

Well, I'll be, Shane thought, recalling his grandfather's favorite old-timey phrase.

Charles, standing next to his wife, gave her hand a squeeze. Shane could read pride in the man's face loud and clear.

Beatrice hugged the girls, and they hugged her back. "I love you two."

"We love you, Nana," they said in unison.

"Oh, and one more thing," Beatrice said to them. "The other day, your father told me that your mother would be very proud of who you girls were. And he's right. Your mother would be so proud. And I'm proud too."

Violet and Willow beamed again and threw themselves at their nana for another hug.

Beatrice's eyes were all misty, and she gave them a surreptitious swipe. "Why don't you take your pops out to the backyard and show him how high you can swing while I talk to your daddy?"

The twins raced to the door, Charles laughing as he ran behind them. A nice sight to see.

Beatrice stood up. "I owe you an apology, Shane."

"It's not necessary. Everything you just said to them is all I need to hear and know," he said.

She nodded and was quiet for a moment. Then she looked from him to Ashley and back to Shane. "I suppose you two are dating."

"We're trying," Shane said, reaching for Ashley's hand and holding it.

"That's a good way to put it," Ashley said with a gentle smile.

"Well, it's clear to me the twins adore you," Beatrice said to Ashley. "I have a lot to think about and get used to. But I need to put my granddaughters first—not myself."

Shane extended his hand, and Beatrice shook it with a smile. Hugging her was something neither of them was ready for, which made him chuckle. "You're welcome to come visit us anytime."

"I appreciate that," she said.

Shane eyed the girls' suitcases by the door. "Well, I guess we'd better hit the road."

Beatrice led the way to the yard. She ran—actually ran—over to the girls and knelt down again on the wood chips, also a surprise, and called them in for one last hug.

"Wonders never cease," he whispered. "We both need to remember that when we lose faith about anything."

"I would not have believed any of this if you'd told me secondhand," she whispered back with a smile.

He gave her a quick kiss on the cheek, and then it was time to head home.

Where the road trip would end—and maybe take his romance with Ashley with it.

It was almost 8:00 p.m. when Shane pulled up in front of Ashley's cabin at the McCray Ranch. The girls were fast asleep in the back seat. She didn't like the idea of not saying good-night and goodbye—for now anyway—but she couldn't imagine waking them for that when she'd see them in the morning. She lived a literal stone's throw away from their cabin, and the girls played outside in the mornings, particularly when they didn't have school. Before she started work in the stables for the day, she'd have them give a treat to the horses. The twins loved offering them apple slices and carrot bits. It would be a nice way to ease into things being mostly the same but a little different—back home but with their father in a romantic relationship with her. She thought back to when they'd brought up her marrying their father. Now it was a possibility. Before it had seemed crazy to her—but now she wondered how they'd really feel.

She needed to talk to Shane about how they might react to him having a girlfriend. Sure, they adored her like she did them, but this was a whole nother story. They'd never seen their father with a romantic partner before. Not once in their five years.

And they'd just had a very emotional morning at their grandparents' with talk of their mother.

Suddenly Ashley felt unsure of everything.

"You okay?" he asked, hopping out of the SUV and walking around. He gave the girls a glance. Still fast asleep in their booster seats.

She nodded. It was late, he'd just driven seven hours with only a couple of stops, and this was a conversation that would be better left to tomorrow. How to handle their romance in front of his children would need to be his call.

"I know you were just stuck in a car with me for seven hours, but if you want to come over in a little while..."

She smiled. "I absolutely do want to."

She liked the idea of the continuity instead of each of them going to their separate homes and spending the night apart. She wouldn't stay over, of course.

"I'll get the twins settled in bed and then text you," he said. "I'll miss you for the twentyish minutes we're separated."

"I will too," she said, slinging her arms around him for a quick kiss before dashing up the porch and into her cabin.

As she was about to close the cabin door behind her, she noticed him waiting for her to be safely inside. She loved that about him. Harrington had certainly never done that. Shane held up a hand in goodbye before turning back to the SUV. She slid aside the living room curtains and watched his SUV travel down the gravel road to his own cabin, not wanting to break their connection.

She had it bad for the man, that was for sure.

Ashley took a fast shower and dried her hair, pulling it

back into a ponytail, then changed into leggings and an over-size sweatshirt. Ahh, comfort. She texted her parents that she was back and everything was fine.

Her phone pinged with a text. Her mother, not Shane.

Breakfast out on Sunday with us and then lunch with me and your aunts at the house. So glad you're home, sweetie.

Hi, beautiful, her dad texted a moment later. Sweet dreams and see you on Sunday.

Ashley smiled. She was so grateful for her parents.

And then her phone pinged a third time. Shane. Her heart sped up.

My living room awaits...

A rush of happiness welled up inside her, and she headed back out, walking down the path to his cabin. Couldn't beat the proximity just a quarter of a mile away. It wasn't adjoining rooms at the Bison Creek Lodge or the cabin they'd shared, but she'd take it. She'd been worrying for nothing about how things would be once they got back home. Here they were, back home a mere half hour, and all was well. Okay, fine, a half hour was nothing. But they both wanted to be together again, and that was what mattered.

Shane was on the two-person—or one adult, two little kids—porch swing when she arrived. She sat down beside him, and he put his arm around her shoulders, and in that moment all felt right with the world.

"I think things are going to be just fine," he said.

She smiled up at him and then rested her head on his shoulder. "Me too." She lifted her head and leaned back against the cushioned swing. "I've been thinking. How do you think Willow and Violet will feel about you being in a relationship with a woman?"

"As long as it's you, I think we're A-OK there."

That went straight to her heart.

The cool night air felt so good on her face, in her hair. She closed her eyes and could feel herself drifting off. One giant yawn later, Shane said, "I'd walk you home, but I can't. Plight of the single parent."

She laughed. "I'll be fine."

And as they had one hell of a kiss good-night and she started off down the path, she truly believed it. She would be fine. They would be fine.

The future was theirs for the taking, and against all odds, they were taking it.

Chapter Eighteen

Later that weekend, Ashley carried a big platter of the chicken-and-cheese quesadillas she'd spent the last half hour making to the dining room table in her parents' house. Her mom and her three aunts were hosting a "Welcome back, Ashley" lunch, with just the five of them. Early this morning, she and her parents had gone out to breakfast, and then they'd stopped at the bank to each deposit their checks from the wedding canceler. That had felt good. Mission accomplished.

And then some.

Her dad, her uncle Teddy, who'd filled in as foreman for Shane during his absence, and the two ranch hands were out on the range. Shane had told her that he was going to spend the weekend with his daughters, checking in on them emotionally, particularly after the scene right before they'd left Jackson Hole. He'd mentioned he might even bring up the subject of his love life. Then tonight, Ashley's parents were going to babysit the twins once they were asleep while Shane and Ashley went out on the town—her parents' kind offer. They definitely had an inkling the two were *involved*—and were clearly okay with it even so soon after the debacle of Ashley's wedding.

"So where are you two lovebirds going tonight?" Ashley's

aunt Daphie asked as she set out a bowl of sour cream and salsa.

"Umbertos," Ashley said with a smile she couldn't help. She and Shane had missed out on dancing in Jackson Hole, but Umbertos, everyone's favorite Italian restaurant, was famous for its romantic, low-lit dance floor and slow songs only.

"Oooh, maybe he'll propose," Aunt Lila said, slipping a bit of chicken to each of her little Chihuahuas, who were under her chair in a little fluffy dog bed that went everywhere with Lila.

Aunt Daphie's eyes practically popped. "Are you kidding me? They just started dating like a minute ago! And Ashley could use some time on her own."

"Shane is a great guy," Ingrid said, sitting down and plucking a quesadilla from the platter. "And, my, is he handsome. Hardworking, kind, the best of the best."

Ashley smiled at her mom. "He is definitely all that."

Aunt Kate plopped sour cream on her quesadilla. "Mmm, Ashley, these are fabulous. You'll have to give me the recipe. The chicken is perfectly seasoned."

Daphie gaped at her sister. "That's what you have to say, Kate? You're the one who wanted to haul Harrington into court for breach of expectations and the money. Now you agree with her getting engaged two seconds later? Don't you think she needs time on her own to heal and grow?"

"I was staying neutral," Kate responded. "But I do think Ashley should follow her heart—whatever that means and wherever it leads. A great new romance or time on her own. Only she can decide that, busybody."

Ashley found herself listening hard to the argument that ensued. She had these questions herself. On the one hand, Shane was everything she could ever want in a man. On the other, she had just been through a big emotional up-heaval and felt shaky in a lot of areas, trust being a big one.

Though Shane was very trustworthy. Her mother brought that up immediately and listed all the ways that Shane had been there for the McCray Ranch the past five years, how he never let them down.

Daphie, who was recently divorced and pro alone, medi-tation, yoga and working on yourself and becoming your own best friend, wagged a finger at her oldest sister. "Yes, he's trustworthy. As a *foreman*. We have no idea if he's a good life partner."

"He is a great father," Ashley pointed out, spooning more salsa on her quesadilla. "Devoted, loving, caring, compas-sionate, fair, warm. Those girls are very lucky to have him as their dad."

"Again, a devoted dad doesn't mean a devoted husband. Did Eli not cheat on me even while he attended every one of our son's lacrosse games? Spend two hours every Sat-urday helping him study for the SATs?"

Huh. She did have a point. But in a million years, Ash-ley could not envision Shane cheating on her. On anyone.

"Can we let Ashley enjoy her new relationship without getting all cynical on her?" Aunt Kate said. "If he hurts her, we'll just kill him."

Ashley's eyes widened.

"Jeez, I kid, I kid," Kate said. "I'm just saying, let's give them a chance. He's not Harrington. And Ashley isn't the same person she was last week. She's been through a lot. And she's had some unexpected adventures." She wiggled her eyebrows.

Wow, her aunt Kate was not usually so on the "go for it" side. She was about caution.

"Plus, being in a good relationship so soon will help Ashley see what she deserves, what she wants," Lila added. "Shane doesn't have to be *the one*. He can be the tester."

Which reminded Ashley of everything Maya had said at the lodge on their final night there about landing in a rebound relationship—and not realizing it until she'd met someone she fell very hard for.

"Look," Ashley's mom said to her sisters. "They're dating. They're not getting engaged at Umbertos tonight. They're enjoying each other's company. I think they're great together. And from everything Ashley told me, they bring out the best in each other. That's what's important."

Ashley felt a shy smile come upon her face. Her mother had called not long after Ashley had returned to her cabin from the brief interlude on Shane's porch swing, checking in, making sure she was really okay, and they'd had a good talk. Ashley had opened up. Her mother had made her feel so positive about her romance with Shane.

She'd explore her feelings and take it day by day.

Saying so got her four nods from her wise mother and aunts, and she was satisfied.

"I do think Ashley will make one hell of a mother," Aunt Daphie said.

"Whoa, now who's getting ahead of herself!" Ashley's mom countered. "Though I am ready to be a grandmother. What should I call myself? Grandmère? Grandmama? Granny? Grammy?"

Ashley grinned at her mom. "You're gonna be amazing at it, that's all I know."

"Those precious little girls do need a mother," Lila said, then took a sip of her iced tea.

It was scary enough worrying about whether she and Shane

were the real deal or a road-trip romance. Add Violet's and Willow's hearts, minds and souls into the mix and she had to tread carefully. She couldn't let those girls get hurt because of her.

They talked motherhood in general for the next twenty minutes, all of them seeming to realize that Ashley was getting a little overwhelmed by the conversation. They moved on to local gossip, and soon enough, the quesadillas were gone. They'd been a big hit and there were just crumbs left.

She suddenly had an urge to go riding. Not necessarily to have some time alone to think about all the things her relatives had just said, but to just let everything settle. She needed the fresh air on her face, in her hair, as she and her favorite mare, Gingersnap, rode far out on the property. Ashley popped up. "My dear aunts, I'm going to take you up on the offer to clean up since I cooked—I'd love to go riding right now, clear my head."

They all thought that was a good idea.

A half hour later, as Ashley saddled up Gingersnap, she wondered what Shane and the girls were doing, where they were. She missed them so much. She'd see them tonight right before bedtime—apparently they'd asked Shane if she could come over and tell them a story and tuck them into bed. She'd love nothing more.

And then a romantic night out with their handsome father? Oh, yeah. She was looking forward to both with equal measure.

"Daddy, can we go see Ashley now?" Violet asked.

He smiled at his daughters, who were down to their last few french fries at the burger joint they went to for dinner in town. "Bored of me already?"

Willow swiped a fry in the little mound of ketchup on her plate. "Daddy, you're not boring! But we miss Ashley."

"Ashley's so great," Violet said.

He took the last bite of his burger, his stomach and heart both full and happy. "I agree."

He did love that the girls adored Ashley. He'd spent the entire day with the twins—both in their white cowboy boots, or boot, in Willow's case—and the girls had spent at least half of it talking about Ashley. How fun she was. How pretty. How smart. How nice. *How she'd said those nice things about Mommy.*

He'd been well aware that Ashley had known his wife, that they'd been acquaintances who said hello and stopped to exchange small talk if they ran into each other. But they hadn't really had the chance to know each other well. Both were busy, Liza as a new, exhausted mother of twin babies, and Ashley as the horse trainer, groomer and stable manager of her family ranch. Now, though, the fact that she had known the twins' mother had special meaning, particularly for Violet and Willow. It was thanks to Ashley's memory of Liza that Ashley had been able to get through to Beatrice in a closet in the twins' bedroom at their grandparents' house—which had led to the sweet boots on their feet. A symbol of their rebellious mother, who'd had her own mind, heart and soul.

As Willow tore her last french fry in half and gave a piece to her sister, which warmed his heart, he realized he hadn't brought up the subject of him and Ashley dating. Willow was out of ketchup but Violet still had some on her plate, and she set her plate on top of her sister's so they could share the condiment. He watched them pop the split fry into their mouths and decided it would be premature to introduce his love life in a big way. No one said he and Ashley had to make their romance obvious to his daughters right away. The girls didn't even have to know. If he and Ashley got serious, that would be a different story. But until then, there was no need to bring his love life into *their* lives.

They had been the ones to bring up the idea of him and Ashley getting married, but they were five. They knew a wedding was about a couple staying together forever. But they didn't know much else about marriage—and the topic didn't really seem to interest them, given that they hadn't brought it up again.

At some point, the twins would happen upon him and Ashley kissing, and they'd *know*. He had a feeling they'd be happy about the kissing too. Which made him smile.

"I know Ashley is spending today with her family," he said as they all gathered up their wrappers and cups, "just like you're spending today with your family. But she did say she'd come visit and read you two a story before bed."

"Yay!" they said in unison.

"So let's go home and get into bed!" Willow said, but then glanced up at the still-bright-blue sky. She frowned. "It's definitely not bedtime yet."

"But we can go to bed *early*," Violet pointed out.

Shane gaped at his daughters. "You actually want it to be bedtime so you can see Ashley?"

They both nodded.

Yup, he had a very strong suspicion they would not mind the idea of him and Ashley as a couple. He glanced at his phone, shaking his head on a smile that reflected the warmth in his heart. "You've got about two hours before bedtime. But maybe Ashley can come over early. Let's head home."

The twins fist-pumped and skipped their way to the SUV. Once they were buckled in the back seat, Shane drove to the McCray Ranch, his own heart speeding up at the idea of seeing Ashley. He knew just how the twins felt and then some.

Once they were back at the cabin, they went straight to their bedroom. When he went to see what they were up to, they were both in pj's and in their beds, blankets pulled up to their chins. Wow, these two were serious.

"Can you call Ashley and tell her we're ready for our story?" Willow asked, her favorite lovey under the crook of her arm.

Violet nodded. "Since it's early, she can tell us a *million* stories about Helena the horsey."

Shane laughed. "She'll probably really like that, actually. I'll go call her, okay?"

He went to find his phone, which he'd tossed in the basket on the coffee table in the living room. Just as he grabbed it, it rang.

Anthony McCray.

"Oh, God, Shane. There's been an accident. Ashley got thrown off the mare she was riding. The only good news is that she was on her way back to the stables and was pretty close—Jack actually *saw* her get thrown and called 911 right away."

Shane had frozen at the word *accident*, his breath caught in his throat, his heart pounding. No. No, no, no.

His hand on the phone was shaking. "She's okay, though? Nothing broken?"

"She was knocked unconscious. The ambulance just came and took her to General. I'm headed there now. Her mom went in the ambulance with her and just texted me—no change. She hasn't woken up."

Unconscious. A terrible chill ran up Shane's spine. He couldn't find his voice.

"Come when you can, okay?" Anthony said. "I know you'll need a sitter for the girls."

"I'll be there as soon as I can," he said, his voice shaky, his legs trembling now.

Unconscious. No change...

He started to put the phone in his pocket, but then pulled it out again. He called Jack, the ranch hand who'd seen the accident, and asked if his teenage daughter was free to babysit for a few hours tonight, starting as soon as Jack could drop her off. Luckily, the answer was yes.

"Was she thrown clear?" Shane asked, his heart pounding so loud he wasn't sure he'd even hear Jack's response.

"Yes, thank God. And it happened on the open path. If it had happened thirty seconds earlier, she might have been knocked into the tree line."

He closed his eyes. At least there was that.

Jack assured him he'd drop off his daughter in five minutes, and they disconnected.

Shane had no idea what he was going to tell the twins right now. They'd be upset enough to learn that Ashley wasn't coming to read them a million stories. But if he told them why...

He walked slowly to their bedroom, trying to think, but his head was jumbled. He sucked in a breath and walked in, not sure what exactly would come out of his mouth. Until he had more information, he didn't want to leave them hanging in worry.

Both girls were asleep, Violet's mouth slightly open,

Willow on her side with her lovey tucked close against her. They'd had another big day, so falling asleep early wasn't a surprise.

And lucky for him. He wouldn't have to tell them why Ashley wasn't coming over. Or that he had to go and would be home later. If they woke up while he was gone, the sitter—a bubbly, funny sixteen-year-old named Elly who'd babysat for them before—would tell them he had to go out for a while, and they'd have a little milk and then go back to sleep.

Jack was true to his word and arrived within minutes. Once his daughter Elly was settled in the house, Shane rushed out.

Jack was waiting. "I wish I had more info for you, Shane. Even though Ashley was thrown clear, she seemed to land hard."

Dammit. "What happened?" he asked as he fished his keys out of his pocket. "Do you know? I mean, what spooked the horse?"

"Delivery truck backfired. Scared the bejesus out of all of us until we realized where the deafening sound came from. It's why I was looking around and happened to see the accident."

"Just tell me one thing," Shane called as he ran over to his SUV. "Was she breathing?"

"I don't know, Shane. I'm sorry."

He nodded and took off for the hospital, which was twenty minutes away. Bluetooth read him a text from Ingrid. No change.

That had to mean she was breathing but still unconscious.

A cold burst of fear traveled up his spine and settled around his neck, squeezing to the point that he had to pull over for a moment and suck in some air. He got back on the road, driving as fast as he could without endangering anyone.

Finally, he made it. He parked and ran inside the Emergency entrance, quickly finding the McCrays and Ashley's three aunts either sitting or pacing. He rushed up to Ashley's parents.

Anthony's eyes were red rimmed. "All they could tell us is that she has a sprained ankle. And hit her head pretty hard, but there's no skull fracture."

A sprained ankle. Like Willow. No skull fracture. Both good signs. "So she'll be okay, right? She'll be okay."

"They can't say yet," he managed in a shaky tone, then dropped down in a chair, then bolted up and began pacing. "She's still out."

Ingrid was being consoled by her sisters, but the three aunts looked very worried, and all of them had the same red-rimmed eyes as Anthony.

Please, God, he sent heavenward. *Please.* He couldn't even get out any more of a prayer. That ice-cold fear ran up his spine again, spreading into his chest. He wrapped his arms around his body. *Please, please, please. Let her be okay.*

He dropped down in a chair, dimly aware that he felt strangely numb, the cold replaced by a nothingness. He squeezed his eyes shut.

Bile clawed at his gut, and that chill was wrapping around him. He was ice-cold again and shaking suddenly.

He'd been here before. In this waiting room.

Waiting. Waiting. Waiting.

The last time he was here, he'd lost his wife. *We're so sorry, Shane. We did everything we could...*

His children had lost their mother. Just three months old and motherless.

A blackness threatened to engulf him. He opened his eyes. *Don't lose it*, he ordered himself. *Ashley needs you right now. Keep it together.*

I can't do this, a small, terrible voice whispered in his head, then started echoing. *I can't do this again.*

Chapter Nineteen

Ashley's first thought when she'd learned from the nurse that she'd sprained her ankle and would need a boot was that she and Willow Dawson would match. Her second thought—her head hurt a bit. She'd been unconscious for almost an hour, but she'd been very lucky—the CT scan showed no sign of injury other than a small goose egg. Her ankle wouldn't require surgery.

Her parents had been in, her three aunts, but where was Shane? According to everyone, he'd arrived very soon after her father had alerted him to the accident and had been sitting in the waiting room looking pale and worried. While she'd been unconscious, she'd been allowed to have visitors for just a few minutes, and apparently, he'd come in to see her but had quickly returned to the waiting room. He was still there. Her aunts had left to relieve Shane's sitter, since Ashley would be here overnight for observation and everyone assumed he'd want to stay with her as long as he could. Her parents had gone to the cafeteria to get her soup and hot tea. Now was a perfect time for Shane to come in, for them to have a little time together alone.

She'd asked a nurse to let Shane know she was awake and wanted to see him, but fifteen minutes later, no Shane.

She looked at the analog clock on the wall. She'd been

here for over three hours. She'd been awake for the past hour. Why hadn't he come in to see her?

A nurse came in to check her vitals. She asked if Shane was still in the waiting room and he was. Yes, the nurse had let him know he could see Ashley anytime until 9:00 p.m., which was coming right up.

And then a terrible idea occurred to her.

He'd been in that waiting room before. For news about his wife after the accident.

His twin three-month-olds in their double stroller beside him, both babies crying, inconsolable on and off for hours.

She knew that because her father had told her. She and her mother and aunts had been away on a girls' trip that weekend. But her father had rushed to the ER the moment he'd heard about the car accident. Liza's parents and brother and Shane's family had been pacing, her mother alternating between crying and demanding information on her daughter's condition.

And then the doctor had come out, and her father had taken one look at the woman's face and knew.

Shane had stood up and dropped to his knees before the doctor had even reached him. And then they'd all heard what the doctor had said.

We're very sorry. We did everything we could...

According to her father, Beatrice had collapsed in her husband's arms and nurses had rushed to help them into chairs.

He'd learned the worst news of his life in that waiting room. Had been crushed in that waiting room. His daughters had become motherless in that waiting room.

And now he was sitting in one of those gray padded chairs.

Oh, Shane, she thought. He must be besieged by memories.

She felt fine now except for the slight headache and wished she could go into the waiting room herself and see Shane, assure him she was okay, that she'd been very lucky.

Maybe it was silly, but she believed he was her talisman. He was in her heart and had been with her when the accident happened—even if not physically. The thought was a comfort.

"Ashley?" she heard him call from behind the ringed curtain.

Her heart sped up a bit. He'd come. *Finally.* She let out a breath, so relieved.

"Come on in," she said.

He was as pale as her parents had mentioned, his expression grim. "You're okay, I hear. Except for a sprained ankle and a goose egg."

"Willow and I have matching ankle boots," she said with a smile. "Oh, gosh, you don't think Violet will try to injure her leg to match, do you?" She chuckled—though it wasn't really funny because Violet just *might*.

He put a hand on her shoulder. "Thank God you're okay. Your parents are back—they brought you some food. They're in the waiting room."

He didn't sound like himself. He sounded like a stranger.

"Shane, are *you* okay?"

He turned away for a moment and didn't say anything, then shook his head. "I'm not."

"I understand," she whispered. *This is hard, but say it, Ashley. Talk about it.* "It must bring back the worst memories."

He sucked in a breath and gave something of a nod. "Now that your folks are back and there's only ten minutes more of visiting hours, I'll let them come and say goodnight, and I'll get home and let your aunts go."

He definitely didn't sound like himself. She hoped he'd lean down and hug her, even if that would be difficult to do in their positions, or at least drop a kiss on her lips, on her forehead. But he didn't.

He reached for her hand and held it for a moment and then left. Taking a big piece of her heart with him.

She bit her lip, feeling slightly sick. Worried. Nervous. Scared.

Don't worry, she told herself. *He'll be back in the morning to pick you up. He just needs to get out of here and try to deal with what being back here awakened for him.*

There was an Urgent Care entrance on the other side of the hospital, so he likely hadn't been back to the ER itself in these five years. He would have taken the twins there for their high fevers and minor injuries.

Walking into the ER tonight, sitting in that waiting room for hours...

But her parents had told her that while she'd been unconscious, the doctors said they'd have to wait to assess her when she came to. *We didn't know how bad it was gonna be*, her father had said, tears in his eyes. *If you'd wake up at all.* He'd burst into tears then, her parents clinging to each other. She'd assured them she was absolutely fine, she'd gotten lucky, and they kept saying they knew it but it was so damned *scary.*

She thought back to her and Shane's conversation in the barbecue restaurant in Jackson Hole. They'd talked about risk. Possible loss. How Ashley had wanted a guarantee.

How he'd said, *You think I'd give you up because I fear losing you—to anything?*

Remembering that made her feel much better. Everything would be okay. Like Shane often said, things took time. This would take time. They'd get through it. They were that strong.

She wished she could sleep beside Shane tonight, just holding him, just there for him, her head pressed against his shoulder.

It was going to be a very long night for them both.

In the morning, Shane put the twins on the school bus, then realized as it was halfway down the road that he'd forgotten to put their lunch boxes in their backpacks; the orange and blue soft sacks were both still on the counter, next to the mess he'd left—the packages of turkey and cheese, the mustard for Willow, the mayo for Violet. The packs of mini pretzels. It vaguely occurred to him that he needed to buy more of those; he was down to his last two.

This was how it had been since the twins had woken up. He was so scatterbrained. He hadn't slept much. He'd set his alarm for their wake-up time just in case he was either asleep or out of his mind, as he'd been much of the night. He'd sat out on the back patio awhile, barely aware that he was cold.

And he'd cried—hard. For a good half hour.

What he knew when the alarm had gone off at 7:00 a.m. was that he couldn't do this. Not that he had a choice; *something* had changed when he'd woken up. The raw aching vulnerability had been replaced by something hard. He could almost feel the metal shutter surrounding his heart, protecting it. *Try to get past me*, it seemed to say in a dead voice.

Yes, something had changed. He'd gone numb again, as

he had those first weeks after he'd lost his wife, become a widowed father to two babies. He'd had so much help then—his family, Liza's family. Beatrice's face gray. Charles constantly crying. But the twins—caring for them, holding them, feeding them, rocking them, consoling them—had gotten them all through. Liza's babies had needed them all. That sense of purpose, along with the knowledge that Liza lived on in these precious infants, had saved them.

He'd felt that way this morning when he'd made Violet's and Willow's lunches, when he'd sat down to brush both girls' hair, when he'd reminded them to brush their teeth, when he'd taken a look in their backpacks to make sure they had their take-home folders. There was such comfort in the everyday tasks. His girls were what kept him going, always.

He'd drop off the girls' lunches on his way to see Ashley in the hospital. He'd tell her he couldn't do this. She'd understand. She'd be disappointed, hurt even, but hadn't she said this might just be a rebound relationship anyway? That she wasn't sure they'd last once they got home?

He'd just be cutting it off now. A preemptive move. A necessary move.

He could not care this much about someone else other than his children. He could not love someone again other than his children.

He could not lose another person he loved.

He wouldn't. And the way to do that was not to date, not to love.

Somewhere inside him he could feel another sharp ache, that metal shutter not doing its job. But that pain was another sure sign that he was doing the right thing by taking himself out, stepping away.

He'd do *his* job—as foreman on the ranch. He'd raise

his girls. He hadn't intended to get involved with another woman, and the road trip had let him compartmentalize; it had been a road-trip romance, but now the trip was over. The romance was stopping with it.

He got back to the cabin, and the sight of all the lunch stuff on the counter made him envision his daughters on the bus. They were probably telling their classmates their adventures these past several days, Willow showing off her black ankle boot, Violet fluffing her very short bangs with pride. Both showing off their white cowboy boots. He squeezed his eyes shut for a moment, then opened them and took a deep breath.

He alternated feeling too much and feeling numb.

Yesterday, the subject of dating Ashley hadn't come up with the twins, and now he was grateful. They hadn't even known their father had briefly been dating her. All they knew was that he and Ashley were good friends. And hopefully, in time, they'd get back to that.

Right now, he could see them going back to the relationship they'd had before the wedding. Acquaintances. But that might be the numbness talking. They would always be more than acquaintances, even if they never spoke again. What was between them ran deep, it was in their veins, and it always would be.

And if she started dating someone else and he didn't like what he saw, he'd butt in again. That was who he was. But he wouldn't get involved in her life beyond that. He just couldn't.

He sucked in a breath and cleared the counter, then grabbed the two lunch boxes and headed out. He liked the idea of going to the elementary school, being in the girls' universe even if he was just going to the office. He'd feel them surrounding him. They were *inside* that metal shutter in his chest—not outside like Ashley was.

Then he'd go to the hospital and he'd tell her how it had to be.

Ashley's aunt Daphie was adamant over FaceTime that Shane would arrive with a huge bouquet of her favorite flowers, which were red tulips and in bloom. That he'd be fine this morning, his head and heart in a better, stronger place. If Daphie thought so, it was easier to let herself hope. Plus, her aunt had always believed in the power of a good night's sleep. But her aunt hadn't seen Shane last night, his face, his eyes, his demeanor, his posture. Or heard his voice, which had had a rawness to it that had made her heart ache.

She was sitting in the guest chair in the hospital room she'd been moved to last night, ready to leave, her phone held up to her face to see her dear aunt. She had her discharge papers and was waiting for Shane. He'd texted last night that he'd pick her up and bring her home.

"Plus, he owes you dinner and dancing at Umbertos," Daphie said. "So once your ankle is all healed, he'll have to make good on that."

"I appreciate your new optimism, Auntie."

Daphie smiled. "I believe in you two. I know I was down on you two getting involved so soon after the wedding disaster. But I was coming from my own long line of man troubles. Last night, your parents told me a lot more about the kind of man Shane is. He's exactly who I want for you, honey."

She bit her lip. "I might not have a say, unfortunately. I just have a bad feeling. A scared feeling. And it's telling me that I've lost him. That he's gone, retreated deep, and I won't be able to reach him."

Daphie gently shook her head. "You two belong together. Might take him a little bit to get there again, but have faith. That's my new motto. Have faith."

Ashley smiled. That was hard-won coming from cynical, I-hate-everyone-and-everything Aunt Daphie. "I'll try. Love you."

"Love you," she said.

They disconnected and Ashley set down her phone, peering out the window, which had a lovely view of the parking lot. Ah—she saw Shane's SUV pull in. She got up slowly, walking carefully on her new boot, which she wasn't quite used to, and looked out, dying for a glimpse of her handsome man. Hopefully he was still *her* handsome man.

But he didn't get out of his vehicle. In fact, she could just make out him sitting in the front seat. He didn't seem to be on his phone. He was just looking straight ahead, then down, then out the side window.

Oh, crud. Her stomach dropped. This wasn't good. He had something hard to tell her.

Like, *I can't do this*. She felt it coming, and her eyes immediately welled with tears.

Dammit.

When she dabbed under her eyes and looked out the window again, she could see Shane making his way to the hospital entrance.

Brace yourself, she thought. *This is gonna hurt.*

She could be wrong, of course. Last night was hard on him. The memories. Being in that waiting room, not knowing how she was, if she'd make it… It must have brought a lot of pain back up for him.

But she was fine. Didn't that count for anything?

There was a tap at her door, and she sucked in a breath. "Come on in."

One look at his face, at his eyes, the set of his jaw, his bunched shoulders, told her everything. He *was* already gone.

"Shane, before you say anything, let me say this. I love you."

She paused, hoping to see some reaction, some change in his expression. But there was none.

She quickly continued so he couldn't get a word in to tell her they were over and walk out. "Before the road trip, I wanted to bop you on the head at least twice a week. In the beginning of the road trip, I was an emotional mess, as you know, unsure of everything, so hurt and dejected that I was actually hoping Harrington would see me and want me back."

She almost couldn't believe she'd been in that headspace. But that was oftentimes how heartbreak worked. You could want to earn the love you'd been denied, that had been snatched from you. You wanted the approval. You wanted to feel good about yourself again.

She mentally shook her head. She could barely remember that woman, and it hadn't been that long ago. That was how different she felt now, how strong, how *sure*—of herself, of Shane, of *them*.

"You helped me change, Shane. You helped me find my way back to myself. You helped me believe in myself and my right to go after what I want. Now that I know this, that this feeling is possible, I'll never again accept anything less."

The look in his eyes almost broke her heart. Because the very air in the room seemed to vibrate with the *I'm sorry* that was coming. Nothing she was saying was reaching inside him. He was listening. But it wasn't getting *in*.

"And, Shane, what was said that final morning at the Shaws' house. About risk—"

He was shaking his head. Fast. Meaning he didn't want to hear this, wouldn't hear this.

"Ashley, I *do* remember what was said. I fully remember Beatrice saying that her daughter wasn't doing anything risky when she got into that accident. That it wasn't her fault. You weren't doing anything risky either when you got into your accident. You were trotting back to the stables. A delivery truck backfired and bam—your horse spooked."

"Right, and—"

"And just like that, reckless, careful—it doesn't matter. The risk is in loving someone in the first place. I've got enough of that with two little girls. I can't take on any more. I've always known I couldn't—it's why I never started dating. But you came along and—"

"And now I'm asking you to let me back in. We both had to go through big changes to find our way to each other. We're so *rare*, Shane."

He was silent, then turned to look out the window.

"And like you said—like my aunt Daphie said," she added, "I have to have faith. You've made me believe that real love exists."

"At least I did that," he said in a low voice, turning to face her. "That does help."

"Help you feel better about walking out of my life, you mean?" she blurted out. She knew that was what he was about to do.

"I'm here to take you home," he said. "But I'm also here

to tell you that I can't do this, Ashley. I wanted to. I thought maybe I could. But I can't. I don't *want* to."

"I'm not worth it?" she said before she could stop herself. Her eyes filled with tears.

"You're worth it. Of course you are. But this isn't about that. It's about me being unwilling to go through what I did five years ago ever again. I can't. I've got those girls to raise. You've seen up close and personal how hard that is, how fraught, how everything changes every five minutes. I'm going to just be their dad. No one's—"

"Husband," she said.

He nodded. "I'm very sorry, Ashley. Hurting you kills me."

"What about what you said in the barbecue restaurant, Shane? That you'd never let me go just because you were afraid of losing me. *You said that*."

"That was before…" He trailed off, his expression so pained she wanted to go to him and hold him. But of course she couldn't.

He was lost to her right now. Probably for good.

She felt her heart break, snap in two.

"Is there anything I could say that would change your mind in the fifteen minutes it'll take to get to the ranch?" she asked.

He looked at her and shook his head.

She tried to stifle the sob that rose up in her throat. "Then I can't sit there, in your vehicle, with you so close and yet a million miles away from me. I can't do *that*. I'll call my aunt Daphie to pick me up."

"Ashley—"

"Go before I burst into tears," she said.

He looked at her one last time and then slipped through

the door. She'd thought she knew what heartbreak felt like? She'd had no idea.

She dropped down in the chair and sobbed.

Chapter Twenty

Five days later, Shane was even more miserable than he'd been the day he'd gotten the call from Ashley's father that she'd been thrown. That she was unconscious. That no one knew her condition.

"Daddy," Violet called as she ran from her room in her pj's, her sister right beside her. Shane had tucked them in and turned off the light fifteen minutes ago and had thought they were asleep.

He mentally shook his head to clear it, to be present for his daughters. "Yup, sweethearts? What can I do for you?"

"We have a question," Willow said, biting her lip and looking at her twin.

He tried not to frown. Something in the way they were acting, the hesitance in their voices, made him think this was about Ashley. He hoped it wasn't.

"It's about Ashley," Violet said.

He inwardly sighed.

"Daddy, we were wondering if you and Ashley are still friends."

His heart ached. *We're not friends, actually. We're not... anything.*

Violet nodded. "Because she hasn't come over in a long

time. And we really want her to tell us a bedtime story about Helena the horse."

He knelt down in front of his girls. "Tell you what. I'll ask her if she can tell you guys a story tomorrow night. Tuck you in. I can't promise she'll be able to, though, okay?"

He would ask—for them. And he and Ashley could try to work out some semblance of friendship again. Acquaintanceship, really, since neither of them would be ready to hang out with each other, go for ice cream with the girls, chat about their lives. He certainly wouldn't want to hear about anyone Ashley was dating. Though he had no doubt that would be far off for her.

Or maybe not, he thought glumly. She wanted love. She wanted to start a family.

"She might not?" Willow asked.

She might not. He didn't want to set up false hopes. Or say anything, really.

"Well, I promise to ask her, okay?"

Violet bit her lip and looked at her sister.

They knew, dammit. They knew that something had changed between him and Ashley.

He followed them, tucked them both back in and said, "I'll call her in the morning and ask. I promise."

They nodded and clutched their lovies and closed their eyes.

He kissed their foreheads, wished them sweet dreams and then left the room.

God, his heart felt so heavy. He stood by the sliding glass doors to the patio, looking out at the darkness. At the moon. The stars. Not too long ago he'd sat outside with Ashley sharing that moon and those stars.

Now they weren't anything. He felt like hell.

It's gonna take time, that's all, he told himself. He'd let himself experience something that had been profound and beautiful—a romance with Ashley—and he'd cut it out of his life. Of course it hurt. He just needed to get back to the status quo, his life before the road trip. When everything *had* been fine.

It hadn't been fine, though, he recalled now as he tried to concentrate on inventory in the big barn. The Shaws had been constantly after him. Now they weren't. He'd had all these days of peace, of Beatrice and Charles FaceTiming the girls and overhearing Beatrice say, *Give my love to your daddy.*

She'd never said *that* before this week.

And Ashley had helped set this new relationship with the Shaws in motion when she'd found Violet in the closet in the girls' room. She'd known exactly what to say when Violet needed help with her grandmother, when someone had to step in.

Ashley had. Because she'd been there five years ago when Shane's life had been ripped apart. He and Ashley hadn't been close then, but she'd been there. She *knew*. His history was part of her own memories just because they lived on the same property.

Speaking of which, it had been with absolute dread that he'd texted Anthony McCray the morning after he'd ended things with Ashley.

I ended up hurting Ashley worse than that jerk did. I understand if you need to let me go.

Three gray dots had appeared and disappeared, then re-appeared. Finally, Anthony had texted back. You're the best foreman I've ever had. And besides, I asked Ashley if she was doing okay with you and the girls living on the ranch and she said yes. That at least she'll get to see Willow and Violet and have the same relationship with them as before.

That was true. The girls hadn't known there had been a romance to blow up, and so everything was the same to them. And Ashley, because of who she was, gave nothing away. She was herself with the girls. There was no hidden agenda, no asides, no trying to get information out of them. She cared about Willow and Violet and that was evident. He knew this because he'd come upon Ashley and the girls in the stables twice in the past five days, though Ashley hadn't heard him come in. He'd listened to the way she spoke to them, with such kindness, sweetness. He loved the way she answered their big questions, with such thoughtfulness and care.

At least he hadn't destroyed all that, he thought now.

But the twins had noticed she hadn't come over in the past several days. That he didn't take them over to see her. If they ran into her on the ranch property, that was one thing. But neither side was ringing doorbells.

Little kids noticed far more than adults thought they did.

He *would* ask Ashley to read them a story tomorrow night—for the girls' sake. It was a big ask—that he knew. He'd hurt her badly. But he'd make himself scarce so that Ashley wouldn't have to deal with *him*.

He dropped down on the sofa, staring up at the ceiling, thinking about his video call with his cousin Reed last night. Their conversation had been knocking around in Shane's head in the middle of the night and all day today.

He'd FaceTimed with Reed, a cousin he'd always been close to, after being unable to find any damned comfort in the usual ways. Like sitting outside on the porch or patio in the warming spring air. That was out now since it was something he'd done with Ashley, both on the road trip and back here that first night. Even looking in at his sleeping daughters last night hadn't worked its usual magic. Instead of his heart filling with peace and contentment, he worried that, someday soon, there would be discord between him and Ashley, that the end of their romance would lead to some kind of blowout and the girls would be devastated to lose her in their lives.

He'd paced and then grabbed his phone and texted Reed that he could use some advice. Reed had FaceTimed him right away. His cousin was a detective in Bear Ridge, serving with two of his other cousins, the ones who owned the Dawson Family Guest Ranch. Reed had been through hell and back a couple of years ago but had welcomed love into his life not too long ago and had never been happier. A baby in an infant carrier had been left on his desk at the police station with an anonymous note to care for her for a few days. At the time, Reed could barely look at a baby without shattering because of his past.

Shane figured his cousin would have answers to share about how he'd gotten over his own past to be happily remarried now—and raising that little baby girl.

He'd told Reed everything. How close he'd come to actually thinking he could do this, have a relationship with a woman and love someone again.

Someone he could lose.

Believe me, you know I understand, Reed had said.

A couple of years ago, Reed had married a woman who'd been six months pregnant with her ex's baby. The ex had abandoned her. Reed welcomed that baby as if she was his own. But when his wife had an affair with her ex two years into their marriage, he lost not just his wife but all ties and rights to the child he'd thought of as his own. He'd been so heartsick that he'd packed up and moved hours to Bear Ridge to be near family.

I felt the same way, Reed had added. *Scared out of my mind to let myself care about that little helpless baby that had been left in my care for a few days. Scared out of my mind to let myself feel what I was feeling for the social worker I'd been snowbound with along with that baby. And I almost lost both of them to my own stubbornness, my unwillingness to get out of my way.*

How you'd overcome it, though? Shane had asked. That was what he couldn't figure out. He almost felt like he'd had nothing to do with the decision to break off things with Ashley; that his head and heart had simply ganged up on him and taken over. That metal shutter had gone up and that was that.

Same way you will. I was miserable, like you are now. And I realized that not having Aimee and baby Summer in my life was a lot more painful than worrying about losing them.

That had stuck with Shane all last night.

I wouldn't give you up just because I fear losing you—to anything...

He *had* said that. And yes, it was before he had almost lost Ashley.

He got up and paced. This was so damned painful. His heart felt like it might explode.

Did he hear voices suddenly? His daughters', yes, but another voice. Like Beatrice Shaw's. But that was impossible.

He must be going crazy.

He got up and walked over to the twins' bedroom. He definitely heard them talking.

Then Beatrice Shaw responding.

What the heck?

He pushed open the ajar door with a fingertip. His girls were on their stomachs in Willow's bed—his cell phone, which they must have swiped when they'd come out fifteen minutes ago, on the pillow, their grandmother's face filling the screen.

Had they video-called their nana? Why?

Willow turned and noticed him standing in the doorway. Her eyes widened, and she poked her sister.

"Uh-oh," Violet said. She looked at the phone. "Daddy caught us, Nana."

"Sweeties," Beatrice said. "Let me talk to your father, okay? I'll do what I can, okay?"

"Thank you, Nana!" the girls said in unison.

Do what she can? About what?

"Here, Daddy," Violet said in her most innocent tone. "Nana wants to talk to you."

Willow nodded and took the phone from Violet and handed it to him.

He narrowed his eyes at his daughters. "I'll take this in the living room. You two should be asleep."

"Night night," they said and got back under the covers.

He left the room, closing the door behind him. He went into his bedroom and closed the door, away from possibly big ears that might be trying to eavesdrop.

"Beatrice? What's going on?"

Beatrice's eyes were misty. Uh-oh. What was this?

"The girls told me that something is going on. Or not

going on. That you and Ashley don't seem to be friends anymore. They're worried."

He sucked in a breath and looked away for a moment, then found himself breaking down and telling Beatrice everything. *Just about* everything.

"Well, it was plain as day that you two are deeply in love," Beatrice said. "Why do you think I got so emotional that my five-year-old granddaughters had to talk some sense into me?"

"I can't," Shane said, shaking his head. "I can't go through that again."

"I feel the same way. But I certainly can't cut my son out of my life because he might get into a car accident."

Shane almost gasped.

"I know it's a little different," she added, "but the point is the same. And let me tell you something else."

He was a little scared of what that might be now.

"Liza would have wanted you to find love again. I believe that with all my heart. Charles and I talked about that, actually, the morning you picked up the girls. Liza would have wanted you to give them a mother who'd cherish them as she would have."

Now he did gasp.

"Shane, you know how I've spent the past five years trying desperately to control everything around me—especially my granddaughters. But I know now that I can't. I can only love them. And you."

Was it his imagination or did that metal shutter in his chest creak open a bit? Just a bit.

"You can't control love, Shane. It's wild and wonderful and comes with incredible risk, yes. But it's worth everything. Even the loss. I know that now."

He felt his own eyes getting misty. "Now I do too," he said.

She smiled. "Think on it tonight, Shane. Sleep on it. Or better yet, don't waste another second and call Ashley and ask her to come over. Tell her you have some groveling to do."

I would never give you up because I was scared of losing you—to anything.

Like himself. His own stubbornness.

Stupid dumbhead idiot, he chastised himself.

Ashley was finally going to hear from the man she loved that he had made the biggest mistake of his life and loved her. He had to smile about that.

"I think I will," he said. "Thank you, Beatrice. You just might have changed four lives tonight."

The last time he saw the look that was now on Beatrice's face, in her eyes, was the day the twins were born, when she'd held both in her arms for the first time.

"I'll free up the line so you can call Ashley," she said and disconnected.

He just hoped he wasn't too late, that he hadn't been the final straw, causing her to completely give up on love. Lose her faith in happily-ever-after.

And her ability to believe that he *had* made the biggest mistake of his life in letting her go.

Because he sure had. He knew it now.

His girls knew it.

And he was going to fix it.

Ashley had just come out of the shower when her phone pinged with a text.

Shane.

Could you come over now? I need to tell you something right away but I can't leave. Plight of the single parent, remember? I'm hoping to change that, actually.

Her mouth dropped open. She would not read into that last sentence. She would not read into any of the text.

She typed back: On my way.

What could this be about? She quickly got dressed in jeans and a sweater and towel dried her hair, then pulled it into a low ponytail and hurried out the door. On the path to his cabin, she reread the text.

I'm hoping to change that, actually.

Being a single parent?

Stop speculating, she told herself. *You'll find out soon enough.*

Like right now, because she'd arrived. He opened the door before she could even knock and stepped out onto the porch. He gestured to the swing and she sat. Then he sat beside her. Her heart was so full of hope that she had to hold on to the post to keep herself from falling over.

"I've been miserable since the morning I left your hospital room," he said. "It didn't take long for me to realize that living without you is way more painful than the thought of losing you."

Oh, Shane. She was so touched that she couldn't speak. And she didn't want to interrupt. She wanted to hear everything he had to say before she'd fling herself into his arms.

"I made the biggest mistake of my life that morning," he said.

Her hand flew to her heart. "I've been wanting to hear the right man say that."

He smiled and reached up to touch her face. "I love you so much, Ashley," he said, taking her hand and holding it. He kissed her knuckles, then looked at her. "I'm so sorry for hurting you. I promise to make it up to you every day."

"I love you too," she whispered. "So much. And I love Violet and Willow with all my heart."

"I know it. And so do they. To the point that they kind of engineered this. Do you know they stole my phone and FaceTimed their nana tonight for help in getting us back together?"

She smiled and linked her arm through his. "Those girls. Very smart and resourceful."

He laughed. "We'll be a family. The four of us. And maybe a baby brother or sister for the twins."

She was so moved she couldn't speak.

"We want a baby sister!" a little voice called.

"But a brother would be good too," another one added.

What on earth? Shane popped up and looked in the bedroom window, which faced the yard, just inches from the porch. Big ears, indeed.

"You two might as well come on out," Shane called with a smile.

"Yay!" came two little voices. They came rushing out in their orange striped footie pajamas.

Oh, how she did love these girls. So, so much.

"We're going to be a family?" Willow asked, hope in her eyes.

"And have a baby sister or brother?" Violet seconded.

"Hopefully very soon," Shane said. "If Ashley will marry me."

Three sets of eyes looked at her.

She was so happy, so overwhelmed with absolute joy,

that for a second she couldn't speak. "Oh, I'll marry you. *All* of you," she added, wrapping her arms around the girls.

Shane leaned over his daughters' heads to kiss Ashley. "Okay, now it's like ten o'clock and you two need to be asleep immediately."

"I think we'll sleep really good tonight, Daddy," Willow said.

Violet smiled on a firm nod.

They walked the smiling, chattering, yawning girls to their room, tucked them in and kissed their foreheads. Ashley started to tell them a story about Helena the horse, but three lines in, the twins were asleep.

Tears misted Ashley's eyes. "Just think, now I can do that every night. I'm going to be their mother. It's a dream come true. This is all a dream come true."

He pulled her into his arms and held her tight. "It is. I stopped believing in all that. But now I do. And the girls will too."

She leaned up and kissed him. Her Shane. Her heart.

He turned off the lamp between the twins' beds, and they went into the living room. Again, Shane took her in his arms. Ashley rested her head against his chest, Shane's heartbeat precious against her ear.

What happened on the road trip wasn't going to stay on the road trip. It had been a journey that would last forever.

Epilogue

On the first day of summer, another wedding was being held at the McCray Ranch. This time, the groom was there. Sure, he lived on the ranch, but he'd have walked a thousand miles to get there if he had to. Wild horses couldn't have kept him from waiting down at the end of the aisle for his bride.

Ashley McCray was getting married today. For real. And she had no doubt that the wedding would go off without a hitch, that in just fifteen minutes, she'd be Ashley McCray Dawson.

Yes, she'd practiced writing that name last night in her journal, her heart overflowing.

Ashley McCray Dawson, mama to two precious girls, daughters of her heart. She'd love them with everything she had. As she would their father. Forever.

There was no bridal tent this time. Just a big tree on the McCray Ranch that she was waiting behind with her father. There was no bridal party either. No groomsmen.

Just two people very much in love who would say their vows in front of family and friends. Ashley's parents were there. And her aunts and uncles and cousins, including Miranda and her husband. And of course, the Shaws.

The wedding march started, the traditional one that both Shane and Ashley wanted. Ashley's father walked her slowly down the aisle.

Her eyes were getting teary, and she saw her handsome groom, her Shane, surrounded by his girls, *her* girls too, swiping fast under his eyes. The twins were in their favorite play dresses, colorful leggings underneath. No one's hair was in a chignon, except Beatrice's.

Willow was out of her black boot, as was Ashley, and Violet's bangs had grown so long they had to be cut that morning so she wouldn't have to keep swiping them out of her eyes to see her dad get married.

She joined Shane in front of the minister's podium and then knelt down to hug each girl, who were beaming with happiness.

"Hi, Mama," Violet whispered.

"Hi, Mama," Willow seconded.

Last night, the girls had asked her what they should call her after the wedding. Mommy? Mama? Second Mommy?

Ashley had told them they could choose. Shane had nodded.

"We want to call you Mama," they'd said together, holding hands.

She'd had to hold back tears, but she'd caught a tear slipping down Shane's cheek.

"Mama it is."

Now, as the minister began the ceremony, Ashley's heart was so full as they recited their vows.

And then they had their wedding kiss, Shane slightly dipping her, and there was cheering and clapping.

The new family of four walked back up the aisle, stopping to hug their relatives and friends.

They had a honeymoon to start, right here on the Mc-Cray Ranch, the four of them together. A family forever.

* * * * *